MIND
BLIND

MIND BLIND

LARI DON

KELPIESTEEN

*Many thanks to everyone who took part in
the competition to name one of my characters,
especially Calum Smith who came up
with the winning name, Roy.*

KelpiesTeen is an imprint of Floris Books
First published in 2014 by Floris Books
© 2014 Lari Don

The publisher acknowledges subsidy from
Creative Scotland towards the publication
of this volume

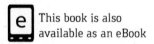 This book is also
available as an eBook

British Library CIP data available
ISBN 978-178250-053-7
Printed in Poland

*To Mirren – this one has always been for you,
and to Gowan – my most influential editor*

I killed a girl today, just after the school bell.

I try to tell myself that I didn't really kill her.

That I didn't mean to, that I didn't want to.

But she's dead.

And it's my fault.

So I killed her.

chapter 1

Ciaran Bain, 30th October

I was shaking with fear, though it wasn't my own fear. I hadn't been scared when I slid past the police surveillance outside the girl's house, nor when I broke in. But as I slipped deeper into the memory of her fear, I started to shiver.

Why had Vivien felt so scared in her own house? If I could understand that, maybe I could find what I was searching for.

I shut the door of the understairs cupboard and knelt down inside, squashed between rows of green wellies and piles of board games.

In the dark, I slipped further into Vivien's memory.

I felt the same bumpy floorboards under my knees that she'd felt. I was kneeling in exactly the same place. She had definitely been hiding here, in this cupboard, when she got grit on her fingertips.

Why had she been hiding inside her own house?

Probably because she didn't want to be caught with her hand in the urn. She didn't want to be seen rummaging in her nana's ashes. I must be on the right track.

I'd broken into her family's house hoping to find the

place she'd been thinking about when we fought in the van, hoping to find what she had hidden.

Vivien had put the light on, so I reached up and pressed the switch. Then I took my gloves off, because what she'd felt on her fingertips might be the key to what I was searching for. I could put my gloves on again if I had to touch anything that would hold a print.

I knew there would now be a line of light shining under the cupboard door, but I was sure no one was around to see it. I couldn't tell exactly how many people were in the Shaw house, because sleeping minds are too blurry for me to count, but there had been no one awake when I broke in. Now I had to risk bringing my whole concentration inwards to Vivien's memories, and hope no one would wake up while I did.

I closed my eyes.

The memory I had from Vivien's mind was so short. She hadn't remembered opening the box, opening the urn or even putting anything inside. All I had was:

Grit on her fingers and the contrast to the smooth light object those fingers had held a moment before. The grit pressing on her fingertips as she twisted the lid back on. Holding the urn with one hand and the box with the other. The weight of the box on her thighs when she put the urn inside. Leaning back against the door to give herself room to bend the box lid over. I leant back too.

She felt guilty, but she was also excited. This memory was full of secrets and hiding. And fear. What was she afraid of?

Then she closed the box.

Where did she put it? Tidying up isn't as exciting as hiding a secret, so she hadn't thought about that when we were screaming at each other.

10

I went even deeper into her memory, hoping to glimpse where she'd planned to put the box.

Knees on floor.

Grit on fingertips.

Box getting heavier.

Door opening...

Had someone seen her?

The door opened...

SHIT!

I crashed out of Vivien's memory, and out of the cupboard.

The door hadn't opened in her memory. It had opened behind me!

I fell backwards onto the floor. I rolled away and thumped into the wall. Then I rolled the other way, panic knocking all the training out of my head.

Who had crept up on me? One of Vivien's family? One of the policemen from the street? Whose fear was I sensing?

I was blinded in the dim hall after the bright cupboard.

Then someone stood on me. A bare foot on my chest.

Now I wasn't just sensing fear, I was reading thoughts and questions. I almost screamed. But I couldn't let the police outside hear me. So I gritted my teeth, forced the panic and nausea down into my guts, and tried to get out from under the foot.

I couldn't escape.

I wasn't being pinned down by the weight of the person, but by their emotions and questions.

I was trapped on the carpet by...

By a girl!

I am so crap.

My eyes were adjusting. I could see her now. This girl had the same dark skin and brown eyes as Vivien, but she was shorter, with wilder hair, and she was dressed in red pyjamas rather than a blue coat.

She was glaring at me. All her questions were crashing into me, through the foot on my chest.

Who is he?

What's he doing here?

Why doesn't he push me off and get up?

How long has he been here?

Did he come into my room?

Oh god. I should have called the police instead of coming downstairs.

I should run.

Why doesn't he run?

I couldn't run. I was trying so hard not to scream that I could hardly breathe.

I am so crap.

She was staring at me, battering me with her thoughts.

He looks more scared than I am.

Why isn't he getting up?

Why is he such a wimp?

Good question. Why am I such a wimp?

I finally dragged in enough breath to fling my arm up and push her foot away.

My sudden movement took her by surprise. She lost her balance, falling awkwardly against the wall.

I leapt up.

We were facing each other across the narrow hallway.

And we were the only people in the house.

Now this girl was awake, I could tell there was no one else asleep upstairs.

Now this girl was no longer touching me, she wasn't disabling me with her terrified thoughts.

Now I was on my feet, I was taller, bigger, scarier than her.

And she was alone.

I grinned at her.

Her head jerked back.

The more confident I looked the more afraid she was.

So I might be able to convince this girl that I was in control. But I knew I was making a huge mess of this job.

chapter 2

Ciaran Bain, 30th october

I'd been seen, which meant I could be identified.

I'd been seen by Vivien's younger sister. I knew her name from the files: Lucy Kingston Shaw.

I breathed out, long and easy. I reached into my pocket for my black leather gloves and slipped them on.

She was really scared now. Perhaps it looked like I was going to strangle her. I had to calm her down, because if she started screaming, the police would hear.

I wiggled my fingers. "Fingerprints," I whispered. "Silly me. Should have had them on all the time."

"You're a burglar?" she whispered back.

I shrugged.

"You're a pretty useless burglar."

Great. She'd known me for less than a minute and she'd already realised I was crap. But that was ok. She was relaxing. Now that I was incompetent, I was less scary.

"Did I hurt you?" she asked. "When I pulled you out of the cupboard? You looked like I was killing you or..."

The word 'killing' jolted her with sudden grief. She was still half-asleep, perhaps she'd half-forgotten about her sister. But she didn't want to discuss that with me, so she kept asking questions.

"Who are you? What are you doing in our house? What were you stealing from under the stairs?"

"Wellies," I said seriously. "You've got wonderful wellies in there."

She almost smiled, then frowned. I could sense her confusion. There was still fear, but less panic now.

She was only a mindblind. I had much more information about this conversation than she did. I should be able to guide it in the right direction.

First, I didn't want her to do anything to alert the policemen, so I needed her to stay calm. Then, while I had a member of the Shaw family all to myself, I could ask her some questions, find out where the urn was, so I could get what I'd been searching for and go.

This girl had already seen too much, so she would probably have to be silenced. I should get information from her while I had the chance.

She was staring at me. She was more awake now, and soon she was going to react rationally to finding a stranger in her house. Soon she was going to call for help. Even if she didn't know about the police outside, when she got scared enough, she'd start yelling for the neighbours.

I took a step away from her, moving along the wall towards the kitchen and the back door.

I smiled again. That didn't help. Perhaps I don't have a very reassuring smile. Maybe I'm better at scaring people. Or killing them, it turns out.

So I said quietly, "I'm not going to hurt you."

That was probably true. My Uncle Malcolm was

15

going to kill her, but I wasn't going to hurt her. Not unless I had to.

I kept my voice gentle and even, smoothing the harsh West of Scotland accent that Londoners tend to associate with TV gangsters. "I can leave now or I can tell you why I'm here."

"You're not really here for the wellies, then?"

I managed a half-laugh at her brave attempt at a joke. "Do you want me to tell you why I'm here?"

She nodded.

"I came here to find one tiny thing. If you give it to me, I'll go away. And if you don't tell anyone I was here, you'll never see me again."

"I'm not giving you anything! How dare you break into my house, then ask me to let you steal something and keep your break-in secret?"

She was getting angry. I didn't need to read her mind to know that, any mindblind would notice. She was raising her voice, stepping towards me, fists clenched.

Her anger was giving her confidence. I had to bring her down a few notches. "Do you want a cup of tea or something?"

"What?"

"Let's sit down. I'm really not going to hurt you. Honestly."

I turned my back on her and walked into the kitchen. It was a calculated risk. If she ran for the front door or grabbed a phone or started to scream, then I could probably get out the back door and over the fence before the police reacted.

But if she followed me, I'd know she wanted to talk to me. Then I could get answers.

She followed me, fear, curiosity and confusion

battling inside her as she padded into the kitchen and switched on the light. I sat down at the table, but she stood by the light switch.

"Do you really want tea?" she asked.

"Yes." Actually I didn't want tea, but it would calm her down to make it.

"Builder's tea or herbal? I can do hemlock, arsenic, belladonna."

I smiled at her poisonous joke. "Ha ha. I'll have whatever you're having. And a biscuit, if you're having one."

"I don't think I'm having anything. I haven't managed to eat much since... em..."

She sat down and put her head in her hands. She was suddenly overwhelmed with grief. She wasn't crying, just lost in sadness and disbelief.

I got up and opened the fridge, looking for something sweet. It was all healthy stuff, no full-strength coke or Irn-Bru or anything useful. I found a carton of orange-and-mango juice, and poured some into a clean glass from the dishwasher.

"Drink this. Sugar will help."

She took a sip, then a gulp, then drained the glass. I refilled it.

I sat down again and we stared at each other. She was a mess. The more awake she became, the worse she was coping. She was grief-stricken, scared, confused and angry. But at least she wasn't dehydrated.

What was I doing? I was talking to Vivien's sister. She'd seen my face, heard my voice. What the hell was I doing?

But I'd done it now. I might as well follow through. If I got the codenames, it would be worth it.

I needed to know how long I had with this girl. I needed to know when her parents were due home.

"Why are you alone in the house? Where's everyone else?"

She was instantly suspicious. "How do you know I'm alone?"

"If your mum or dad or anyone else was here, you'd have shouted as soon as you found me. Why have they left you on your own?"

"Because I told them to. Because I didn't want to go and sit in another depressing room hearing people cry and I didn't want them hugging me and telling me I'm the future now and I'm sick of it already and I told them to go out if they had to talk to Grampa, but I would stay here and get some peace and quiet and they could be as long as they liked and I wouldn't care, and Mum didn't want to leave me so I said if I had to spend one more minute being guarded and watched then I'd just go out and find my very own murderer!"

She glared at me.

Wow. I didn't need to read this girl's mind. She would tell me all her thoughts for free if I asked the right question.

"Have I?" she demanded.

"Have you what?"

"Have I found my own murderer?"

I went cold.

"Did you kill my sister?"

She couldn't read my mind. So I should say, *What? Has someone killed your sister?* I should act surprised.

But I didn't answer. I didn't act anything. I just stared at her.

"Did you kill my sister? Did you kill Viv?"
I looked at my hands in their black gloves.
"Did you?"
"Yes."

chapter 3

Lucy Shaw, 30th October

He killed my sister.

When he fell out of the cupboard, I was too shocked to connect the break-in with Viv's murder. I'm not sure I even remembered about Viv, to begin with. I was too busy being scared for myself and confused about him to remember that the worst possible thing in my whole world happened this week.

Once I realised that the two crimes coming so close together couldn't be a coincidence, I didn't expect him to admit it. But now he had admitted it, what was I going to do?

I couldn't let him just sit there at our table, grinning at my nervous jokes and calmly admitting he'd killed my sister. I had to make him pay.

I was standing up by the dishwasher and lifting out the knife before I even thought about *how* to make him pay.

He sighed. "Don't be silly. Put that down."

"I'm not being silly. You killed Viv. I'm going to kill you right back, you murdering bastard."

He actually laughed at me. "You can't kill me."

"I can."

He stood up and moved away from the table. "No. You can't. Really. You're not going to get near me with that. I might be a crap burglar, but I'm quite good at... other stuff. Put it down or you'll get hurt. I don't want to hurt you."

"Why not?"

"What do you mean, why not?"

"Why don't you want to hurt me? You *killed* my sister!"

He looked at his hands again. "I didn't actually kill her. I wasn't there when she died."

"You said you killed her."

"I sort of killed her. It was my fault. I took her to the man who killed her. I made the stupid mistake that meant she had to die. But I didn't actually break her neck. And I don't want to hurt you."

I didn't believe him. I didn't believe that he hadn't killed Viv or that he didn't want to hurt me.

I lifted the knife. I didn't know how to use it, except for chopping onions and peppers, but it might make him keep his distance until I decided what to do next.

I didn't get to do anything next.

He moved so fast.

He stepped over to me, kicked my wrist, caught the knife as I dropped it, put it back in the dishwasher, then sat down.

I fell against the kitchen unit, rubbing my wrist. And shaking a bit. "You bastard."

"Sit down. Knives aren't going to help either of us. Sit down and calm down."

I didn't want to do anything he asked. I didn't sit down. And I couldn't calm down.

Now I was completely awake and really scared.

I was alone with the person who had killed my sister.

I thought about running for the phone or the door, but I remembered how fast he'd moved a moment ago. I thought about screaming, but who would hear me?

Then I thought, if he was going to kill me too, at least I could find out why Viv died first. I wasn't satisfied by the 'random attack' story the police had persuaded Mum and Dad to believe. And if he really didn't intend to hurt me, then I should gather evidence so I could get justice for my sister.

I looked at the boy properly for the first time, past his confident smiles and leather gloves, so I could describe him to the police, if I got the chance.

He looked younger than Viv and possibly older than me, so maybe fourteen or even fifteen. He was clearly Scottish, with all those rolled 'r's, but he wasn't pale and freckly like the MacDonald twins in my year. His tanned outdoor skin, light blue eyes and straight blond hair made him look like a baddie in an old WW2 film, or a Viking berserker. Northern, cold-hearted and slightly nuts.

He shook his head at me, as if he knew I was memorising his face.

I tested my voice, hoping it wouldn't shake. "Tell me why you took her to a man who killed her. Tell me what mistake you made. Tell me why you're in our house. Tell me everything."

"First you tell me when your parents are due back."

I glanced at the clock. It was after 1 a.m. "They're at my grampa's. They could be back any minute." Maybe if he thought Mum and Dad were about to walk through the door, he would go away.

Rather than getting up and leaving, he frowned and

looked out of the window. "No, they won't be back in the next few minutes. There's time for you to tell me what I need to know."

"I'm not going to tell you anything."

"That's your choice. I'm not going to force you." He shrugged. "Your sister had something that she promised to destroy, but she hid it instead. If I find it and remove it, then the people who killed her won't come here looking for it. So I need your help."

"I'm not going to help you!"

"Ok. I'll be off then." He stood up. "And the man who killed your sister will probably knock down your door sometime tomorrow. Good luck with him, Lucy."

That was almost as much of a surprise as the kick. "You know my name?"

"I know everything, except where your nana's ashes are."

"What?"

"Vivien hid what I need in your nana's urn, in the understairs cupboard."

"She hid something in the ashes? Gross!"

"Yeah. But clever."

I nodded. "Viv is always... was always... But why would she hide something in the ashes? Why didn't she just hide it in her sock drawer? Why would she do something so... disgusting and disrespectful?"

"She was probably afraid of the people who might come looking for it."

I shivered. "So who was she hiding it from?"

"I suppose she was hiding it from me. From me and my... the people I work for."

"Who are you? Why did she hide something from you? What did she hide?"

He shook his head. "I've given you answers, now you give me answers. I didn't find the urn under the stairs. Where is it?"

I didn't want to give him any useful information, but this answer might get him out of my house. "It's not here. Mum didn't like it in the house, it gave her the creeps. So Dad said someone else would store it until next year."

"Next year?"

"We're going to scatter Nana in the sea, in the same place my great-granddad was scattered, on their wedding anniversary, next spring."

"So who's got it now?"

"I don't know."

"You don't *know*?"

I was telling the truth, but there was no way to prove that to him. And now, for the first time tonight, he looked angry.

chapter 4

Ciaran Bain, 30th October

Was she telling the truth? Did she really not know where her own great-grandmother's ashes were? I couldn't tell for sure without touching her, which I didn't want to do. But she wasn't planning her words like a liar.

"I really don't know," she repeated. I sensed slight panic, but no deceit.

"So who might have it?"

"Dad might have given it to Grampa, because he's nearest. Or Uncle Vince might have taken it, because he's got more storage space than Grampa."

"If your grandfather is nearer, I'll go there first. Give me both addresses, though."

"I'm not giving you their addresses! I don't want you and your murdering gang anywhere near my family."

"Lucy, the man who did kill Vivien already has those addresses on file. That's where I got *your* name and address. If I don't go now, on my own, then he'll go, with all my... with lots of others, as soon as he works out what she hid and where."

"How is that worse than you going tonight? Am I meant to think you're good news and they're bad news?"

I smiled reassuringly.

She wasn't reassured.

"What harm can I do? On my own?"

She rubbed her wrist.

Oops. I shouldn't have shown off with flashy kicks. She now had a very good idea how much harm I could do on my own.

"Come on, Lucy. I didn't attack you, you tried to attack me! I won't hurt anyone. I'll just search their cupboards and leave. Trust me."

She didn't trust me. Fair enough. I didn't trust me either.

I sensed her make a sudden decision.

"I'll go."

"What?"

"I'll go. I'll find the urn, then give it to you. If I do that, will you leave us alone?"

"Yes. No. No!" I hadn't seen that one coming. "I mean, yes, once I have what's in the urn, I will leave you alone. But *no*! You can't go. Don't be daft."

I suddenly had a clear picture of this skinny girl, shorter than me and younger by the looks of her, in a dark house, searching under the stairs. Then I saw her hauled out by Malcolm, and Daniel putting his foot on her stomach.

I'm not a fortune-teller. I read minds, not the future. But I knew that Malcolm or Mum would drag everything out of me as soon as I went back, then my family would start searching for the codenames too. If they found this girl in their way, Lucy would be the one who'd get hurt.

The only way to stop all of the Shaw family being killed was for me to get the codenames tonight. Then

I could protect this family, protect my family, maybe even protect my own future.

Though it was probably too late to protect Lucy.

She'd seen my face. Her sister had been killed for seeing my face.

So it probably was too late for Lucy. But I could try.

"Are you thinking?" she asked. "It looks like hard work."

"You can't go," I repeated. "It's not safe."

"*You're* not safe. I suppose we could go together, then I can stop you stealing anything, damaging anything, hurting anyone..."

"Yeah? You can *stop* me doing anything, can you?"

"Maybe I can. You're all cocky now, boy, but I knocked you down pretty good in the hall."

I couldn't let her know how she did that. "You took me by surprise, that's all."

"So here's another surprise. We're going together. We'll find the urn, you'll get your mysterious *thing* and you'll go away." She glared at me, completely determined.

I needed those addresses. What was the most efficient way of getting them?

I could take off my gloves, grab Lucy and demand her grampa and uncle's addresses. She was probably too stubborn to tell me voluntarily, but I might be able to read something useful while she was concentrating on refusing to tell me. I wouldn't get the exact postal addresses – she would only think those if she was actually writing them down – but she'd probably visualise the streets and the houses.

However, we're not meant to let targets know we're mindreading, so I'd have to hurt her, twist that sore

27

wrist perhaps, as an excuse for touching her. But if I hurt her she'd scream, which would alert the police.

Also, if I touched her, I'd read the thoughts behind her grief and fear, and I might scream louder than her. Then she'd see exactly how much of a wimp I was.

So it was the rational decision to let her lead me to the right house.

And if we found the codenames and if I persuaded Malcolm and Mum to let me brief them verbally, perhaps they wouldn't find out that Lucy had seen me. It was unlikely, but it was the best chance I could give her.

So I nodded.

"Let's go now then," she said. "Before my parents get back."

"Don't be daft! How will your parents react if you're not safe in bed when they get home?"

She didn't want to agree with me, but she shrugged.

I glanced at the window. "Anyway, it's not going to be quick or easy getting out of here. There are two policemen watching your house."

"There are police watching us? Why?"

"Probably hoping for evidence that one of you killed Vivien. Suspecting the family is easier than doing real detective work."

She was horrified. "But *you* killed her! I'll tell them that right now."

She headed for the front door.

"Lucy, stop! If you drop me in it now, your entire family will be in danger!"

She stopped. Right by the understairs cupboard.

I spoke softly. "I know you want someone to blame for Vivien's death, so you can tell the police about me later, if you want. But wait until I get the secret safely away. If you shout for the police now, you'll see me in handcuffs, which I'm sure would make you happy, but then *my* family will come searching for the secret."

She raised her eyebrows as I said 'my family'. I was probably telling her too much, but the truth might scare her into doing what I wanted. "Yeah. My family. There are lots of them, they're all bigger than me, and if you hand me to the police they'll be very annoyed." Probably. Or maybe they'll be relieved to get rid of me.

She was balancing revenge and caution, trying to decide which was more important.

But I couldn't wait for her decision, because suddenly I sensed...

Exhausted grief.

Desire for comfort.

Worry.

Her parents, moving at driving speed up the road.

Even worse, slightly further away, I sensed sharp wakefulness. More police, two of them, following the Shaws.

"Your parents! They're nearly home!"

"How do you know?"

Shit, I'd broken one of the basic rules: knowing stuff I shouldn't know. "Em... I think I hear a car. Get to bed. I'll be... where can I hide?"

"You're not hiding in my bedroom!"

"Damn right!"

She looked around frantically. "In the study!" She pointed at the door opposite the cupboard. Then she said, more calmly, "I'll come and get you once they're in bed." I sensed a sliding deceit behind her words. She was already trying to think of ways to make my night even more difficult.

"Wait until they're asleep," I said. "Be patient."

We nodded to each other, both agreeing, both plotting.

By the time the key turned in the lock, Lucy was running upstairs and I was closing the study door.

I crouched under the desk and waited.

I sensed the Shaws' weariness and their concern for Lucy. One of them clumped upstairs to check on her. I held my breath, hoping she wouldn't mention finding me downstairs. But she must have been in bed, pretending sleep, because the adult felt relief and love.

Her parents were both exhausted. They pottered around taking off coats and shoes, then, after a few minutes of doors opening and closing, toilets flushing and lights clicking off, the house was quiet.

No one was asleep yet, but I couldn't wait any longer.

chapter 5

Ciaran Bain, 30th October

Now that everyone was in bed, I could start to search again. The urn wasn't in this house, but perhaps I could find the addresses of the houses I had to search next.

I switched on my torch and opened the top drawer of the desk. It was filled with notebooks and printer paper.

The next drawer contained pens, compasses and rulers.

The bottom drawer held old CD roms and dusty cables, as well as a multipack of slim silver flash drives. The pack had been torn open and there was only one left inside.

I tipped out the single flash drive and weighed it in my hand. Did it feel familiar? To be sure, I had to go back into Vivien's memory again.

I was spending a lot of time in this dead girl's head, much more time than I'd spent with her when she'd been alive.

I hadn't spent that much time with her, because the grab had only taken a few minutes and the getaway had been fast too.

Ciaran Bain, 28th October

The whole job had felt weird and unsettling right from the beginning.

At the briefing, I had sat at the back, as far away from everyone else as possible. I don't like sitting too close to anyone, even people I've known all my life. I don't want to sense their emotions, even if they're feeling the same emotions as me.

So I hate briefings, I hate parties, I hate car journeys, I hate sharing a bedroom and I only ever touch another human being by choice if I'm trying to beat them in a fight.

I sat at the very back of the room, my chair pushed hard into the corner, while my mum clicked information up onto the big screen, and my Uncle Malcolm talked us through the job.

I watched the screen, but I also watched my cousins nodding keenly in front of me. I could sense their desire to impress the senior readers. All except Roy, who was worried about something (possibly the welfare of the target); his little brother Josh, who was nervous (probably because this was his first job outside Scotland); and Daniel, who was confident he didn't have to impress anyone because his dad already thought he was wonderful.

All this felt entirely normal. What felt weird was the information we weren't getting.

Uncle Malcolm gave us details about times, locations and escape routes, and handed out a pile of maps, but there were no details about the background of the job, nor the intended outcome. He showed us pictures of the target, but didn't tell us why the client wanted the target grabbed.

This lack of detail suggested it was a rush job. I'd guessed that already, when all the younger generation were summoned from Scotland at short notice.

A team of senior readers had come south earlier in the month. Mum and most of my uncles and aunts had vanished in the middle of the night a fortnight ago, rushing down to the Surrey warehouse we use as a base for our regular London operations.

They'd left all the teenagers behind, with only Aunt Rose and Uncle Greg in charge of training, which meant hours of martial arts with Aunt Rose and hours of getting in touch with our feelings with Uncle Greg. But we had plenty of time to skive off too, which meant lots of fishing and football during the day and lots of pizza and action films at night.

None of us had had a full night's sleep or eaten any fruit and veg for a couple of weeks.

Now here we were, after an overnight drive down in three uncomfortably packed people carriers, about to take part in a grab that clearly hadn't been fully thought through.

But I couldn't say that. I'm only a foot soldier. I don't get to question the bosses' decisions. I don't even get to do the exciting stuff. I just hang about at the back, picking up any mess. No one trusts me to do more than that.

Though the briefing was sketchy, it was clear why they needed the fourth generation of readers in London. We were the best team for this job.

Because the job was to identify, follow and grab a teenage target as she came out of school. Half a dozen strange adults hanging about the school gates would have been suspicious, but half a dozen teenagers would blend in perfectly.

So we were shown pictures of the target, and a map of her usual route to her flamenco class, with an 'x' at the spot where Daniel and Martha would grab her and put her in the van, as well as the locations of the back-up van and the senior readers' cars, and the safest routes back to base.

That was it.

My mum stood up. "Come on. We need to be there before the bell goes." We grabbed our equipment and left the briefing room, which was really just a large shed in the middle of the warehouse. All our bedrooms and offices are in boxy little portacabins scattered around the cold grey space.

We climbed into two blue people carriers and two white vans parked near the shuttered front doors, and drove off.

I was in the second people carrier. Laura sat in the front with my mum. Becky, Roy and Josh sat in the middle. I sat in the back, on my own, as usual, wearing my black leather jacket and gloves, as usual.

It's not a fashion statement. Leather gives me some protection. Not against emotions, nothing can stop them getting through, but against the thoughts I read whenever I touch someone. Leather is much better than fabric. With another animal's skin between me and the rest of the world, it isn't quite so overwhelming. Perhaps I'll get a motorbike when I'm old enough, so I can wear black leather from head to toe for the rest of my life.

I sat on my own, studying the map. After about twenty minutes, Roy turned round and flicked the corner of the printout. "Nearly there, mate. Are you ready?"

We checked we had all the essentials. Cash, in case we got stranded. False ID, in case we got lifted. Masks, mobile phones and microphones. Then we all pulled on stripy green-and-blue school ties, badly knotted and deliberately squint.

We couldn't hang around outside the school before the final bell – we'd look like truants. Also Malcolm said that the target was never first out of the door. So we stayed in the vehicles until we heard shrill ringing, then got swiftly into position.

All four teams were in place by the time pupils started to come out of Winslow Academy's wide green doors and down the dozen steps to the street.

Team 1 was the grab team – Daniel and Martha, Malcolm's kids and the most efficient readers in our generation. They were out of sight, in the alley, inside the van driven by Uncle Paul, our usual getaway driver. Both of them were already masked, waiting to leap out and grab the target as she went past.

Team 2 was the follow team – Becky and Laura, Roy's big sisters. They were waiting at the bottom of the steps. Teenage girls don't expect to be followed by other teenage girls, so Becky and Laura walking behind the target wouldn't make her suspicious. Neither of them were strong readers, but all they had to do was follow a target in plain sight.

Team 3 was the advance team – two readers leaning against a wall further down the road. No one expects to be followed by someone in front, but if you can anticipate where a target is going, you can keep ahead of them and make sure nothing gets in the way of the job. The advance team was Roy, who can't read worth a damn but is smarter than the rest of us, and Sam, who can read well enough but lacks Roy's brains.

Team 4 was the loser team, just there to pick up rubbish.

I was in team 4. Obviously. Me and Roy's little brother. Like all Auntie Susan's kids, Josh is a fairly weak reader, and he's only just turned twelve. So he's the rookie and I'm the wimp. Team 4. Team Loser.

Josh and I were stationed opposite the school, to watch the pupils leaving and to act as the main contact with the senior readers, so the active teams didn't have to walk and talk at the same time. Once the target was en route, we'd circle round to the other end of the alley, so we could clear away any evidence after the grab.

We were the bin men. But at least we were out on the job this time, rather than sitting back at base doing homework.

Normal boys hanging about outside a school would probably moan about their parents or make admiring comments about passing girls. But we were wearing throat mikes and earpieces, so our family could hear every word we said. We would only talk if it was relevant to the job.

I said, "You all set?"

Josh answered, "Yeah."

And that was it. Male bonding on the job.

Josh stood beside me fiddling with his phone, while I perched on a low wall, leaning against a lamppost. I was trying to look casual, but I also knew that standing upright might be a bit of a struggle in the next few minutes. Because we were now watching a stream of kids coming out of Winslow Academy.

Dozens of them, then hundreds, pouring out of the doors, barging around each other, then hanging about at the bottom of the steps. Most of the kids were wearing ties, but this wasn't a school with blazers, so there was a colourful mix of denim jackets, cardigans, hoodies, duffel coats and even a few unfortunate anoraks.

I could see them, and hear them yelling and chatting.

I could sense them too.

I could sense every single emotion, of every person in that crowd.

Waves of emotion were crashing into me, knocking me off balance.

More pupils flowed out of the school and the crowd started to push across the road towards us. I was struggling to breathe through the overwhelming weight of their advancing feelings.

I hate crowds. I don't enjoy being close to my family, but at least their feelings are familiar. This was like being attacked by an army of strangers. All these new emotions battering up against me, swirling around in my head, pushing me backwards...

"You ok?" asked Josh.

I was clinging onto the lamppost, hugging it.

Then my mum's voice in my ear, alerted by Josh's question. "Are you ok, son? Can you cope, do you need me to take you home?"

This was so humiliating. Everyone was hearing this.

"I'm fine, I can cope."

I loosened my grip on the lamppost. I let the wall and the lamppost support me. I let the waves of people's feelings tear into me and over me, and I did cope. But only just.

I concentrated on looking for the target. Lots of the girls walking down the steps looked similar to the girl in the photos, so I was looking at bags too, assuming that however fashion-conscious a girl was, she probably only had one schoolbag.

But I kept being knocked off-balance by the increasing number of kids swarming out of the school, radiating more feelings straight at me.

At least most of the emotions assaulting me were positive. Relief at getting out of school. Pleasure at seeing friends. Excitement about the free hours ahead. There were ripples of sadness from lonely kids and spikes of aggression from boys squaring up to each other. But it was mostly happy feelings slamming into me. That was probably better than an angry crowd or a grieving one.

Then I saw her. So did Josh. He lifted his hand to point at her.

I kicked him. I prefer to kick than hit. With strong boots and thick soles, fewer thoughts get through.

So I kicked his hand down and muttered, "Don't point, you idiot."

Then I said more formally, "Team 4, target spotted."

Because there she was. In the blue coat she'd been wearing in two of the surveillance pictures. With the same stripy schoolbag on her shoulder. Walking down the steps, laughing with a friend.

The target.

"Are you sure?" asked Malcolm.

"Yes," I said.

"Confirmed," said Josh.

"Team 2 confirms sighting," said Becky.

"Then do your job," said Malcolm.

So we did.

Becky and Laura waited until the target got to the bottom step and turned left, then they wandered casually after her.

"Team 2 following," I said quietly.

I checked further down the road and saw Roy glance round at the target.

"Team 3 keeping ahead," Roy said, then he and Sam started walking down the road, kicking an empty can between them.

"Target is following expected route," I said. "Team 3 ahead and Team 2 behind. I'm not sensing suspicion or fear from the target. She's calm and happy."

She was happy. She was chatting to her friend, on her way home from school.

I nodded to Josh and said, "Team 4 heading for the alley."

"Good move, son. Well done," said my mum, carefully not using any names.

Malcolm snorted. "He's not doing anything special, he's just following my plan."

I grinned. My mum was a senior and very loyal member of the family firm, but every time she praised me, it seriously annoyed Malcolm. Her encouragement and Malcolm's irritation gave me the energy to jump off the wall.

As the overwhelming crowd of kids began to thin out, Josh and I turned the opposite way from the other teams.

We were going to sprint right round a large residential block to the other end of the alley our target used as a short cut to her dance studio. However, we didn't want any witnesses saying, "Oh yes I saw a couple of lads running like they'd robbed a bank," so Josh held his jacket loosely in his left hand and I whirled round, grabbed it from him and ran off.

"Hey! Give that back!" And he chased me.

So people just saw a couple of kids fooling around.

As we sprinted round one corner, then another, I knew from the calmness of my family's distant feelings and the silence in my ear that it was all going to plan.

If the target did what she'd done last week and the week before, she'd walk to the next street corner, say goodbye, then as her friend went one way, the target would go the other, through her shortcut.

But then I sensed a jolt of surprise and concern, coming from several cousins at once.

I heard Laura's voice sharp in my ear. "There's a problem."

"What?" asked Malcolm.

"Target didn't turn off at the alley you identified. She's still walking down the road with her friend."

Josh stopped running. I didn't. I turned and beckoned at him. Even if the job was changing, we were no help to anyone hanging about here on the pavement.

"Keep following," ordered Malcolm. "Everyone stick to the plan. She might turn back."

When Josh heard that, his footsteps speeded up behind me. I dropped his jacket and increased my speed. I wasn't going to wait for him.

I could sense his frustration behind me. But I kept running. He wouldn't catch me. Like all my cousins, he's fit, but he got that way by playing football and working out. I just run as often as I can. So I outpaced him easily. Not to win a race, but because I was trying to do my job.

If I remembered the map right, then the target's change of routine might mean my location was more important than originally planned.

I didn't stop at the end of the alley containing the van and Team 1. They didn't really need me. I kept running to the next alley down.

I heard Becky's voice. "They're chatting on the next corner. I think they're saying goodbye. Yes, they're splitting up."

There was a pause, then Roy murmured. "She hasn't turned back. Hold on. She's turned right. She's walking along the next alley down."

"Shit," said Malcolm. "We don't have anyone there."

"Yes, you do," I said. "I'm at the end of that alley. I can grab her and hold her for a few minutes, if you send the second van here."

"Don't you dare, boy! Don't be stupid. You can't handle something that complex. We'll have to pull out and try again later this week."

"No," my mum said. "We can't afford to wait any longer. I'm sure he can do it. Driver 2, get the back-up van there, now. That's an order."

I didn't listen to Malcolm's response. I was going to do this anyway, whether Malcolm and Mum agreed about it or not.

Because I had just seen the target 100 metres away, at the other end of the narrow alleyway.

There was no one else around. I couldn't see anyone. I couldn't sense anyone. It was just her and me.

"I can see her," I said quietly. "I can get her."

41

I stepped into the dark shadow behind a row of wheelie bins and pulled a thin black mask from my jacket pocket.

I waited to do my job. I waited to kidnap a girl.

chapter 6

Ciaran Bain, 28th October

Before I knocked her out and threw her in a van, I'd better be sure this was the right girl.

I recalled the briefing photos. Dark skin. Short neat black hair, almost shaved to her skull. Small ears close to her head. Wide-set brown eyes. Narrow mouth, which had been chatting and smiling in all the photos we had. Perfect brace-straightened teeth. Not tall, but with a dancer's build. No martial arts experience, though, Malcolm had assured us.

Just a girl on her way to a dance class. Walking straight towards me.

I didn't have any doubts at all about what I was doing.

I've had lots of opportunity to look back at the thirty seconds I waited in that alley. And I know that, at the time, I didn't have any doubts at all.

I wanted to be good at my job. I wanted to prove myself to Mum, to Malcolm, to my cousins. To myself.

I didn't think about the girl at all, except to check that she was definitely the target. I didn't think about her feelings, except to check that she was calm as she walked towards me, swinging her stripy schoolbag.

I had no doubts about what I was going to do.

There was silence in my earpiece. No one was arguing now. What was the point? I was either going to do this right or make a monumental mess of it.

I waited.

She was so close I could hear her footsteps.

So close I could hear her breathing.

I pulled on the mask and checked my gloves.

And I stepped out.

I sensed her sudden shock at seeing a masked figure in front of her.

I checked her face. Yes. This was the right girl.

I grabbed her arm with my leather-covered left hand and sensed immediate piercing fear. Before I could buckle under the weight of her terror and before she could get a breath to scream, I aimed my right hand at the side of her neck, just below her ear.

I struck one sharp blow. The girl collapsed.

I held her as she fell, then let her slip gently to the ground. I checked all around. Still no witnesses.

"I have her," I said. "Get the van here *now*."

I dragged her behind the bins and waited for Kerr to drive the van round. He's just turned seventeen and is desperate to prove he's as good a driver as his dad. So he pulled up right beside us, and was out of the cab and opening the back doors in less than a minute.

I picked the target up, holding her close to my chest, which I couldn't have managed if she'd been conscious. I slid her along the floor of the van and climbed in myself. Kerr chucked her bag in, closed the doors and drove off smoothly.

"Target in van," I reported. "Target unconscious and in the van."

Kerr said from the front, "Van proceeding back to base."

I heard Mum's voice. "Well done! I knew you could do it!"

Then Malcolm, less enthusiastic. "Let's see if you got the right girl and if you can get her home in one piece, boys. Radio silence now and everyone back to base."

I took off my earpiece, my mike and my gloves, and settled down for a long ride home.

That's how I killed her.

Chapter 7

Ciaran Bain, 28th October

I killed her because I took off my gloves and started doing my homework.

I knew she hadn't stayed unconscious. I sensed her mind get sharper when she woke up ten minutes after the grab. She tried to slow her terrified breathing, to convince me she was still out cold. She didn't fool me, but I didn't think she was any danger. I could sense her trying to stay calm by thinking rather than panicking. Fair enough. At least she wasn't crying. But unless she could dance her way out of a moving van, she wasn't going anywhere.

So I let her pretend to be unconscious. I stopped concentrating on her and started practising my weakest skill: I started doing my homework by trying to build a wall against other people's emotions.

And I almost managed it. That's why I didn't notice her change of focus until she moved.

Until she leapt across the van and pulled my mask off.

I grabbed at her, my bare hands gripping her arms, pressing against the muscles under her coat, forcing her away from me.

And one of us was screaming. Not her. Not the kidnapped girl locked in a moving van. She didn't start the screaming.

I started it. I was screaming.

That's why I'm useless. I always overreact to other people's thoughts.

I was screaming at her as I held her away from me.

Then she started yelling back at me.

We were both screaming with shock and panic and regrets, screaming right in each other's faces.

I couldn't think while I was so close to her, while I was touching her.

So I dropped her. I opened my hands and dropped her. Then I shoved at her with my boot, pushing her towards the metal wall at the front of the van. She scrambled away from me across the ridged floor.

I stopped screaming, and started thinking again. I realised she still had my mask crumpled in her hand.

I took two steps towards her and leant over her, bracing myself against the van wall, trapping her in the corner. I didn't touch her, but I got as close as I could bear. I whispered, "Don't tell them you saw my face!"

Kerr must have heard our screaming competition from the cab, but he mustn't hear what I was saying now.

The van was slowing down.

"Don't even *think* about seeing my face."

She whispered back, "Why? Will you get into trouble? Do you want *me* to protect *you*?"

"No! You need to protect yourself. If they know you've seen me, they might..."

The van was turning right, slowing even more.

47

She was puzzled, shaking her head.

I held out my hand. It was trembling. I am such a wimp.

She slapped my hand away and I jerked back from her hatred.

The van stopped. I moved nearer to her again and whispered, "Give it back!"

"I'm not giving you anything."

"The mask, you idiot. Give it back."

She shrugged and threw the mask at me.

I fumbled it on, whispering one last time, "Don't think about my face."

The door rattled open.

"What was all that noise?" Kerr was wearing his mask too. "Were you wrestling or snogging or what?"

"She tried to reach the doors. I stopped her. No problem."

I didn't look back at her. I jumped out of the van and walked away. If I didn't think about her pulling my mask off and she didn't think about my face, we might be alright. She might be alright.

So I walked away.

I went to my room to work on my essay on drug smuggling routes.

And I left her to die.

Even on the far side of the warehouse, I sensed the decision. Deciding to kill a target is serious enough for everyone to sense the senior readers' doubt or guilt or excitement. I knew who they must be discussing, so I threw my laptop on the bed and ran out of my cabin.

I ran across the warehouse and crashed into the outer room of the Q&A suite. The door to the inner room was shut, but I could sense the girl's fear thrumming out of it. I'd been trying to ignore her fear when I was writing my essay, but this close it was overwhelming.

Half my family were in the outer room, all in masks for questioning a target. Shit. So she wasn't just a hostage. They'd been questioning her, reading her thoughts as well as her words. She wouldn't have been able to keep anything secret.

"It was just for a second!" I yelled at Malcolm. "Not enough to identify me. And she hasn't seen any of you."

My family can argue without words, but we usually speak out loud, because we all read minds in different ways and at different strengths.

Malcolm answered me. "I saw your face in her head, Bain. Clear as piss in snow."

Kerr pulled his mask off. He was training here today. Apparently I wasn't old enough, or not controlled enough, for the Q&A suite. Kerr said, "I heard your conspiring little voice in her ears. *'Don't tell them. Don't even think about it.'* How stupid can you be? How stupid do you think we are?"

"We already know how stupid Bain is," sneered another voice: Daniel, also training in Q&A, though he's only a month older than me. He stepped towards me, trying to intimidate me with his size. "But we don't know whose side Bain is on. Hers or ours?"

I ignored Daniel. I tried to make a sensible case for not killing the girl. "She's only a teenager, Malcolm. She can't be a threat to anyone. She must have given you whatever information you need, so why don't you just let her go?"

But Malcolm wasn't arguing with me. He was simply

telling me how it was. "Too late, Bain. She's seen you. You made such an impression, she could draw the police a perfect picture of you."

Mum turned round from the keyboard, her frustration and disappointment cutting into me. "Malcolm's right. It's too late. She's too dangerous. Especially to you, Ciaran."

I could keep arguing, but once Mum and Malcolm agree on something, it's inevitable.

There was nothing I could do. It was too late.

I didn't see her again.

I didn't even open the door into the inner room. What would be the point?

I walked away. From Malcolm ordering me to stay, from Mum ordering me to come back. I just walked away.

Her name was Vivien Mandeville Shaw.

She was sixteen years old.

And I killed her.

chapter 8

Ciaran Bain, 28th October

I walked away from her fear and from its inevitable end.

But I couldn't go far dressed like this. I'd leapt off my bed in nothing but jeans, t-shirt and socks. I didn't even have shoes on. I rushed into the changing rooms beside the dojo and gym, to grab a pair of running shoes from my locker.

I was lacing the left shoe when I sensed someone approaching. Someone radiating bewilderment, someone without the business-like certainty of the group in the Q&A.

Roy pushed through the door, looking like a rugby player who's been kicked in the head once too often, all big shoulders, squint nose and confused face.

He's not as dumb as he looks. He's the only one of my cousins who bothers to sit proper exams and he passes them all. But he's such a useless mind reader that he spends a lot of time confused about real life.

"What's going on? There's a horrible feeling and I can't pin it down. Have you done something stupid again, Bain?"

"They're going to kill her."

"Who?"

"The girl we just grabbed. They're going to kill her, any minute now."

"Why are they going to kill her? She's only sixteen. She can't be a player. Isn't she a hostage, someone's daughter or something? Why do they need to kill her?"

"It's my fault, Roy. I let her see my face in the van."

"You idiot. You absolute idiot."

"I know. I was practising blocking emotions and I got it right for once, so I didn't notice her working up the courage to attack me. She pulled my mask off and got such a good look at me that everyone in the Q&A saw me in her head. And my face in her head is a death sentence. I'm getting out of here before it happens."

Both shoes were laced now. I stood up.

"You can't just walk away," said Roy. "Can't we stop them?"

"I did try, but Mum and Malcolm both agree she has to die."

"Can't we go in there, grab her and get away?"

I was shaking my head, when Malcolm's distorted voice boomed through the intercom: "Boys, boys. If you're thinking of doing something heroic, stop it now. I can sense your plotting from here, so you should know that the Q&A door is locked, and all my loyal family are around me. Settle down and get used to it."

Secrets are hard to keep in my family. Conspiracies are difficult to hide.

The intercom buzzed and went silent. Roy and I looked at each other. I shrugged. He sat down and put his head in his hands. He'd been happier when he was confused.

I banged out through the door. I probably still had a few minutes to get clear.

I'd never actually been responsible for anyone's death before, but I'd been on base during a couple of deaths. I'd responded much worse to the targets' terror than anyone else in the family.

So even though I hate being on the streets surrounded by people, I knew it would be better than the moment of someone's death. Especially someone who was so strong in my mind.

As I ran out the side door, I wasn't sure who I hated most.

I hated myself, obviously, because I'm useless. If I hadn't taken my focus off her in the van, she wouldn't have to die.

I hated Vivien, for pulling my mask off. Everyone knows you don't look at your captors' faces if you want to live. Stupid suicidal girl.

I hated my Uncle Malcolm, because he treats me like some crap he's stepped in.

I hated Mum, for giving me this horrendous genetic gift.

I hated Daniel, because he's the kind of son my mum should have had.

I hated Roy, for being so reasonable all the time.

At that moment, I hated pretty much everyone.

So I ran. I just ran away. It's the only thing my dad gave me. A good strong running away gene.

I didn't even know who was going to kill her. Or how. I didn't want to know.

I put as much distance between us as I could, but

I didn't have time to run far enough. So I sensed the moment she went from simple fear to spiralling highs of panic.

She had been afraid before, but she'd been keeping it under control, because she hadn't been afraid enough. She probably thought she'd been as scared as it was possible to be in that van with that weird screaming boy. But now she knew she was about to die.

I didn't know exactly what my family were doing. Perhaps they'd opened the door and she could hear them talking about disposing of her body. Perhaps they'd walked in with a body bag.

I don't know what she heard or saw. But I know what she felt. I sensed all her confusion burn away in the white heat of the one thing that matters. Life, and losing it.

I was walking now. I couldn't run any more. Her terror was making my knees weak. I was reeling all over the pavement, trying not to bang into other pedestrians. I was aware of their emotions, but they barely registered above the terror in my head from the girl in the warehouse.

Then Vivien Mandeville Shaw stopped.

Her terror just cut out. It didn't fade. It didn't stutter. The volume didn't slide away. It just stopped.

She had been the loudest, strongest, most violent emotion for miles around. And then she wasn't. She just wasn't there any more.

I'd felt her die.

For a moment, I felt the freezing silent nothing of death. Just as she felt it, just before her mind switched off.

I wasn't walking any more. My legs had given way. I was sitting on the pavement, propped up by the greasy corner of a chip shop.

Now her terror was gone, I could sense everyone on the street.

I could sense the disgust and curiosity of people staring at me as they went past, probably assuming I was on drugs, or drunk on a Monday afternoon.

I should go back to base now. She was dead. I wouldn't have to feel like that again. Not until next time we found a mole in a people-smuggling chain, or an undercover cop in a drugs gang, or next time someone we questioned started to guess how we knew so much, or I made a mess of my job and condemned someone else to that sudden complete end.

The chip shop wall was digging into my ribs, and I was struggling to breathe, sinking into the river of critical emotions around me. So I dragged myself up and started to walk.

I didn't walk back to base. I staggered towards the nearest peace and quiet, which turned out to be a golf course. I walked past the clubhouse, followed the boundary fence behind a screen of trees between the course and the road, and climbed over a dragged-down section of wire the local kids must use to get in.

Then I headed for a wide tree in a patch of smooth grass. I crouched against the trunk and tried to calm down. A few gently competitive golfers were wandering round the course, but it was less stressful than a busy street.

I took a few deep breaths, and tried to work out what had gone so appallingly wrong with my day.

It wasn't a surprise that my family weren't law-abiding citizens. I'd known that for years.

My family's been in this business since the Second World War. It was my great-grandfather Billy Reid who took us out of the fortune-teller's booth, stopped making an exhibition of himself and started using his skills in other ways. He offered information gathering, bodyguarding and identifying his clients' enemies. Even, for a higher price, getting rid of those enemies.

Spying on the mindblind, for the mindblind.

My family didn't worry about breaking laws that weren't written for people like us. We never explained our methods to our clients. We kept it in the family and trained our own staff, from the nursery up.

But I'm crap at it.

I'm not crap at the reading. I'm stronger and more accurate than any of my cousins. I'm not crap at lock picking, martial arts or any of our other basic skills, either. But I am crap at using those skills in the field, because I can't get close to the targets.

I can't stand being attacked by people's feelings, being ground down by their thoughts. I can't keep my mind on the job when I'm being assaulted by other people's fear and pain. It's not like I care. I don't *care*. I just can't help being crushed by it.

I was trying to learn to handle it, to stop it distracting me at the time or destroying me afterwards. That's what I was practising in the van. Building a wall against Vivien's emotions, so I didn't sense her fear.

So what went wrong?

Easy. I shouldn't have done my homework in the van, and I certainly shouldn't have taken my gloves off.

But no one else in the family would have freaked out like that when she touched them, no one else would have started screaming at the terrified thoughts crashing about in her head: her worries about her family, and had she dropped her phone, and sorry to her gran, and grit on her empty fingers, and a maths test she wouldn't need to revise for if she really was being kidnapped.

I had kept her feelings out, which let her attack me; I had let her thoughts in, which stopped me defending myself. I'd made a total mess of it. But she was the one who died.

Uncle Greg says I can learn to control my overreactions. It's not that I'm useless, he says, it's just that I'm more sensitive.

I've asked him not to say that in class though. The first time Greg said I was 'sensitive', Daniel bought hypoallergenic mascara and sensitive skin make-up remover, and left them on my pillow.

Most of what Uncle Greg says in the classroom is no use to us anyway, because he won't get involved with the illegal aspects of our business.

I already knew I was too sensitive to operate in the real world. People thought I was on drugs when I was out on the street. I had to sit on a golf course to breathe properly.

No one could show me how to cope. Mum found reading easy and enjoyable, so she couldn't understand why I hated it. Uncle Greg saw our skills as a gift and wanted me to share that optimism. Roy was such a useless reader that he couldn't grasp why it affected me so much.

If I couldn't learn to control my overreactions, then I would never be any use to my family. But even though

I was useless, I knew I should head back to base. I didn't have anywhere else to go.

I was about to stand up when I was suddenly aware of sharp and dangerous emotions, newly arrived outside the golf course.

This wasn't honest competition between golfers. This was the intense concentration of a hunter.

Someone was hunting near the golf course.

Who was the hunter? And who was the prey?

chapter 9

Ciaran Bain, 28th October

Who was the prey?

I was the prey. Of course.

Who was the hunter? Daniel. Of course. He was here to catch the little runaway and take me home.

But I wasn't going to let my family use me as a training exercise.

I may be crap at some of this stuff, but I'm not as useless as the mindblind. I was not prepared to be the target in a grab.

Daniel and I are technically the strongest readers in the fourth generation. I can sense emotions over longer distances, but Daniel is better at pinpointing location, which makes him a more efficient hunter. We're both very accurate thought-readers too, but Daniel edges it on points again, because he doesn't scream, faint or throw up when he reads someone's mind.

Also he's taller, bigger, stronger and fiercer than me.

But I've got my dad's running away genes, and I hoped that would help in a chase.

Daniel hadn't sensed my exact location, he was checking out the golf course because I usually run to the nearest green space.

He'd brought a team with him, but I couldn't tell who yet - probably his wee sister Martha, and his sidekicks, Kerr and Sam. Would he have all four Patersons with him too? Would he really expect Roy to join in with the inevitable end of the hunt?

Because I knew what Daniel would do if he caught me. The senior readers wouldn't mind one of us coming home with a few bruises and minor broken bones, if we all learnt a useful lesson. Especially not if I was the injured one. Efficient violence is a skill our family teaches, rather than discourages.

So I needed to get away before they worked out where on the course I was. If I played this right, I might manage to avoid a kicking *and* get back to base before them. I could be lying on my bed like a good boy doing my essay when they all trudged in, having failed today's test.

But I didn't get up and run right away. Once they were closer, I could tell how many cousins were there, and which way I should run.

I might even be able to work out if I could cheat. Because I was unlikely to beat Daniel and the rest of the fourth generation if I played fair.

As they got closer, I counted eight minds, most of them relishing the excitement of the chase. But one familiar mind was anxious and uncomfortable. So Daniel had brought Roy.

Now they were at the clubhouse. Was I worth the cost of eight teenagers playing 18 holes? No, they were going to break in too.

There was a moment of focus as Daniel instructed his troops, then they moved around the fence towards the trees.

I got up. They would find the bent wire soon, and by the time they got in, I needed to be hiding in the tall grass at the edge of the course, not out here in the open. I sprinted towards the fence.

This was a risk: I was running towards cover, where I'd be hidden from their eyes, but I was also running towards their minds, and the nearer I got, the easier it would be for them to sense me.

However, I had a plan. I was going to try an experiment. No, not an experiment, just an idea I'd been considering recently. We can't cover our emotions like we can cover our thoughts, but I'd been wondering if I could deliberately change the emotions I gave out.

Daniel and his team would be searching for prey feelings, victim feelings, possibly even fighter emotions, and the familiar mind of their pathetic cousin.

So all I had to do was pretend to be someone else.

All I had to do was feel like a golfer.

As I ran, I imagined myself starting a round of golf, grasping the club, swinging it. I felt a bit bored, slightly frustrated, mildly competitive.

I made it to the rough without any of my cousins recognising my mind. I dropped to the ground just inside the fence, 100 metres from the broken section. I lay in the long dry grass, feeling smug. I was trying to feel smug like a middle-aged golfer though, not smug like someone getting one over on his cousins.

They were so close now, I could hear Daniel's voice as he bossed them about.

I concentrated on mild golfy thoughts – a ball curving away from me, hole in one, checked trousers – as Daniel sent Martha, Kerr and Sam away from my hiding place, past the clubhouse, and announced

61

he would lead Laura, Becky and Josh in the other direction, towards me. He left Roy, the one Paterson he never trusted, to guard the exit he was sure I was nowhere near.

Then Daniel strode towards me, with three Patersons behind him. And I realised I'd made a massive mistake.

I couldn't stay in the grass feeling like a golfer, because golfers don't lie down when they're playing. If Daniel sensed someone in the rough grass, he'd come over to investigate. Then he'd beat me to a pulp.

So I had to make my mind invisible. I had to stop thinking or feeling at all.

I'm not sure how I did it, but I found the nearest nothing in my head: the dark quiet nothing of Vivien just after she stopped being afraid. Just after she stopped feeling anything. Exactly when her thoughts and feelings switched off.

I dived into the moment of her death.

I joined Vivien in her dark nothing.

So I didn't feel the earth under me, the danger passing me, the grass tickling my nostrils. I didn't feel anything.

Eventually I became aware of just one sensation. The feeling of grit under my fingers. Hard poky dry cold grit.

But my fingers were touching the earth. Soft, slightly damp earth. Not gritty at all.

That tiny difference between Vivien's memories and my surroundings pulled me out of her death.

Then I was lying on the ground again, brutally aware of my heaving stomach and thumping head.

I flexed my mind cautiously. All the good readers – Daniel, Martha, Kerr, Sam - were now too far away to sense me. I'd been hidden in Vivien's death for as long as it took them to walk to the other side of the course.

I could sense other readers too. Further away, outside the fence.

Bloody hell. My uncles. At least three of them.

What were they doing here? Were they judging this as a field exercise? Marking Daniel on his leadership? Or assessing me, to see if I'd lost control completely? I hoped they hadn't detected me trying out forbidden new techniques.

I double-checked. The family were too far away to sense me, as I shivered and retched.

I lay in the grass, wondering what I had just done.

Did I *think* myself dead?

I'd better not do that again. If the sensation of grit on Vivien's fingers hadn't woken me up, I might have shared her death forever.

But it had worked. Daniel had walked right by me without sensing my emotions at all, because at the time I was feeling nothing.

As my head and stomach settled, I sat up. Now I'd better get off this golf course.

Was Roy still guarding the bent fence?

I recognised the nearest mind and grinned.

I wasn't going to cheat. I was going to ask my best friend to cheat for me.

I stood up, put my earthy hands in my pockets and strolled towards the fence.

"Hey mate," I said softly.

"Hey."

"So, what about kneeling down and doing up your shoe, or nipping into the trees for a piss, and letting me past? Accidentally of course."

Roy is the worst reader in the family. He's not

63

bothered about his marks in training exercises, because he's not planning on a career in the family firm. So of course he would let me past.

But I could sense his answer.

He was miserable. He was miserable that he'd been put here, miserable that I'd asked him to break a direct family order, miserable about how he was going to answer.

He didn't have to shake his head for me to know.

"You're choosing Daniel over me?"

"It's not Daniel's hunt. It's Malcolm's hunt."

That made complete sense and no sense at all.

The uncles weren't watching Daniel hunt me. They were hunting me themselves, sending Daniel and his team in like beaters, to flush me out.

Why were the senior readers hunting me? Just because I'd kept going when Malcolm and Mum ordered me to come back? I had no time to wonder. I had to get away.

But Roy couldn't let me past.

Roy's current strategy was to survive our family long enough to get out when he was eighteen. So he couldn't directly disobey Malcolm, not even to help me.

We both knew that he should keep me here and call for back up.

We stared at each other.

We're both readers. He's a useless reader and I'm crap at everything, but you don't need to read minds to know what your best friend is going to do.

I grinned at him. He frowned.

Then I turned my back on him and ran.

I sensed his indecision. Would he yell out, tell them I was here?

No. He smashed through the grass after me. His long legs caught up with me and his hand stretched for the back of my t-shirt.

Then, with perfect timing, he stumbled over his own big feet and thumped to the ground behind me.

I laughed as I ran off. Let Malcolm try and sort that one out. All he'll get is the truth of Roy refusing to let me through, and of Roy tripping and falling when he chased me.

But now I was running *away* from the best exit.

So I ran towards the only other way off the course. The clubhouse.

Then I sensed a thump of recognition. Someone had spotted me.

chapter 10

Ciaran Bain, 28th October

I'd been spotted by Kerr, on the other side of the clubhouse. He must have sensed my confrontation with Roy. Or maybe he'd heard Roy hit the ground like a tree trunk.

I could see him now, running to block my way out. And he was nearer the clubhouse, so I wasn't going to get off this golf course unless I knocked him out of the way first.

I'd already tried to cheat my way out. Now I'd better start fighting dirty.

I stopped running towards the exit and started running straight at Kerr.

This might seem either brave or stupid. But getting a thumping from Kerr would be better than getting a thumping from Daniel, who fights to hurt rather than simply to win. Also there was an even chance I might beat Kerr.

So I ran straight at him.

He stopped beside two elderly ladies in beige trousers and grabbed a club out of one of their trolleys.

The women shrieked. That would bring the rest of the family.

Kerr was standing between me and the exit, and between me and the rest of the women's clubs. In the dojo, he and I were well matched. But now he had a weapon and I had nothing.

Kerr was laid back, grinning at me, hefting the club in his hand. He just had to stop me getting to the exit before Daniel and his team got here.

I slumped and let him drive me back a couple of steps. I was stumbling backwards, carefully feeling almost defeated, but also trying to circle nearer to the clubhouse exit.

Kerr laughed. "I'm not that daft, Bain."

Let's see if you are, I thought as briefly as I could. He swung the club at my head. I ducked to the side and he swung again. Now he was driving me away from the clubhouse, towards the 18th hole.

A couple of men in pink diamonds and yellow stripes yelled from a distance, "Get off the fairway! It's dangerous!"

He swung again. I ducked again. Closer to the hole, closer to the flag.

"Calm down, Kerr. We're attracting attention." I didn't say too much, because he reads by voice rather than touch. As I spoke, I thought of the golfers looking at us, the golf balls aimed at us. I needed him to believe I didn't want to be going in this direction. He swung again and I ducked away.

He was herding me. I'd better resist. I jinked one way, then tried to run the other way.

Kerr lashed out. He'd sensed I was planning something, so he anticipated the change of direction and caught me on the shoulder.

Shit! That *hurt*.

But at least he thought the swerve was what I'd been planning.

And suddenly I was running, away from Kerr and his golf club, towards the 18th hole. I needed him to chase me towards this boring bit of golf course, so as I ran I concentrated on feeling fear, pain, defeat, not on what I was running towards.

I reached the flag poking out of the wee round hole. I grabbed the flagpole and ran round it, hand high on the pole, like using the banister to swing yourself round the bottom of the stairs.

Then I yanked the flag out of the ground.

And aimed it at Kerr.

His surprise was almost comical. He hadn't seen a weapon when I was running towards the flag, he'd just seen a bit of golf landscape.

He was already skidding to a halt on the grass. Shame. I'd hoped he would run straight onto the flag, like a jousting knight onto a lance.

Now we were squaring up to each other. He had a puny little golf club and I had a nice long flagpole.

I jabbed the pole at his chest and he danced out of reach.

He was still confident, because even though my flag would probably beat his club in the end, that wasn't what mattered. What mattered was speed. If I didn't get past him to the exit in the next minute, I wouldn't beat him at all.

Because I could sense the rest of them, closing in. Roy resigned. Daniel angry. The uncles still watching from a distance.

All Kerr needed to do was to keep me here.

He slashed out at the flag, hoping to break it. But I

whirled the pole out of the way of his swing, brought it right over his head and cracked it into his left shoulder.

We were both hyped now. This wasn't a training bout. We were really trying to injure each other.

And my family were getting closer. I needed to finish this fast.

I threw the flagpole up and over, then caught the muddy end. Kerr got in a hefty blow to my ribs while my defence was up in the air, but then I had the red flag under his nose, tickling, teasing.

He bellowed, lifted the golf club over his head and slashed it down, straight at my skull.

I ignored the club, and drove the flagpole towards his chest, shoving him backwards. The club kept crashing down, but he jerked it back as he stumbled and it missed me by a couple of centimetres.

He was off balance. So I held the flag firmly and ran at him. But I didn't aim the pole at his body, I aimed at the ground, and as the tip hit the grass, I forced it deeper, gripped the end tight and let my speed carry me up into the air.

I let go when the flagpole pointed straight up, and I soared towards Kerr. I kicked my left heel solidly into his cheek, and as he screamed and fell away from me, I landed on the smooth fairway grass, found my balance and ran.

I didn't look back. I could sense his disorientation. He didn't know which way was up; he couldn't possibly chase me.

I shouted cheerfully to the two old ladies as I ran past, "He's dropped your club at the 18th!"

But then I saw what was ahead of me.

Sam in front of the clubhouse door, Josh and Martha

standing either side. They were blocking the exit and leaving me out here, exposed, ready for...

Daniel.

Daniel was sprinting at me from my left.

Kerr had done his job: he'd kept me on the course long enough for the ring of cousins to tighten round me.

I swung round to face Daniel.

He was grinning as he slowed to a jog.

I knew what I should do.

I should surrender.

I should give up and give in. I should pretend I thought this was a game. Put my hands up and say, *Well done guys, you got me. Full marks. Now let's go home.*

It wasn't a game, though. It was the next round in a battle Daniel and I had been fighting since we were babies.

It was a chance for Daniel to prove yet again that he was the top dog, that I was the runt.

But if I surrendered, he'd just laugh and lay into me anyway.

So, fight and get beaten up, or surrender and get beaten up. Tough choice.

Daniel could sense my dilemma, my confusion. I could sense his pleasure and anticipation.

He was only a few steps away. Not even jogging now. Just walking. Slowly.

Daniel works out for fun, not just for fitness, so he's building bulgy muscles, which he decorates with tight t-shirts. And he has shoulder-length black hair that he actually thinks looks cool pulled into a pony-tail.

I fixed a picture in my mind of him tying a pink ribbon in his hair, then caught his eye.

He scowled. "Don't play the fool, Bain. My dad

wants a word about that job you ruined. So come on home."

I opened my mouth to say, *Yes. Ok. Fine. I'll come home, just don't hurt me.*

But I could sense his happiness at beating me yet again. He was enjoying his victory already.

So I said, "No. I'm not coming home just because you say so."

He laughed. "Are you going to stay out here with the mindblind, the people who make you cry and faint and puke? Come on home, like a good boy."

"I'll come home in my own time. Why should I do what you say? You're not my boss."

"Not yet."

"Not ever, Daniel Reid."

"No? Your mum might think you can run the firm some day, her clever little reader. But however strong your reading is, Bain, it's no use if you can't get near a target without collapsing. You're never going to run this firm. I'm the next lead reader. And when I'm in charge, you won't have a job. If you can't work with us and you can't live with the mindblind, where will you go?"

I couldn't fault his logic. It was the discussion Roy and I had all the time.

We were circling round each other now.

What was I doing? Even if I beat him - and in a lifetime of bouts in the dojo I had never done that - there were plenty of other cousins near enough to grab me. Was I showing my uncles that I could do something right, even if it was only getting beaten up bravely? But that was damaging the family too. With all the golfers watching, someone must already have called the police. This was just another example of how I was a danger to the family.

The most immediate dangers to me were Daniel's eyes and hands.

Kerr reads by voice, I read by touch, Daniel reads by eye contact. So I couldn't let him look directly into my eyes and see my thoughts.

I couldn't let him grab hold of me either, because if he touched me, I'd get a headful of his vicious thoughts.

I had to beat him quickly, before he got his hands on me or caught my eye.

He's big, but he's fast too. His mum was a martial arts champion in three different disciplines before she married Malcolm. She's tried to be even-handed in teaching us her skills, but Daniel is the one with the most natural talent.

We were still circling. I heard Roy shout, "Stop pissing about, guys. We're too visible, we have to get off this course."

"What a day you're having, Bain," murmured Daniel. "Your first clinch with a girl. Shame it was a wrestling match, not a snogging match. Then your first accessory to murder. And now you're going home for your first..."

My first what?

He'd broken off, because the uncles were coming. We could sense them.

Daniel laughed. "Don't get your hopes up. My dad wants you talking, but he doesn't need you walking. Let's see what I can break before they get here."

Daniel lashed out at my thigh with his right foot. I jumped back.

While he was off balance, I aimed a high kick at

his chest. But I was too tentative, because high kicks against good opponents are risky, so I didn't commit my full weight and I didn't connect.

Damn. A good first shot had been my best chance.

I kicked out at his ankle, hoping to use his higher centre of gravity against him. But he shifted his weight onto the other foot, swung away from my blow and kicked at my thigh again. I jumped away, but even as it glanced off, I could feel the kick's power.

I kicked back, but Daniel was stepping out of range every time I got an angle.

He attacked my thigh again. The same kick, for the third time. Daniel was too arrogant, letting himself get predictable. I swung away from it easily.

And swung right into his trap. He hadn't followed the kick all the way. He'd swung round too, and was waiting for me. He grabbed my bare arm and twisted it with his bare hands.

I collapsed under the weight of his hatred for me and the strobe-lit show of tortures he was imagining as he shoved me to the ground.

He let go of my arm. But I didn't get up. I couldn't. Even ten seconds of the *Ways to Hurt Bain Show* was enough to knock me flat for ten minutes. But I'd read what he was planning next, so I managed to roll up round my face, belly and balls, while he landed thunderous kicks on my back and legs.

At last I could sense the uncles running close enough to see us.

Malcolm was yelling, "Stop, you idiot! I need him conscious!"

Daniel took one more swing, an earthquake of a kick to my left shoulder, then stepped back. "He's all yours,

Dad. I only bruised him a bit. He wouldn't come home when I whistled."

"Get him up."

No! I struggled to my knees. I didn't want anyone else to put their hands on me. I stood up. Then I limped away, like a good boy, between my uncles Hugh and Paul, sensing unfamiliar worries from both of them.

I started to walk to the clubhouse and the car park beyond. But Malcolm snapped, "Not that way, you little traitor, there are CCTV cameras and too many witnesses." So I followed him towards the fence, hardly listening when he told Uncle Phil to wipe or swipe any tapes that could ID us or our vehicles, hardly caring when I heard police sirens in the distance.

In a fog of pain and confusion, surrounded by almost a dozen uncles and cousins, I clambered over the bent wire, fell into the back of a car and was driven home.

Back home to Mummy.

When we got back, there she was, all nail varnish and neat blonde hair. I had sensed her exhausted worry most of the way back from the golf course. But when she saw me come home bruised, bloody and muddy, all I could sense was her irritation. She thinks I'm pathetic.

I fell out of the car. I wanted to crawl over the cold floor to my own cabin in the far corner of the base. But I pulled myself upright and turned to Malcolm, who had driven back in the other car. We hadn't spoken since he'd called me a traitor.

"I was going to come back," I said to his expensively tailored chest. "You didn't need to let the dogs out."

"You disobeyed a direct order. I had every right to send them out."

"Now I'm back. And I have every right to go to my room and have a shower."

Except I didn't have any rights at all. Not in this family. Not unless Malcolm said so.

He shook his head. "We have questions for you, Bain. We needed answers a couple of hours ago. You denied us those answers by throwing a tantrum and running off. So get your arse over to Q&A and start opening your nasty little mind to your Uncle Malcolm."

Chapter 11

Ciaran Bain, 28th October

So that was the other 'first' Daniel had meant. My first time in the Q&A suite. But probably not for my first training session.

Malcolm laughed at my hesitation. "It's ok. You won't see her dead body in there. We dumped her behind the bins in the alley, with a snapped neck and a ransacked bag, like the victim of a random attack. You won't ever have to see her again."

Except I saw her every time I closed my eyes.

I didn't want to be dragged to the Q&A suite, so I limped the length of the warehouse, followed by everyone who'd just been hunting me.

The cousins were calming down after the chase and the fight, but the uncles were still anxious. Why? What was worth all this fuss?

When I stumbled into the Q&A suite, Malcolm turned to the line of cousins behind me. "Off you go to the gym and train harder, so next time I set eight of you on one puny target you don't make such a song and dance of catching him."

Daniel was horrified that his dad had criticised him publicly. I got a blast of his resentment and hate, before he marched off. He'd give me an even more serious hammering next time he found me alone.

But I wasn't alone now. I was in the Q&A suite, standing in the white outer room, facing nearly all the senior readers.

Malcolm. Mum. Phil. Hugh. Not Paul, he was with Kerr in the first aid room. Not Susan, she'd never liked questioning. And none of the aunts and uncles by marriage. They'd brought money, martial arts, contacts or surveillance expertise to the Reid family, but none of them could read minds. So none of them worked in the Q&A suite.

Malcolm gestured to the darkened room beyond. I tried not to panic. Surely he didn't want me to go in there?

I sensed his desire to humiliate and punish me. But I stayed where I was, looking at the floor. It was the safest place to look.

Because I also sensed Mum come over all mother tiger, protecting her cub.

She stood at the door to the dark room, arms folded. "No, Malcolm, that's not necessary. Do my son the courtesy of asking him a straight question and you will get a straight answer."

Malcolm was equally determined. "That's what I would have done, if your son had been available to give me answers when we needed them. But he disobeyed my direct order when he left base. I need to know what he's hiding."

"Then look in his eyes, Malcolm, and ask him here. You don't need to scare him or torture him. You just need to ask him."

I was still looking at the floor. I didn't want to go

through that door and be strapped to that chair. But I wasn't going to beg.

I didn't need to. I had my Mum to beg for me.

Malcolm stood in front of me. "Bain, look at me."

This was the dangerous bit.

Malcolm, like Daniel, reads by eye contact. If you want any privacy without covering your thoughts, which takes a lot of effort, you can't look my uncle in the eye.

It's even harder to hide what you're thinking from others in the family, like Kerr, who can read thoughts from a voice. That's useful on surveillance, because voice readers don't have to touch a target or catch their eye, they just need to be near enough to hear the target's voice. But compared to readings with eye or skin contact, their pictures aren't as strong, their reading isn't as specific and accurate.

Now I had all the skills facing me. Mum reads by touch, Malcolm reads by eye, Phil and Hugh read by voice.

This had happened to all of us as kids. Who broke the TV? Who broke Josh's leg? How much did those trainers cost? Asked a direct question by a senior reader, with your wrist grasped, or your eyes held, it was impossible to hide anything. They would detect a cover go over and demand you take it down. And if you tried to think a lie, you had to build the lie round the truth.

None of us has ever managed to lie to our family when asked a direct question.

So I knew that whatever answers Malcolm wanted, Malcolm would get. Particularly because, unlike the time Roy and I broke Josh's leg trying to see if it really is possible to get out of a bedroom window using sheets tied together, I didn't know what I'd done wrong. I didn't know what I should be covering up.

I still hadn't looked up at Malcolm's eyes. But he already knew I was scared of that dark room, and we all knew Mum was determined to keep me out of it.

Malcolm needs my mum. He's the boss of the family firm, but she's the brains. She's developing techniques to make sense of the confusing information we gather when we read people's minds. It's possible to read a clear word or picture yet totally misunderstand what that word or picture means to the person you're reading. Mum says it's like getting a screen grab, without being able to access the hard drive.

However, Mum is excellent at taking what everyone in a team reads and senses, putting it all together and drawing the most likely conclusions, so Malcolm can't antagonise her unnecessarily. That's probably the reason I haven't been thrown onto the streets, or thrown out of a window, already.

She was standing her ground. She wanted me questioned *here*, not in the inner room.

Malcolm nodded. "Alright, Ciaran. We'll do this here. But if I detect any attempt to cover your thoughts or to lie to me, then I will have you in that chair in that room before you can draw breath."

Mum pulled an office chair into the middle of the room.

"This is informal," said Malcolm. "He doesn't need to be tied down."

She shrugged. "I'll have to touch him, Mal. He won't be able to stand."

I could sense her embarrassment. I am embarrassing. Weak. Sensitive. A wimp. Her only son, and I don't live up to any of her expectations.

Malcolm frowned. "Sit."

I sat. Malcolm crouched in front of me. Mum stood behind me. Hugh and Phil stood either side.

Malcolm ordered, "Eyes!" and I did what I hardly ever do. I looked straight into my Uncle Malcolm's bright blue eyes.

Mum laid her hand on my left shoulder. I tensed. She had woven a cover round her thoughts. Maybe she hoped that would help me cope, or maybe she was hiding something from me.

But she was so close, her emotions overwhelmed me. Her immediate worry about this job, her anger at how Malcolm treats me. Her love for me, which always makes me squirm.

I was moaning already.

"Don't be such a wimp!" snapped Malcolm. "Concentrate!"

I nodded.

"I need to know about the girl," he said. "We killed her this afternoon because she could identify you, then we realised we didn't have the whole story. Even with us team-reading and your mother putting it all together, something vital might have slipped through. But it was too late to ask her again, because we'd already killed her, which was entirely your fault. Then Kerr told us you'd communicated with her during the grab. If you read anything else from her, you can repair the damage you did. So tell me about the girl."

He stopped. My turn.

"What? What do... you need to... know?" I gasped.

Mum was so proud of me for trying, but so embarrassed that it was such an effort.

"Did she talk to you?"

I nodded, but couldn't force any words out.

I felt Mum's hand tighten on my shoulder. My pain was hurting her. We were making each other worse.

I couldn't think properly, couldn't put sentences together, when someone was so close to me. I shoved Mum's hand off. I pushed tears out of my eyes and into my hair with the back of my hand, trying to hide them.

"Can't you read him without me, Malcolm?" Mum was almost in tears too.

"You're the best at joining the dots, Gill. We need you to see what's in his head."

"I have an idea," I whispered quickly, before my mum put her hand on me again. "If that girl said or thought something the client needs to know, I do want to fill in the gaps. I can't do it like this though. If I have to think and remember and talk and feel Mum on my shoulder, all at the same time, I can't give coherent answers. I can't even breathe. But I'm not a target who mustn't know you're reading my mind, so you don't need to hear it in words. You can just read me while I remember what happened."

I sensed Mum's pride. I was trying to overcome my weakness and she appreciated it.

Malcolm nodded.

Mum put her hand on me again. I gritted my teeth. She was willing me to cope. I didn't want to let her down. I tried to sit still. I tried not to scream. I kept staring at Malcolm.

"Remember everything," said Malcolm.

And I did. I had far too much of Vivien Mandeville Shaw in my head, so I spewed her out. Everything she did. Everything she said. Everything she thought. Every mistake I made.

I remembered everything from the moment she grabbed the mask and I grabbed her. I ignored myself screaming inside my own head and concentrated on her. She was yelling back, but fighting too. Pushing, pulling, struggling.

Did she do that? I didn't notice at the time. I was holding her too tight. She was trying to get away and I didn't even notice.

She was screaming, "Let go!" She was thinking it too. *Let go, you horrible boy*. Horrible boy? I suppose I am. Crap at my job. Sensitive. A wimp. And horrible.

She was demanding that I let her go. She was fighting. I was holding her away from me and screaming at her.

In the van, I was freaking out. But in the Q&A, I was remembering every detail. I felt like I was being battered inside my own head, but I could do this. I could remember this for my family, for the client. I wasn't completely useless.

I was finding all her chaotic thoughts in my memory. Thoughts which had been crashing into each other, breaking off halfway through...

She was worrying about her phone. She knew it was stupid to worry about a phone when she was being kidnapped, but had it fallen out of her coat pocket or was it safe in her school bag...?

She was thinking that unless I let her go soon she wasn't going to get a chance to revise for her maths test tomorrow. Then she laughed inside her head, because she was going to ace the test anyway, so it was a bit unnecessary to get kidnapped just to avoid revising.

All of a sudden, she was afraid: a deeper darker fear than her present fear of me and the van, but a fear she only half admitted, a threat she didn't want to believe in.

A sudden avalanche of jumbled memories. Old boxes, new newspapers, arguments and promises, ambulances and tears.

Then a single solid memory. She was remembering saying bye bye and sorry to her nana, and putting a black-and-gold vase in a cardboard box, and I felt grit on her fingers, harder and darker than the...

Then she was thinking about her family. She hoped her little sister wouldn't come and meet her after dance class, wouldn't walk along that suddenly dangerous alley...

She thought about her mum and dad and how worried they would be. She nearly lost it, nearly burst into tears. Then I dropped her.

"Again!" Malcolm ordered. "Run it again!"

So I dragged it out of me, again and again, for Malcolm.

Her courage, her stupidity. The mask. The maths test. The vase. The sister. The age we screamed at each other.

I sensed my mum's concentration and her disappointment at my mistakes. I sensed the uncles all around me, Hugh and Phil digging into my moans, Malcolm piercing my eyes. I felt Vivien in my head screaming and worrying about her family. And my family round me, forcing me to open myself wider than I could bear.

I know I screamed for them to stop. I know they didn't stop.

Malcolm stared at me, yelling, "Keep your eyes open, boy! Don't you dare close your eyes at me!" I forced my eyes wide.

I twisted in the chair. My mum's hand stayed on my

shoulder, sending waves of searching into me. Ripping through me. Slicing me apart.

I gave them everything. I didn't try to keep anything back. I didn't know what to keep back. I didn't care anyway. I had no one to protect, nothing to fight for.

I gave them the feeling of my mask in her fist. The pressure of my fingers on her arms. The grit under her nails. The way she looked at me when I asked her not to think about my face.

I gave them everything. Even the moment I walked away and left her to die.

Then I threw up. Malcolm must have seen it coming. He leapt out of the way. But it splashed onto Hugh's shoes.

Suddenly it was over.

Mum let go. Malcolm turned away.

The four readers nodded together for a moment. I sensed relief from them, a release of fear.

"That's enough, Ciaran," said Mum. "I know you gave us everything. I think it's enough. Thank you and well done."

Malcolm threw me a towel. "Clean up after yourself."

They walked out and left me. Shivering, retching, with a floor to clean.

chapter 12

Ciaran Bain, 30th October

I leaned against the desk in the Shaws' study. I rubbed my shoulders, then fumbled in my jeans for chewing gum. The Q&A had been more than 24 hours ago, and I'd brushed my teeth a million times since, but I still couldn't get the taste out of my mouth. And I couldn't forget Mum's grip on my shoulder, forcing me to remember.

I weighed the flash drive in my hand. I wrapped my fingers round it.

Yes. This was what Vivien's gritty fingers had felt empty of. This was what she'd hidden in the urn.

I stood up straight, and brought my mind back to the present, checking on the surveillance team outside and the family above me.

Only two minds were active upstairs now. Lucy, cycling from anger to grief to curiosity to impatience to anger again, and a half-awake parent drifting off and jerking awake with renewed horror every couple of minutes.

I searched the study shelves, hoping I could find an address book and get out before both parents were asleep and Lucy came downstairs to either accompany me or try to deceive me. I didn't find anything useful. So I turned the computer on, but there was no file with family addresses, not even a Christmas card list.

Lucy Shaw, 30th October

What was I doing?

Had I really suggested sneaking off in the middle of the night with a boy I didn't know? With a boy who had broken into my house?

What was I thinking?

I would admit, though not to his face, that he might be almost cute. With that blond hair, smooth tan and silver-blue eyes.

He might be *almost* cute. Apart from the fact that he killed my big sister.

Whatever he looked like, it wasn't wise to head off into the night with him. It wasn't safe, it wasn't sensible. But what was the point of playing safe? Vivien was always sensible and safe, top marks and gold medals. Look what happened to her. Maybe I had to take a few risks, in order to find out what this boy did to Viv, and to make sure he got the punishment he deserved. If violence and crime and death could find Viv on the way to her flamenco class, then I wasn't safe anywhere, and hiding from it wouldn't help. Perhaps I needed to go out there and face it.

I leapt under the duvet when I heard Dad's feet on the stairs, rolled over so my back was to the door, and tried to breathe more slowly. My heart was racing, but he wouldn't hear that.

The door creaked open. He tiptoed in and put his

cold outdoor hand on my forehead. He murmured something. I tried not to listen, in case it was more sentimental nonsense.

As he walked out, I heard him sniff. I have tissues by my bed, the ones with lotion to stop your skin peeling when you're wiping your nose a lot, like when you've got a bad cold or someone has murdered your only sibling. I blew my nose quietly and wiped my eyes.

I heard them both go to the loo and brush their teeth, then they went to bed. Once they stopped whispering, I got up again.

I found my darkest clothes: black jeans; dark top, inside out so the picture on the front didn't show; black Converse, which I hadn't cleaned recently, so the white bits were all muddy; and the navy hoodie Mum hates because she thinks it makes me look like a criminal.

I tied my hair back, then grabbed my keys and purse out of my bag, and put them in my pockets.

I picked up my phone and looked at it. I should just dial 999 right now. I slid it into my back pocket. I could dial 999 any time I liked. Any time I thought he was holding out on me or a danger to me.

I opened my door and sneaked downstairs. I heard a sob from my parents' room. Mum was still awake. But I didn't turn back. I hoped the boy could hear her crying, then he might stay hidden for longer.

Because I'd changed my mind about teaming up with a murderer. I'd decided to do this myself. I would walk right past the study, keep going silently to the back door and get out on my own.

If I ran all the way to the centre of Winslow and all the way home, perhaps I could get back with the urn and whatever it contained before he realised that I'd left without him.

I wasn't keen on leaving him here with Mum and Dad, but I was even less keen on taking him to Grampa's house, like Red Riding Hood escorting the wolf to her granny's.

The study door stayed closed as I sneaked past. I smiled. He wasn't that smart, then.

I tiptoed through the kitchen, then into the extension, heading for the back door.

And he grinned at me.

He was standing there, his arms folded, a self-satisfied smile on his face. Blocking the back door.

"Sneaking off?" he whispered. "Without me?"

I shrugged.

His grin got wider. "Don't ever try to deceive me, Lucy. I'll always be one step ahead. And how were you planning to get past the police?"

I wasn't convinced anyone was out there, but I didn't say that. "I have a perfect right to walk out of my own house."

"In the middle of the night?"

I shrugged again.

"There are four police out there now," he whispered, "because two more followed your parents home. I can't get both of us past that many. Even though you're little and skinny, you still don't look enough like a stray cat to sneak past them."

He thought I looked like a skinny stray cat? What an arrogant prat. "Of course I can get past them. I'm half your size and I don't glow in the dark." I pointed to his golden face and pale hair, then my dark skin and black hair.

He took a thin black hat from his pocket and pulled it over his face. Not a hat, a balaclava.

I shivered. He suddenly looked really scary. Not cute at all.

But I said, as calmly as I could, "Terrorist chic. What else do you have? Machine gun? Bomb?"

He pulled the mask up, leaving it lumpy on his forehead. "No. But I am tooled up for this and you aren't."

"What tools will get you past the police? Poison darts? Sleeping gas? How did you get past them on the way in?"

"I can move with the dark, blend into the background, that sort of thing. But it's too risky for you to try to sneak out. If they see you, they'll just get more suspicious of your family. And I've got a better chance of getting past them on my own, without you trailing behind me."

"No. You've got a better chance of getting past if you take me with you."

"Oh yeah? Why? Have you got magic invisibility wellies?"

"No. I've got a way out of the garden. Are they watching the whole street, or just our garden gates and walls?"

He looked like he was concentrating, listening to something. He couldn't *hear* people out there, could he? Maybe he was delusional, maybe he thought he had superpowers.

"There are two watching your front gate and two watching the back gate, but they can probably see right up and down both the street and the lane. There isn't any way out but my way, and you can't do my way."

He was so sure of himself. I wanted to show that he wasn't the only one who could sneak about at night.

"There is another way. Next door's shed backs onto the side of our garden, like it's part of our fence, and there's a loose plank. We can go through their shed, into their garden, then over their low wall into the next garden and so on until the end of the block. See, local knowledge beats criminal experience every time!"

He smiled at me. "Ok! That's good. Can you show me?"

We opened the back door and crept into the sharp outdoor air of the garden. Then I realised we would be visible from the front when we were crossing the grass to the shadows by the shed.

"Getting across the grass..." I whispered.

He nodded. "I'll distract the team at the front. You get to the shed as fast as you can, then stay low and small at the base of it." He pulled his leather gloves on and his balaclava down, then leant close to me. "Wait for me at the shed, Lucy. Don't go without me."

I nodded, and crept to the corner of the extension.

Then I heard the familiar hollow thud of a wheelie bin overturning and a cat's yowl. I sprinted across the grass. I reached the shed wall and crouched down, breathing hard. Not from the run, but from the excitement and adrenaline.

Where was he? Was he still at the other side of the house, playing skittles with bins? No, he was back at the corner already, looking towards the road.

I followed his gaze. I saw a car parked in the street and two people who had just leapt out of it. A woman from the driver's side and a man from the passenger's side, both looking over to our driveway. The man was shaking his head, speaking into a mobile phone, then he got back into the car.

The boy was right. There *were* police outside my house.

I was shielded from the car by the plants in the flowerbed. But how was that boy going to get across the open grass? Did he want me to create a distraction for him?

Before I could signal a question to him, he vanished.

He just vanished.

Not into a puff of smoke. Not swirling a cloak round himself.

Just gone.

It wasn't completely dark. I could see the flowerbeds in the front garden, and the patio tables and the fruit bushes at the back. But even though I knew he must be somewhere, I couldn't see him.

I spent about ten minutes watching the deep grey shapes for movement or a silhouette, then suddenly he appeared behind me. How had he got there?

He was good. Scary. But good.

"You waited. Sensible. Now show me this secret way through the shed."

"You show me how you did *that*!"

"No. Trade secret. You wouldn't have the patience to learn. Or the incentive."

"Why not?"

"Because you haven't spent most of your life scared out of your..." He stopped and bit his lip.

Aw. Poor thing. There must be a hard luck story there, some sort of Jacqueline Wilson family disaster. But I wasn't going to give him the satisfaction of asking him.

He grinned. Like he knew I wanted to know. Sod him.

"Show me the way, Lucy."

I ran my hands over the planks at the base of the shed. I don't play Amazon warriors or spies or cat burglars any more, so I haven't been in the shed for years. I was hoping Mr Nicolson hadn't nailed the plank down recently. I'd look like a total idiot in front of this boy if the plank didn't move. Or if either of us was too big to fit through.

He was a bit taller and wider than me. More like a leopard than a skinny stray cat. Or a mountain lion, with that blond hair. But even with his leather jacket on, he wasn't bulky. If I could still fit through, he probably could too.

Then I found the right plank.

It's an old shed. Not a garden centre prefab job, but built from planks nailed together. Clinker built, Uncle Vince says, like a ship, overlapping to make it solid and watertight.

But the plank third from the ground was only nailed at one corner. It was secure unless you pushed at it but, when we were small, Viv and I discovered we could swivel it up inside the shed. Then it stayed up, friction and the tight nail holding it steady against the upper planks, so we could post ourselves like letters through the gap.

I pushed slowly and gently. Surely it used to move more easily than this? Then I remembered. When I was about ten and still playing games in the garden, but Viv had pretty much stopped, the nail at the top corner worked loose and the plank kept slipping down and hitting me as I went through. So my big sister crept into the shed and used Mr Nicolson's own hammer to tighten in the nail again.

Vivien did that for me. I can't remember if I said thank you to her. I can't even remember the last thing I said to her on Monday morning. The last thing I ever said to her...

"Concentrate, Lucy," the boy whispered behind me. "Concentrate on this just now. If you get too upset, we won't be able to find the urn."

Was my grief that obvious? Even in the dark? With my back to him? I hadn't sniffled, had I?

I put more pressure on the plank and it slid round like the hand of a clock moving from 9 to 12, vanishing inside the shed.

I didn't want him to go first, in case he got stuck and blocked my way. So I slid through, head first. I landed awkwardly, just in front of the ancient lawnmower. The shed smelt familiar: sweet grass, old oil and rusty nails.

I rolled out of the way. Then, in the dim streetlight coming through the shed windows, I watched as the boy's shape came through like a Chinese dragon, all coils and smooth twists.

He didn't land on the floor. I don't know how he did it, but he didn't even get his jacket dusty, and he was standing straight while I was still pulling myself up on the handles of an old filing cabinet.

He turned round and eased the plank down. "Good escape route. You must have had fun when you were wee! Now, when we leave the shed, follow me exactly and don't say a word."

"You're not the boss," I objected.

"Yes I am. How many houses have you broken into?"

"None. I only break into sheds."

"So I'm the boss, because I have more experience. Be quiet and follow me."

I didn't think a background as a burglar was something to boast about, but I decided not to argue. The more information he gave me about his background, the more evidence I'd have against him. So I nodded.

He pushed the shed door open slowly, slower than a snail moves. He can't have broken into that many houses if he always does it in slow motion. He laughed softly. "Don't be so impatient. Rushing leads to mistakes."

"Just get on with it, Obi Wan."

But I'd worked out how he'd moved invisibly in the garden. It wasn't magic, he just moved so slowly that anyone looking for him was bored to death.

Then he slipped out through the door and I followed. We ran round the back of the Nicolsons, over their wall into 27, round their greenhouse and into 25 and 23. Eventually we clambered over the railings onto Swan Road. We crouched on the pavement.

He pulled his balaclava off and grinned at me. "Scared yet?"

"That was fun!"

"It's even better if you're being chased. So, which way to your grampa's?"

"Oh no. Now you follow me. Now I'm the boss."

chapter 13

Lucy Shaw, 30ᵗʰ October

Now I was the boss, I started running towards the town centre. I heard him whisper behind me, "Slow down..."

But I kept running. Actually, I accelerated. It wasn't my fault if he couldn't keep up.

Then he grabbed me.

He yanked on my sleeve, swung me round and pushed me against the wall. Then he stepped away quickly, like I was toxic or something.

"Slow down!"

"Why? Am I going too fast for you?" Football training keeps me pretty fit. Maybe he really couldn't keep up.

"Running is too obvious. Witnesses remember people running. Walking is safer, so walk briskly. And from now on, please do exactly as I say, or you'll get us both arrested."

Getting him arrested was entirely my plan, but not yet. So I walked. He stayed two steps behind, which suited me. We turned a few corners and crossed a few deserted streets, then as we walked under a streetlight, he stepped in front of me, walking backwards. He looked at me, my face, my hair, my clothes, then he frowned.

I kept walking, straight at him, faster forwards than he was backwards. He sidestepped and started walking beside me. But not too close.

"You look different."

"From when?" Had he been watching me? Stalking me?

"From earlier. In the house. Your hair. It's not as..." He paused.

Yeah. My hair is getting a bit out of hand. It's either turning into a political statement, a 70s retro look or a thorn bush, depending on whether you're my grampa, my friends or my mum. And when I get out of bed, it is wild.

Now my hair was tied back, I must look different.

He was still staring. "You look older. How old are you?"

"Fourteen."

"Fourteen! You're never fourteen!"

"Yes, I am."

"Just turned fourteen?"

"No, I've been fourteen since the summer. Since June."

He frowned again.

Then I got it. "How old are *you*?"

"Fourteen. As well."

"Uh huh. When were you fourteen?"

He shrugged. "Last month."

"September! September the what?"

"September the none of your business. You don't want to know *anything* about me."

"Ha! I already know something. I already know I'm *older* than you!"

"Not by much."

96

"By enough."

"I'm bigger though. Bigger, faster, stronger. And scarier."

We'd stopped walking. We were glaring at each other across the width of the pavement. Any minute now we'd be arm-wrestling or seeing who could spit further.

"You're not scarier! You should be scared of me. I'm the one you confessed to. I'm the one who can get you arrested."

"That's why you should be scared of me, Lucy."

"I'm not scared of you," I said firmly. I started walking again, towards the centre of Winslow, which isn't the centre of much. But it's got shops, a cinema, a library, a police station.

I turned left and took us away from the centre again.

"You're doubling back, Lucy. Are you double-crossing me?"

"I'm avoiding the police station."

"Ok, lead on."

Once I'd worked out a different route, I said, "My turn now."

"What?"

"You've asked lots of questions. Now it's my turn. What's your name?"

"I can't tell you my *name*! I need to find what I'm looking for, then vanish."

"You said I could call the police and put them on your trail once you had your secret."

"You can try. But I run faster than any middle-aged policeman, and once I'm out of sight, if they don't have my name, my date of birth or any other personal information, they'll never find me."

"But what can I call you?"

He raised his eyebrows. "You could call me Boss."

"No way! Burglar Bill perhaps, or some other codename."

He jerked back from me suddenly. Then he laughed. "Ok. Whatever. Call me whatever. I'll be gone as soon as we've found the urn anyway, so you can call me whatever you like."

I shrugged and led him safely towards the town centre from the east side, heading for the car park beside the shopping centre.

I knew I should be leading him straight to the police station. He had killed Viv, or helped someone else kill her. Why wasn't I turning him in?

Did I really believe in the big scary man who would attack us all if this boy didn't take his little secret away? Did I even believe this boy had killed Viv?

I wasn't sure what I believed.

He seemed to have far too much information about our family, and he had skills they don't teach at school: criminal sneaking about, kicking knives out of people's hands, second-guessing what everyone was doing.

He was weird. He was scary. But was he a killer? Despite his confidence and his bossiness, compared to most boys at my school he was polite and reserved. He never even came close to me - except when he was attacking me, obviously - like he didn't want to invade my space. And he claimed he was protecting my family by taking away this secret.

Was he dangerous? I didn't know. So I should stay with him until I had more answers.

He coughed, to get my attention. "Where does your grampa live?"

"I'm not telling you until we get there."

"I need to know *before* we get there, so I can look out for another surveillance team."

I sighed. "We're a couple of minutes away. He's in the flats just up from the library." I marched on, across the empty car park.

"Stop!" he hissed.

I stopped. I didn't want him to grab me again. "What?"

"Is your grampa's flat in that red block on the corner?"

I nodded reluctantly. We could see the top two floors over the low shopping-centre roof.

He took the lead. I was following again. I'd given away all my power when I told him where we were going.

Instead of crossing the open car park, he walked briskly to the shopping centre, then moved slowly under the shadowy cover of the jutting roof. When we reached the corner he peered round to get a view of the street and of Grampa's door diagonally across the T-junction.

He nodded and eased back. "Someone's watching his flat too."

"How do you know?"

He gestured. "Look."

I peered round and saw a car, with someone sitting in the driver's seat, parked on the other side of the road opposite Grampa's front door.

I stepped back. "You're right. But how did you know, before you looked?"

He stared at me and flexed his fingers in his stupid gloves. "It's obvious. If they're watching your house, they'll be watching his too." He glanced round again. "This guy's on his own. Even so, it's not going to be easy to get in that front door. Is there another door?"

"There's a back door. But there might be someone watching the back too."

"There isn't. Em. I don't think there is. This guy is here alone, waiting for the police who followed your parents to come back. At least, that's what makes sense."

I thought it was a hugely dangerous assumption. But if he wanted to take the risk, that was fine by me.

"How do we get to the back door?" he asked.

"There's a lane further up the street." I pointed to an entrance before the next block of red-brick flats.

"That won't work. The bloke in the car has a clear view of the lane. Are there any other access points to the back?"

"*Access points?* Do you mean 'ways in'? Access points! You're not training to be a health and safety consultant are you?"

But he was already turning away from me.

"Hold on." He looked round the corner. "He's on the move."

"How did you...?" I was starting to wonder about all the things he knew before he looked, but I didn't ask any more.

I knelt down and looked round the corner too. I saw a tall man in a suit shut the car door and walk towards the lane.

"He's checking the back," said the boy. "Follow me."

He sprinted along the front of the shopping centre to the flower shop opposite Grampa's flat. I followed as fast as I could.

He crouched in the doorway of the shop and gestured for me to do the same. "Just in time," he grinned, pulling his balaclava down.

From our position in absolute darkness, I saw the policeman emerge from the lane and return to his car.

"That was too close," I hissed once the car door had thudded shut. "He could have come out when we were still running."

"We had time. He went round to check no one was going in the back door. Surely that was obvious."

"It wasn't obvious to me!"

"That's why I'm the boss. And the next time he checks the back, we'll go in the front."

Then he shut up. Just closed up. Crouched there, utterly still and utterly silent.

I copied him. Still and silent.

We waited.

Soon my left foot was getting pins and needles. My nose was itchy. My right knee was cramping up.

But as my eyes adjusted to the dark, I could see he wasn't twitching a muscle. Musical statues was clearly another of his criminal skills. So I stayed rock-still too, biting my tongue, clenching my fists, digging my nails into my hands.

Then he laughed, very quietly.

"What?" I whispered.

"It's not a competition! If you need to move, it's ok to move. We're in the dark, he's in the light. He can't see us. Anyway, if you get cramp, you'll seize up when we run. So find a comfier position and stop trying to out-macho me."

I flexed one foot at a time and rolled my shoulders. When I wasn't so uncomfy, I started wondering if the wreaths for Viv's funeral were already being made up in the shop behind me.

"Any minute now," he interrupted my thoughts. "Get ready."

Then the policeman got out of the car, walked across the road and into the lane.

We jumped up and sprinted across the road. When we reached the door I dug about in my pocket for the keys. But the boy grinned at me and pushed the door with his foot. "It's not locked."

We both stepped inside, closing the door quietly behind us. And I walked up the stairs, not sure if I was protecting my family or betraying them by leading this boy to my grampa's flat on the first floor.

Feeling like a traitor, I unlocked the door and let the wolf in.

chapter 14

Ciaran Bain, 30th October

So I walked into the second Shaw house of the night. I hadn't heard of this family three days ago, now I was on a guided tour of their residences.

I knew far more about the Shaws, their past and their connection to my family than this girl could ever guess. But I hadn't found out about them in a briefing. I'd had to find out for myself.

Ciaran Bain, 29th October

I'd been desperate to prove I could bounce back after my mistake with the mask, my thrashing by Daniel and that brutal Q&A by my mum and uncles. So when we were called for another briefing the next morning, I turned up all showered and combed and shiny.

Malcolm, the great mindreader, must have been thinking about something else, because he spluttered coffee all over his laptop when he saw me come into the briefing room.

"Bain! What are you doing here?"

"I'm working. I thought the briefing was for everyone."

"You actually think you're working again today, after the almighty mess you made of yesterday?"

I looked round at my cousins. "They're working and they made a mess of yesterday as well. They took far too long to grab one puny target, remember?"

I didn't meet Daniel's eyes, but I sensed his growl of anger.

Mum swivelled round from her computer. "Why shouldn't he go, Malcolm? He didn't make a mess of everything yesterday. He did extremely well on the grab, much better than you expected, right up to his mistake with the mask. And we need everyone on this job, so we can track this undercover cop in Georgie's supply chain, then get back to our main job. So why shouldn't Ciaran go?"

"Because he's a danger to himself and everyone else."

"Nonsense. He'll be fine on a simple job like this."

All the fourth generation were looking at their shoes, pretending not to notice the bosses having an argument.

"No, Gill. Yesterday he wrecked an essential grab, he ran away and he fought with his family in public."

"Yes, he ran and he fought, showing more initiative and guts than you ever give him credit for. Then when you dragged him home, he showed his loyalty by answering all your questions. He's the most talented and sensitive reader in the fourth generation. The family needs to train him, not sideline him or destroy him."

"Talented? He *screams* when he touches a target. What use is that?"

I wanted to hide under the desk. I could sense everyone's contempt past my own burning embarrassment.

But Mum kept on and on. "I am working on it. Greg is working on it. Ciaran is working on it."

"You're not working on it fast enough. He's a danger to any job, however simple. He may have some talent, but he has no control. He can't read anything important without throwing up or sobbing like a baby. We can't draw attention to ourselves like that. Ours is a quiet subtle skill, not a performance."

"He won't get better without practice. Put him on this job, Malcolm."

"But, Auntie Gillian, what if we have to terminate the target?" Daniel asked smoothly. "What if Bain goes gooey again about being close to a death?"

I stepped forward. "Bring it on, Daniel. I've tracked targets before. We've terminated targets before. I'll do it again. I'm not questioning our methods."

Malcolm slammed his laptop shut. "But we're questioning your skills, Bain. Every time we set you practical tests, you fail spectacularly. Every time you fail, you put the family in danger. So you stay on base and do your homework, while we go out and earn a living. And you're not rejoining my team until you show that you're both trustworthy and competent. That's my final word on the subject."

He shouted over my mum's protests. "I'm not wasting any more time arguing with you, Gill. You're his mother; you can't see what a liability he is. Come on, everyone, out to the cars. We'll brief you on the way."

I sensed Mum's defeat, as she stood up and followed Malcolm and the rest out of the room. I wasn't worth fighting for.

I kicked her chair across the floor.

Then I noticed her computer was still on. Humiliated

by losing the argument, she had left without logging out. The system was still open at her high security level.

I hooked the chair back with my foot and sat down at the keyboard. But I wasn't planning to do homework. Not official homework anyway.

I typed in: **Shaw.**

Just out of curiosity.

I wanted to know why a sixteen-year-old schoolgirl had created more stress for my family than any undercover cop or gang war.

I found a Shaw folder. But it wasn't Vivien Mandeville Shaw. It was Ivy London Shaw. That made sense. Targeting a teenager was probably designed to put pressure on someone older and more influential.

I opened the Ivy Shaw folder. The first file by date was an article from an English local newspaper. Then there was an update file on tracing and tracking people called Shaw. Two Shaw Q&As: an undercover interview of the whole family, and the individual one of Vivien. Then Mum's report on the Q&A of her only son. I wasn't sure I wanted to read that. Vivien's target profile, which I already knew contained no details of the wider job. And the master file: the objectives of the job.

I opened the master file.

Client: Reid family.
Budget: Fee and expenses ceiling – unlimited.
Aim: Trace and track Ivy London Shaw, née Glass. Find evidence relating to Billy Reid. Eliminate everyone who has read it and destroy all evidence.

I almost closed the file and left the room right there. The Reid family as a client? Doing a job for ourselves? Unlimited budget? Where's the profit in that?

And finding evidence about Billy Reid? Our great-grandfather, the founder of the firm, the man who ran away from the circus? Billy had been dead for seven years. Why did we need to protect him now?

But if this was about family, that explained yesterday's overreaction. I'd messed up a job that wasn't about a client, it was about the family.

The wise thing to do would be to close the folder, go into the gym and sweat my curiosity away. I should forget I'd seen this.

But what could that schoolgirl yesterday, with her maths test and her worries about her little sister, have to do with Billy Reid, who died peacefully at home in Lanarkshire before she was even at secondary school?

I clicked the newspaper file.

It was a scanned-in feature page from the *Winslow Chronicle*, the folds and creases visible on screen.

There were two photos. One of a slim young black woman in an old-fashioned white coat, standing stiffly, holding a clipboard. One of a much older woman, sitting elegantly on a white metal chair in a conservatory.

She was the same woman. The first was captioned, Dr Ivy Glass, High Hall College, 1943. The other, Ivy Shaw, née Glass, at home in Winslow, 2013. The headline was:

LOCAL SCIENTIST DISCOVERS POWER OF THE MIND

Secret wartime research revealed by her family

Oh shit. We'd been exposed.

Then I looked at the date. The article was written in July, three months ago. If we'd been exposed, the authorities were taking their time getting to us.

I read the article:

Local granny Ivy Shaw is now happiest at home with the exotic Caribbean plants in her Winslow conservatory, but 70 years ago she was a brilliant young scientist helping Britain's war effort against the Nazis.

She worked on an amazing secret government project, only now being publicly revealed, as her proud descendants discuss her original notes exclusively with the Winslow Chronicle.

Dr Shaw was a researcher at High Hall College, Cambridge, specialising in psychology and neuroscience. She worked on a top-secret project for military intelligence, investigating whether any British subjects had special mental powers that might help the Allies.

She examined mediums (who claimed they could speak to the dead), fortune-tellers (who claimed they could see the future) and psychics (who claimed they could read minds) to establish scientifically whether any of them genuinely had these powers.

"Obviously," says James Shaw, her grandson, "if mediums could talk to the dead, soldiers' spirits might be able to give useful information to tacticians; and if the future could be predicted, the outcome of battles could be known; and if psychics could read minds, that would be useful in intelligence gathering.

"But," laughs Mr Shaw, a local optician, "my grandmother proved that without a gullible audience and stage props, these carnival performers weren't able to make more accurate guesses about the future, or about what dead people had known, than the ordinary students she used as controls. And almost all of the psychics were no more accurate about what she was thinking or what symbols she was seeing on hidden cards than the controls were. She concluded they were conmen and could be of no use to the war effort."

The *Winslow Chronicle* pressed him and his keen daughter Vivien about whether Ivy found ANY people with these powers, as Mr Shaw had said she proved they were lying in ALMOST every case.

Vivien Shaw, Ivy's great-granddaughter, who attends Winslow Academy, answered: "My nana said one man seemed to have more than average accuracy, in a negative way. One man got so many answers wrong that she wondered if he knew the right answers and was deliberately giving wrong ones. The number he got wrong was far more than could have happened at random."

When asked who this mysterious man was, Miss Shaw couldn't answer. "Nana says it's her responsibility to keep the real names confidential. They all have codenames in the file, and the man she thought was covering up correct answers was called 'Lomond'.

"She wondered if Lomond might have been interpreting body language, or even somehow detecting electrical impulses from nerve-endings in the brain, and then deliberately giving wrong answers so that he wouldn't be recruited as a spy.

"But she wasn't allowed to continue her research, so she never discovered the truth behind his unusual pattern of answers."

James Shaw explains why our local liar-detector

hadn't told anyone about this wartime work before. "It was top secret, so the files were probably destroyed after the war. My grandmother only kept her own working notes."

Vivien adds, "It's a shame that my nana didn't get funding to finish her research after the war. She became a biology teacher, and inspired lots of other scientists, but she never got any acknowledgement for the work she did exposing these charlatans."

When asked if she wants to continue her great-grandmother's work, Vivien says modestly, "I'm studying maths and science at Winslow Academy, and one day, perhaps, if you give me an MRI scanner and a few mediums and fortune tellers, I could show that the way their brains light up proves they're lying rather than using impossible magical powers."

Her father smiles proudly at her. Another Winslow scientist in the making.

I scrolled back up. They had pictures of the scientist Ivy Shaw, but no quotes from her. Had she died before the article was written? No, they'd have described her as "the late Dr Shaw". Was she senile? Was she just shy? Vivien certainly hadn't been shy on her behalf.

But the danger to my family was obvious.

The man Ivy Shaw thought might have been covering up genuine mindreading skills must have been Billy Reid.

Lomond was my great-grandfather.

I thought back to the family legends we were told as kids.

Billy hadn't been conscripted as a soldier in the Second World War because he'd had rickets as a child, so he kept working as a fortune-teller and psychic with the travelling fair during the summer and in variety theatres in the winter.

Then he was jailed as a conman, because a scientist forced him to lie to save himself from being used as a secret weapon, and by the time he was released he'd decided he would never work for anyone else again. He wouldn't be a bottom-of-the-bill entertainer any more, he'd use his skills to be a bodyguard and a spy.

That was how the family firm started. Billy set up a protection and intelligence firm using his own skills, and then the skills of his sons and his grandchildren.

Now some local rag was announcing that he actually had been a mindreader.

The article revealed the codename, rather than his real name. But if that codename was linked anywhere, on any report, in any notes, to the surname Reid, then the family had to get it and destroy it. Or none of us would be safe. Because we all knew that if the authorities got hold of us, we'd be handed over to scientists and treated as freaks all over again.

But Vivien had said goodbye to her nana. I knew that from her thoughts in the van. This article was three months old and I suspected her nana had died since.

If the scientist who had uncovered Billy's secret was dead, was the danger over? Or if Vivien's nana was no longer guarding her subjects' privacy, had the danger only just begun?

I opened the trace-and-track file, to discover what had alerted my family.

A tabloid paper had picked up on the local article and started investigating. They'd dropped the story when they realised Ivy Shaw wasn't going to talk to anyone. But the journalist's initial Google searches about psychics and the Second World War had jangled our virtual tripwires, and we'd followed the trail back to the original article.

That's why the senior readers had hurtled down to London. To track Ivy Shaw.

I was right: the file confirmed she had died of natural causes, just after the article in the *Winslow Chronicle*.

Mum had posed as another journalist and interviewed some of the family as soon as the senior team arrived down south.

I clicked on the audio and heard Mum's voice, introducing herself as Louise Allan, a freelance journalist. She was using a soft Irish accent – she says the only useful things she ever got from my dad was the skill of faking different accents.

She asked the interviewees to introduce themselves, for levels on the digital recorder.

"I'm Reginald Shaw, Ivy Shaw's son."
"I'm Reginald's older son, James Shaw."
"I'm Reginald's younger son, Vincent Shaw."
"I'm James's younger daughter, Lucy Kingston Shaw. My older sister Vivien isn't here, she's got a debating competition at school. Anyway, she doesn't think we should talk to you, not now Nana's dead. Did your recorder pick all that up?"

I sat back hard when I heard Vivien's sister. There was nothing wrong with Lucy Shaw's voice. She had a perfectly nice middle-class BBC English voice. But she sounded like a happy and alive version of Vivien.

112

Exactly like and completely different from the terrified girl in the van.

I shivered and clicked on Mum's transcript instead. The first part of the interview covered the same ground as the local article: Ivy came from Jamaica to study, then she did vital war work, she became a teacher, had a family, and now her family think her work should be recognised, blah blah blah...

There were also notes under each answer from Uncle Hugh, who posed as a photographer so he could act as a truth-tester. Voice readers aren't great at reading specific thoughts, but are really strong on telling whether someone is lying.

Then I got to a highlighted section. Here Mum had asked if they knew the real names of any of the subjects.

Each of them in turn said, no, their nana never let anyone see the last few pages of her notes, the appendix with the full names.

My mum pressed them harder:

Q: Why did she forbid you to read the last pages?
Reginald Shaw: My mother was determined that the names were to be kept confidential. These are real people and no one has the right to invade their privacy.
[truth]
Q: But surely they're all dead now?
Lucy: We can't assume that. Nana only died this summer and some of the subjects were younger than her.
[truth]
Q: Even if you plan to keep it confidential,

as your great-grandmother wished, will you read the whole report sometime in the future?

Lucy: We can't. We burnt her notes.

[truth]

Q: That's very dramatic! Why?

Reginald: She didn't want anyone following it up. Some of the subjects were humiliated by what she had done. Maybe they really believed in their spirits and their powers. And some of them were charged with fraud. She didn't want it dragged up again. My mother was angry about the *Chronicle* article and made us promise to burn the notes without reading them. So we promised and we burnt them.

[truth]

Q: So none of you ever read the end of the report? Might anyone else have a copy of it? Who else worked on this project?

Reginald: Her assistant, Adam Lawrie, didn't have access to all the information. She never trusted him with her notes, she preferred to be her own secretary, to keep her own secrets.

[truth]

Q: And what about the rest of the family? Your wife, Mr Shaw, or your other daughter, did they read the notes?

James Shaw: No, my wife isn't that interested, and I'm sure Vivien didn't read the full report either.

[truth, but also hesitation and protective,
defensive feelings]

Q: Are you sure? I'd love to speak to her, if she did.

114

Lucy: No, she didn't. Viv was really keen on keeping the notes, though, because she thought they represented the truth of science. She didn't want to burn them. She had a couple of arguments with Nana, that last week, about not wanting the notes lost forever. But Nana was so determined that Viv promised in the end. She definitely told me that she was annoyed she'd never had a chance to read the whole report, though.

[sincere, but hearsay]

Q: When and where did you burn the report?

Reginald: My mother had a heart attack the week after the *Chronicle* article, then passed away quietly a few days later. We put the pages in the coffin and cremated them with her. It seemed fitting.

[regret, sadness, truth]

Q: So all the pages of the report were burnt with her? How did you feel about that?

Here Mum must have held the microphone up to everyone individually, so Hugh could test the truth of their response.

Reginald: It was what Mum wanted.

[truth]

James: I was happy to see the back of it.

[truth]

Vince: Me too.

[truth]

Lucy: It was my nana's funeral. I couldn't care less about some old bits of paper.

115

[truth]

Q: Returning to her fascinating research, I wondered about Lomond, the man Dr Shaw thought was hiding a skill that really existed rather than pretending a skill that didn't. Have you been tempted to find out more about him?

Lucy: My nana said that he seemed like a dangerous man. Clever, ruthless and selfish. So I don't think I'd like to meet him. And if he could read people's body language or emotions or whatever, then Nana wondered whether those skills were hereditary, handed down in families, because fairground businesses are usually family businesses. So if they're anything like him, we probably wouldn't want to meet his family either.

[truth]

Q: Do you mean there might be mindreading FAMILIES out there?

Shaw Family: (General laughter.)

[awkward but genuine]

Vince: It's unlikely, isn't it? But it's a huge shame that my grandmother never got the opportunity to continue her research.

[truth, resentment]

The interview tailed off there, partly because the Shaws were arguing about whether Ivy Shaw was refused research funding because she was Jamaican, because she was a woman, or because the war was over, and partly because my mum had everything she needed.

I read the end of her report:

Conclusion. The notes were burnt and none of the subjects we interviewed have read the names. However it's not possible to be sure about the motives or knowledge of the older girl, Vivien. She may have deliberately avoided this interview. The answers given by her younger sister indicate that Vivien showed most interest in the report and was least willing to destroy it. Her family believe she didn't read the report, but she may have lied to them. It would be suspicious to set up another newspaper interview, so we need a different strategy to discover what this girl knows.

And Mum's recommendation: Grab Vivien Shaw. Q&A her, discover whether she has our founder's name anywhere in her head, and if she has, terminate her.

Chapter 15

Ciaran Bain, 29th Oct

I felt a wave of relief. If they'd planned to kill Vivien anyway, her death wasn't my fault after all. Except, probably, she didn't have the name in her head. Probably my family had been about to let her go, until they realised she had my face in her head. Probably it was still my fault.

If I checked Vivien's Q&A, perhaps I could find out for sure.

Malcolm was asking the questions this time, while Mum worked on her new way of laying out Q&As. Underneath the verbal answer, readers add the emotions, thoughts, memories and pictures they picked up, so Mum can see all the connections.

Q: Don't panic, Vivien. We just need to ask you some questions. If you're completely honest with us, we won't hurt you.

  [Target emotions: terror, confusion.]
Q: We're working for the government, just like your great-grandmother did.

[Relief at the word government, sharper fear
    at mention of great-grandmother.]

Q: All we need to know is what you did with the notes your great-grandmother made when she was working for us in the war.

Vivien: We burnt them.

[Careful truth.]

Q: How did you burn them? In a bonfire?

A: We burnt them with her body. They were cremated.

[Pictures in head – yellow papers on white dress under brown hands. Bright flowers. Coffin on conveyor belt. Urn in box. Truth, truth, truth.]

Q: Did you read them before you burnt them?

A: No. I was crying too much.

[Truth. Tears on flower petals. Tears on paper.]

Q: Did you read them earlier, when your nana was alive?

A: Yes. Some of them. She was angry we'd told the local newspaper, so she took them back before I read them all. I only read the first 100 pages. There were at least 50 more.

[Truth, fear, anger. Memory of her nana shouting about confidentiality.]

Q: Why did you burn the papers?

A: She made me promise.

[Truth.]

Q: Did you keep your promise?

A: Yes.

[Truth, but a moment's hesitation, pictures of coffin and crematorium urn.]

Q: Did you read all the pages of the research before you burnt them?

A: No.

[Truth.]

Q: Did you ever read the last pages?

A: No.

[Truth.]

Q: Do you know the names of any of the subjects?

A: No.

[Truth.]

Q: Why did your nana want you to burn them?

A: Because she thought the research subjects had a right to anonymity.

[Truth. Memory of shouted words: "ethics... human rights..."]

Q: Why did you argue with her?

A: I said that science should never be totally destroyed, that people's names could be protected, but the science should be made public.

[Truth. Target calming down. She's confident she's right. She's less afraid.]

Q: Why didn't she agree with you?

A: [Delay in answering.]

[Fear again.]

Q: Come on Vivien, why didn't she agree?

A: She said it was dangerous. She said one of the subjects had threatened her, so she didn't want these notes made public. She was a frightened old lady and I didn't want to make her any more scared. So I promised to burn them.

[Truth. Memory of tears and hugs.]

Q: And were you frightened?

A: Of course not. Why would I be? This research

was seventy years old. The subject who had threatened her must be very old now. Old or dead. I wasn't scared.

  [Lie. Target is terrified. She's trying to answer carefully but she's remembering her nana, tears on her face, hands trembling. And her own hands, shaking, opening a box.]
Q: Who threatened her? Which of the subjects?
A: I don't know any of their names.

  [Truth. The last pile of pages in her mind. Regret that she never read them.]
Q: But you know their codenames. Who threatened her?
A: I don't know.

                [Lie. Absolute lie.]
Q: That's a lie, Vivien. Who threatened her?
A: It's not a lie.

                      [Lie.]
Q: Yes, it is. Which subject threatened her? I know she told you...

            (Target shakes her head.)
  (Lead questioner orders applied pressure, first level.)

I closed my eyes. 'Applied pressure' means pain, designed to force answers from the target's voice or mind. I didn't want to read any more. But Vivien had to sit through it, the least I could do was read it.

  I opened my eyes again.

      [Target: pain, fear, pain, terror.]
Q: I said we wouldn't hurt you if you were honest with us. Are you ready to be honest with us?

A: Yes! Please stop! Please!

[Terror. Pain. Surrender.]

Q: Who threatened her?

A: Lomond. Lomond threatened her. He said his family would destroy her family if she ever mentioned his real name or researched this field again. So she didn't. She resigned, moved away, got married and changed her name. She was so scared she hid. That's why I promised to burn them, because I didn't want her to be scared any more.

[Truth. Guilt. Memories of tears on Nana's face, hanky scrunched in her hands.]

Q: Thank you for being honest with me Vivien. So now tell me, did you ever read the page with the codenames?

A: NO. I didn't. Please believe me.

[Truth.]

A: I believe you, and because you're so good at telling me the truth, Vivien, just tell me again, where are the notes?

A: We burnt them. They're ash, they're in the urn. It's true.

[Truth.]

Q: All the notes? Every page?

A: YES!! Please don't hurt me again. All her notes are in the urn. Everything is in the urn.

[Truth. Not even careful truth. She's panicking, telling the truth. The urn is heavy in her hands, and the report is in the urn.]

A: Please believe me. I didn't read it. It's all in the urn.

[Truth.   Absolute truth.]

Q: Calm down, Vivien. I do believe you.
A: Why do you believe me now, when you didn't believe me before? Are you...? Are you reading my THOUGHTS? Is that why he said...?

[A clear picture in her mind: Ciaran Bain,
unmasked, saying, "Don't even THINK
about my face."]

That was when the Q&A stopped in chaos.

The conclusion, hastily typed later, was that she hadn't read the full notes, that she didn't know the name of Billy Reid. But Mum had added a final line:

SERIOUS OMISSION — we never
asked about copies!

That's presumably when they decided to hunt me down to find out what I knew. So the logical file to read next was the Q&A of family liability Ciaran Reid Bain.

It was typed in by my mum, and it was very neat and tidy. You've got to admire her commitment to her job. Last night I was shivering on my bed with vomit down my t-shirt and she was typing up an account of my torture. Thanks Mum.

I loosened my grip on the mouse and looked at the first lines.

"Let go, you horrible boy!"
[Screaming, yelling, fear.]

It was Mum's account of everything they'd sucked out of me about Vivien. I could see the words - phone, sister, mask - but I didn't think I could live through it all again, so I scrolled down to the end.

Summary: In a moment of intense emotion, Ciaran established a connection with the target. The only concrete thought about Ivy Shaw was the target's farewell to the urn containing Shaw's ashes, confirming the report is also ashes in the urn. There was no mention of copies. There was no sense of hiding a name or knowledge of a name.

Conclusion: All evidence indicates the Reid family name is still hidden and the family is in no danger.

Three options for future action:
1. Leave Shaw family alone
2. Establish passive watching brief
3. Search their houses and question other family members to ensure no loose ends.

Proposal from Gill Bain: watching brief.
Proposals from other senior readers: tbc.

I wondered what the others' proposals would be. Then I memorised a couple of details from the track and trace file, closed the folder and erased the records of my access. Roy's dad, Dougie, our IT expert, could uncover my trail easily, but only if he knew he should be looking. And probably I would give my family no reason to check up on me.

Probably I'd never think about the Shaw family again.

chapter 16

Ciaran Bain, 29th October

I lay on my bed, trying to enjoy my day off. But I couldn't stop thinking about the folder I should never have opened, the secrets I should never have uncovered.

Now I knew why the senior readers had needed me so urgently after Vivien died. They needed to know if I'd read anything about copies. Now, after studying my memories of her thoughts, my mum and uncles were convinced there weren't any copies.

They believed they were safe.

But I wasn't so sure that they were safe. That *we* were safe.

Not because of any pictures or words or emotions I'd read or sensed. But because of something I'd felt in my fingertips, something that wasn't in anyone's Q&A reports because no one else is as *sensitive* as me.

I'd felt grit on Vivien's fingers when she was saying sorry and goodbye to her nana. I'd thought she was holding a vase at the time, putting it safely in a cardboard box. But someone in the Q&A had recognised it as a crematorium urn.

Now I knew what I'd found in Vivien's head and felt on her hands.

An urn full of ashes.

And grit on her fingers.

Why would that moment have been so strong in her mind that even a second-hand memory brought me back from her death on the golf course?

Her memory was so strong, because the grit wasn't dirt.

It was ash.

She had grit on her fingertips because she'd been digging into her nana's ashes.

That's not a feeling you would forget easily. Your great-grandmother's burnt bones under your fingernails. No wonder Vivien couldn't help thinking about it, when she thought about death, about fear, about what she might have to hide from people who'd kidnapped her.

And what did she have to hide? Nothing, surely, apart from copies of that report.

I felt again, in her memory, that one other sensation in her fingers. Not something in her hand, but the absence of something. Emptiness in her fingers, contrasting with the grit. The absence of something light and slim and smooth.

If I copied a file, I wouldn't end up with a pile of photocopies. I'd scan the pages and save them on a flash drive. A light, slim, smooth flash drive.

If Vivien had made a secret copy on a flash drive, I thought I knew where she'd hidden it.

Deep down in her nana's cremated ashes.

Gross. But effective. No one was likely to root about in burnt bones and flesh. No one but me.

Because suddenly I wanted to see if I was right, if I could protect my family's secret.

And I wanted to do it on my own.

But I wouldn't be able to search for the copy until it was dark, and I'd have to hide my intentions until then or Malcolm would stop me.

So once my family were back, high on the success of a job I hadn't ruined, I had to hide my thoughts and my emotions.

We can all hide our thoughts, by ringing the inside of our heads with a thick layer of personal privacy. It's one of the first skills we learn, but the cover is hard to maintain. Also it's like shouting 'I HAVE A SECRET!' It's fine for adults to keep thoughts private from kids, and having secrets is expected around Christmas and birthdays. But apart from that, covering your thoughts is considered suspicious.

The best way to avoid letting anyone know my plans was not to let anyone read my thoughts at all, by staying well away from my family. I also had to avoid giving out emotions like excitement or deceit, which might prompt someone to check up on me.

So I decided to live in the present for a day, not worry about the past or plan for the future. I finished a book Roy had raved about, played a computer game I'd borrowed from Josh and fell asleep listening to my own favourite music. I just acted like a teenager trying to avoid his family.

Late in the evening, I sensed someone heading for my corner of the warehouse. I live next to the laundry rather than beside everyone else's sleeping quarters, because I sometimes have screaming nightmares if I've spent time near the mindblind.

It was Roy, walking towards my isolated corner. We hadn't spoken last night, because I'd been too bruised and upset to unlock my door for anyone. This time, I let him in, then flopped back on the bed. He turned off the music, sat on the chair in the other corner of the cabin and muttered, "Sorry."

"What for?"

"For not letting you off that golf course."

"S'ok."

After a pause, I asked, "Did Malcolm give you a hard time about falling over?"

"No. They were too busy with today's job. Anyway, it was an accident, wasn't it?"

"Yeah. Thanks."

"S'ok."

Roy stretched out his legs, taking up most of my floor. "You alright?"

I showed him the bruises from Kerr's golf club and Daniel's boots, then shrugged.

"What about the Q&A?" he asked.

I shrugged again. "It could have been worse. I didn't have anything to hide."

We both glanced at the door, automatically.

I laughed. "Really! I didn't have anything to hide. It was just, you know, them reading me, and Mum with her hand on me."

Roy winced sympathetically. "So what's next?"

"Back to work as soon as Malcolm calms down, I suppose."

"Is that really what you want?"

"What else can I do?"

Roy raised his eyebrows, a whole friendship's worth of good advice and irritating nagging in his eyes.

"Not this again!" I snapped. "It's ok for you, you can stand in a bus queue without collapsing. You could hold hands with a girl without throwing up, if any girl was daft enough to let you. You can be normal. I can't. You can live a law-abiding life if you want. I can't. I can't survive outside the family, so I have to live by *their* rules, not by everyone else's laws."

"Even if you know they're wrong?" he said softly.

"Yes. Because... I'm scared of out there. I'm scared without the family around me. And you're no better, Roy, because if you didn't care about family rules, you'd have let me off that golf course."

"Give me a break. I'm only fifteen. I have to live by their rules now, so they feed me and give me somewhere to sleep. I don't fancy living in a children's home or on the streets. But once I'm old enough to get a place at uni and a job to support myself, I'll be off. You have to decide, Bain, are you staying or are you going?"

"There's no decision to make. I don't have a choice. I can't survive out there, so I have to stay here."

"You *could* survive out there, if you practised."

This was such a ridiculous suggestion that I ignored it and started hunting under my bed for nearly clean socks.

But Roy wouldn't shut up. "You ran away from the family yesterday. Why don't you run a bit further, see what happens?"

"It's not that easy. Look at us right now. You're my best friend, and we can't even talk about this unless you're on the other side of the room. How could I possibly cope with other people? So I'll never get away from this family."

Roy leant forward enthusiastically. "What if you

knew you could live out there? What if we could show that you can?"

"For how long? An hour? I stay out that long on jobs, and you see what state I'm in when I get back."

Roy pulled a rolled up sock from under the chair and lobbed it at me. "I bet you could do a day. Two days. Three days. If we grabbed some money and took off for a weekend, then came back with you still on your feet and still grinning, then they'd stop bullying you. Because Malcolm would realise that you're the strongest reader *and* you can survive out there. At the moment they kid themselves that you're not the best reader, because all they see is your over-sensitivity. If you can conquer that, by surviving a day or so outside, they'd have to respect you. If we can test that, if we can prove that..."

I jerked back. "Roy, are you suggesting we *experiment* on me, to see what I can cope with?"

We both glanced at the door again. 'Test', 'experiment' and 'science' were obscene words in our family.

Roy nodded. "Just because old Billy had a bad experience with science, shouldn't mean we're all forbidden to study biology or psychology or neuroscience, or to test the limits of our abilities. It's absurd, it's backward looking, and it's why we're trapped in the criminal underworld. So yes, Bain, I think we should *experiment* on you."

I shivered. "Please don't call it that, Roy. But you think we should do this... thing... together?"

"Yes! Of course!"

I shook my head. "But if I can't survive out there all on my own, it doesn't prove anything. If I can't do it myself, I have no choice at all."

"That's true. So, will you do it yourself? Will you see if you can cope out there on your own?"

"Maybe. Some day. If they annoy me enough."

"Yesterday they made you an accessory to murder, hunted you, beat you, then tortured you until you threw up, and that didn't annoy you enough?"

I shrugged and threw the sock back at him. "Maybe I'm getting used to it."

Roy stood up. "I'll never get used to it. I hope you don't either."

He left, his disappointment and anger still vivid after he'd slammed the door. I lay back down.

No one in the family would be concerned about emotional ripples from another rerun of our argument. They knew Roy wanted out, they knew I was useless, they knew we moaned. If they felt tension from my room, they'd just shrug and assume we'd grow up eventually.

This was the perfect time for me to think about my half-formed plan for the night, because my doubts and excitement would be camouflaged by the aftermath of our argument.

Was I really planning a lone ranger expedition to the house of a girl my family had murdered yesterday, to check out a hunch about where she might have hidden a flash drive of notes made by her great-grandmother about my great-grandfather seventy years ago?

Why was I even considering it?

Because it was *my* information and I wanted the credit? Definitely.

Because I wanted to show I was better than my family thought I was? Probably.

Because I might be less fatal to Vivien's family than Malcolm would be? Possibly.

Or was I actually doing what Roy advised for once, and finding out whether I could survive among the mindblind on my own? I didn't really know.

But if I was going to do this, I had to get off base undetected.

chapter 17

Ciaran Bain, 29th October

I checked the clock. Nearly 11 p.m. Everyone on base was winding down, going to bed, watching telly. I didn't think anyone was alert enough to notice me leaving, so long as I left without any loud noises or loud emotions.

I took a pile of cash out of my drawer. We always carry paper money on jobs, to buy ourselves out of trouble or take a taxi home.

I was already wearing black, because I usually do. I stuck the basics in my pockets: lockpicks, ID in someone else's name, balaclava, my phone and a small torch.

Then I breathed deeply, and tried to forget my nervousness, excitement and doubt. Once I felt calm, I left my little room and walked through the warehouse quietly and boringly. I sensed the blur of sleep and the zone-out of late-night relaxation, no sudden alertness.

I reached the side door and eased it open casually, like it didn't matter much to me. I slipped out of base and shut the door gently behind me.

No one yelled after me. No one texted to ask what the hell I was doing.

I was out. On my own.

And once I'd caught the bus to Winslow, I felt almost relaxed.

Working on busy public transport makes me ill, but late-night public transport is almost bearable. The driver is concentrating on his job, and the few passengers are likely to be reading or listening to music, living through other people's emotions.

The night bus to Winslow took more than half an hour, which gave me a chance to think in privacy. I ran through my plan. Check the Shaws were asleep, break into the house, find the urn, rummage about in a dead old lady's ashes for a flash drive I was only guessing was there, break out again without waking anyone up, then return home in triumph.

But I had to know where to look for the urn, or I could be crashing about their house all night.

Where do you put your dead nana? In the attic? On the mantelpiece?

I'd have to use Vivien as my guide. I closed my eyes and welcomed her in again. Regret, goodbye, apologies, grit on fingers, heavy urn, twisting the lid, cardboard box corners digging into her legs. She was kneeling on the floor, putting the box on the bumpy carpet.

Kneeling on carpet didn't seem likely in an attic. Nor in a living room, where you'd probably put the urn on a table, rather than the floor.

She was in a dusty, narrow space. Too small for a room or even an attic, probably.

On the bus, I couldn't fully concentrate on that moment in Vivien's head, or I'd lose track of the real world and I might miss my stop. But I could think this through logically. Where else did people keep cremated ashes? A boxroom? The cupboard under the stairs?

I smiled. Under the stairs is where people keep stuff they don't need that often. Christmas decorations. Summer holiday luggage. Dead relatives.

Under the stairs felt right for an urn and right for Vivien's memory of a narrow space, with dust and carpet. So I would search the understairs cupboard first.

Ciaran Bain, Midnight, 30th October

I got off the bus once it had passed the school, the alley and the police tape, but a couple of stops before the Shaws' street. I didn't want anyone to remember me getting off near their house.

I walked down the main road for a few blocks, took a left turn down a leafy avenue, then a right turn onto the Shaws' street. It was a wide road, with decent-sized houses in their own big gardens. The Shaws lived at number 31.

I passed a gate with a curly metal 79. Now I could count down to 31 without checking every gate.

77.

75.

I kept walking: hood up, head down, earphones in. Just a teenager heading home.

It was now past midnight, and there were very few lit windows. But the Shaws had just lost a daughter, so they might still be awake.

I counted down to 57.

55.

Then I sensed a quick snap of alertness.

Someone had noticed me.

Someone was watching me.

Someone awake, alert, suspicious.

Someone professional. Not a girl worried about a boy following her, nor an old lady worried about being mugged. Someone who was coldly and professionally focussed on why a teenager in black was walking down this street.

The alertness seemed to be coming from a car parked further down the street, on the other side of the road, with a head silhouetted in the driver's seat.

Someone sitting in a parked car, on a residential street, late at night.

Someone on surveillance?

I kept walking, but moved my hand up to the side of my face to fiddle with my earphone. I walked past the car, past number 31.

I maintained my steady pace, glancing at the houses, gardens and walls as I passed. I reached the corner, then turned right, out of sight.

I stopped and took a couple of deep breaths.

I'd never been watched like that before.

I'd never detected someone on surveillance, not someone outside my family. But it felt so familiar. Boredom, alertness, sudden excitement when something happens, then boredom again.

I'd been seen.

Shit. I'd taken such a stupid risk coming here.

I should just go home.

Or I could go round the back.

I walked on, looking for access to the back gardens, and wondering about the man staking out the house. He was probably police. Perhaps they were guarding the family in case of another attack, though I was sure

Malcolm had made Vivien's death look like a random attack. Perhaps they suspected someone in the family and were watching in case her dad lit an early bonfire or her mum sneaked away with bin bags of evidence in the middle of the night.

As I moved closer to the back gardens, I sensed someone else waiting and watching. Of course. The other half of a surveillance team, in the back lane.

I really should just go home.

With two policemen on watch, there wasn't an easy way in. But I'd already noticed a difficult way in.

It wasn't flashy and it certainly wasn't fast. I used the cover of a tree overhanging a neighbour's shed roof and almost an hour of painfully slow movement to creep into the Shaws' garden. I used my lockpicks to open the Shaws' back door. Then I was inside Vivien Shaw's house, and I knew exactly where to look for the urn and the codenames.

And all of that had seemed like considerably less trouble than crossing Winslow with Vivien's sister, so she could let me into her grandfather's flat.

Chapter 18

Lucy Shaw, 30th October

We walked into Grampa's flat together and the boy pulled the door shut behind us.

Grampa had left a small light on in the hall, but that didn't mean he was still awake. He always leaves it on. He used to claim it was so the elves could see to fix his shoes at night, but I suspect he's scared of the dark too.

I crept up the hall to the bedroom door, heard snoring, and strode back towards the blond burglar. He put his finger to his lips.

"It's ok," I said in a low tone. "Grampa sleeps really deeply. When we were little and stayed overnight here, we had to jump on his bed to wake him up for breakfast."

He nodded. He trusted me. Foolish. I was telling the truth, but he'd no way of knowing that.

He pulled off his scary hat and smiled at me. "Well done. You did fine on the way here, for someone with no training. Now, let's search the most obvious places first. Where's his main cupboard?"

I pointed at the coat cupboard.

"Is there a mantelpiece?"

I pointed at the living room door.

"Can you think of anywhere better for storing your nana's ashes?"

I shook my head.

"Right. You look in the cupboard, I'll start in the living room."

My search didn't take long. The cupboard was only big enough for coats, shoes, a red umbrella and a pile of leaflets. No urns, no skeletons in the closet, not even any wellies.

I shut the cupboard door and went into the living room.

The streetlight was shining through the half-open blind. The boy was standing in the middle of the room, arms crossed, staring at the fireplace and mantelpiece, which were covered in...

"Books! There's nothing here but books! Your grampa likes to read."

"Read, uh huh, and write."

"He wrote these?"

"Some of them." I pointed to the line of books on the mantelpiece. "History. Politics. History of politics. Politics of history. People power. Black power. He lived it and wrote it."

I waved my hand at the ceiling. There was no room for art on the walls, because they were covered in bookshelves, but the ceiling was plastered with posters from ancient revolutions that still hadn't happened.

I stood to the side of the window and looked carefully out. The unmarked police car was still there, the tall man sitting inside.

I could fling the window open and yell for help.

But this boy was running rings round the police and clearly had been for days. Also he was giving me answers to some of my questions, often without meaning to. If I screamed "Help, police!" now he might get away. And, even if the police caught him, they might not get as much information from him as I was.

Once I had enough answers, though, I *would* shout for help or dial 999.

I turned back and watched the boy run his hand along the line of books my grampa had written.

He pulled out the slimmest one and read the title. "*Black Gowns: Ethnic minorities in British academia, 1900–1975*, by Reginald Shaw, PhD."

"Nana's in that one." I walked over, opened the book and pointed to the dedication:

For Dr Ivy Shaw, my mother, who was a fine scientist but who didn't want me to name her in this book, claiming she wasn't worthy to be in such exalted company – a modesty I hope the black students and teachers of the future will not share!

He sighed. "She was trying to hide."

When he flicked through the book, a cream envelope fell out. We both dived for it, but he got it first, before it even hit the floor. He grinned, then held it out so we could both read it.

The address was handwritten:

Professor Adam Lawrie
High Hall College
Cambridge University
CB1 2MB

He turned it over. My nana's name and address were printed on the back, but the flap was still stuck down.

"Why would your grandfather use this as a bookmark?"

"In this book? Grampa was probably impressed she was still corresponding with people at the best universities, even after she left to be his mum and teach at the local school."

"But she wasn't corresponding with this professor, was she? Or at least he wasn't corresponding with her." He flipped the envelope back over and pointed to a pencil scrawl beside her neat handwriting. *Return to sender. Addressee no longer at this address.*

The boy turned it over again and slid a nail under the flap.

"That's private correspondence!" I said. "Put it back."

He shrugged. "It's ancient history anyway." He put the envelope back in the book and the book back on the shelf. "Ok, Lucy. Where else could the urn be?"

So we split the flat up.

I did the bathroom.

He did the kitchen.

I did the study.

He did the spare room.

Then he stood guard in the hall while I crept into the bedroom and poked about under the creaking bed as Grampa snored.

Ciaran Bain, 30th October

I waited until she was concentrating on her search then returned to the living room and took *Black Gowns* off the mantelpiece. I let the envelope slide out and stared at the name on the front.

141

I looked at the faded postmark. 1 9 6 8.

Why would Ivy Shaw be writing to her wartime assistant more than twenty years after the research project ended?

I ripped the envelope open and pulled out a one-page letter.

Dear Adam,

I can't stress enough that your insistence on continuing with this line of research is dangerous and unethical.

I may not have been clear enough in my previous letter. I say that Lomond is dangerous and you say you are not afraid of one small, uneducated man. So I must be more explicit. Lomond blamed me for his imprisonment and when he was released, he tracked me down to my own home and he threatened me. He said that if I ever told anyone his real name or researched psychics again, he would find me and kill me. He said that this threat would last forever. If I had children, and if they broke the silence, then his children would hunt my children down and kill them. I believed him, Adam. He was a very convincing man, whatever his size and his education.

That's why I left the university, why I moved to London, and why I married so fast, in order to change my name. I hid my notes, I hid myself, and I have stayed hidden. I only wrote to you because I heard rumours of what you were doing from my last contact at the laboratory and I wanted to warn you.

Please, Adam, the experiments you're conducting are dangerous. Dangerous for you, if Lomond or his like ever hear of it. Dangerous for the subjects too. From your brief description of the limited 'success' you have had, I believe you are trying to force the human mind past its natural boundaries, without proper consideration of the implications for society nor of the human rights of your subjects. So I would advise you, as your former mentor, to use your considerable skills to follow another line of research.

Please be careful.

Yours sincerely,

Ivy

So that's why Ivy was so scared and why she passed that fear onto Vivien.

Billy Reid was in his nineties when I knew him, but even then he was a powerful and violent man. He must have been terrifying when he was young. Especially standing in her own home, threatening to murder children she didn't even have yet.

It had worked, though. Ivy Shaw kept the secret right up to her death. But now she was dead, it was leaking out.

I reread the last paragraph. What was Professor Lawrie's research? What was his 'success'? Who were his subjects?

I pushed the letter back in the envelope, then folded it and shoved it in my pocket.

Then I sensed Lucy jerk to a stop, her quiet search halted by a discovery. It must be the urn! I stepped out into the hall.

Lucy Shaw, 30th October

As I searched the bedroom, I couldn't help thinking about Viv.

There were no family photos up in this flat, but it

was filled with pictures for me. Viv sitting in front of the unlit fireplace, reading one of Grampa's books. Viv in the kitchen, trying recipes from fair trade calendars. Viv bouncing on Grampa's bed, when we were small.

As I opened the wardrobe, I was wondering: *What did someone so sensible and open as Viv have to hide?*

I nearly fell into the wardrobe. Because suddenly I knew.

I stood up and marched into the hall.

"Did you find it?" Then the boy stopped smiling and backed away from me. He stumbled into the living room. I followed him and shut the door.

I knew what he was looking for.

Nana's report. Her obsession with that damn report was the only thing Viv ever got in trouble about.

The boy had said Viv was meant to destroy something and we all promised Nana we would burn that report. So maybe Viv had kept it.

I remembered there were codenames at the end of the report, and I thought about how he'd jerked away from me when I said I'd call him a codename.

And all the stuff he seemed to know, before it was possible for him to know it. What those policemen were going to do, where they were. That I was grieving, that I was uncomfy, even that I had just found something.

"You knew I'd found something in the bedroom, didn't you? How did you know *before* I came out?"

"It was obvious," he blustered, "you came out looking so..."

"I didn't find the urn. But I did find something in my head. An answer. And you know all about finding answers in people's heads."

He went pale. Even paler than normal.

"You're Lomond, aren't you?"

"What?"

"I know who you are. I know what you can do!"

"Keep your voice down!" He looked nervous. As nervous and wobbly as when we first met, when I'd floored him with barely a touch.

So I wondered if I could knock him down again...

"You're Lomond."

"I am not!"

"You're a fortune-teller."

"No, I'm not!"

"Yes. You can see the future. You can see when the policeman is about to get out of the car, when I'm about to come out of a room..."

"Yeah," he grinned, shakily. "I can see you're about to make a complete idiot of yourself, Lucy."

"I know you're looking for Nana's report. You think Viv hid some digital version of the report in the urn. The report about fortune-tellers and other fairground frauds. The report about the man codenamed Lomond, the one Nana thought was trying to pretend he couldn't read minds. That's you, isn't it? Lomond."

"Aye, right. I thought we'd agreed I'm younger than you. How could I be in your nana's seventy-year-old report?"

"See! You even know when she wrote it! You are Lomond."

"I am not Lomond. How can I be?"

"Ok. You're not *him*, but you're like him. You can read minds, can't you? And you're trying to hide the truth about him. Is he your grandfather?"

"This is all nonsense. You surely don't believe this.

Your nana was a scientist. She spent her time *disproving* this sort of thing."

"So why do you want to keep her report a secret? That has to be what you're after. The only person in my family with any secrets was Nana. And the only person in the family who paid those secrets any attention was Viv. And she's been murdered. So I know it's that report you want."

He shrugged.

"I know there's a memory stick or something in that urn with a copy of her notes."

He looked away.

"I know it's Lomond you're trying to protect."

He bit his lip.

I took a step towards him. "And I know *exactly* what I think of you."

It didn't matter what mysteries there were to solve, what questions there were to answer. All that mattered was that he had killed my sister. All that mattered was punishing him.

So I grabbed him.

I darted my hand in where his jacket was unzipped, I grabbed his shoulder and I thought as loudly as I could without opening my mouth.

You bastard. You murdering thieving lying cheating bastard. Killing my sister, breaking into my house and terrifying me, to protect a secret from last century. I hate you.

He dropped to the floor, falling out of my grip. I knelt down and put my hand on his collarbone again.

I thought police cars, prison cells, courthouses, lawyers, iron bars, nooses and razor blades.

He started to tremble, his eyes staring at the ceiling,

his mouth clamping shut to keep in the screams I could feel shaking his ribcage.

I thought of Viv in this flat, reading, cooking and laughing. I wanted to cry. But I wanted him to cry too. I wanted him to suffer. I hated him. So I thought about hatred as hard as I could. Hatred. Punishment. Death.

I didn't know exactly what I was doing, but I knew it was working. He was shivering, sweating, whimpering. So I gripped his shoulder tighter and thought harder. About the police, about prison, about how I was going to destroy his future. But I couldn't help seeing Viv.

I was trembling too.

So I let go.

I scrambled away and leant against the couch, then I watched him, to see if he could get up.

I didn't care. I didn't care if he never got up. I didn't care if I had fried his brain or stopped his heart. I didn't care.

Chapter 19

Ciaran Bain, 30th October

I couldn't move.

I'd never had someone think hate at me like that before.

Even after she stopped, I couldn't push my eyelids up or lift my head. I wasn't sure I could breathe.

I couldn't sit up.

I had to sit up. I couldn't let her see how much she'd destroyed me.

She knew, of course. I could read that when she was doing it. She knew what she was doing to me. I could still sense her now. Her anger, her hate, her curiosity, scratching on the raw parts of my mind.

I dragged myself up. I turned my back on her. I needed time to get my face, my head, my self back in order.

What a stinking, stupid, spectacular mess I was making of this.

This was absolute proof that I couldn't survive out here on my own. I'd only spent a couple of hours with this girl. My first extended contact with the mindblind ever and I'd given her all the clues she needed to work out who and what I was.

I could have made it easier by wearing a t-shirt saying 'mindreader', but only slightly easier.

When I was anticipating all the surveillance team's moves, was I giving my own team clear instructions, or was I just showing off?

And when she was having doubts, feeling scared, grieving, why didn't I just let her suffer, rather than trying to distract her? Did I actually think her mental health was my responsibility?

I'd realised she knew too much when she said the word 'Lomond'. But I didn't realise what a dangerous mess I'd made of the night until she touched me.

Until she forced into me:

Grief

Pain

Revenge

Hate...

Hate is a powerful emotion even at a distance. But when it was so close, backed up by thoughts, pictures and memories, her hate had been overwhelming.

Only the fear of the police outside and her grandfather across the hall had prevented me screaming, prevented me begging her to stop.

I could sense her behind me, watching me. I was wrapped round my knees, my back to her.

I had to get this over with.

I turned round.

We looked at each other.

She didn't look much better than me.

She'd had to think all that poison in her own head to get it into mine. And she'd been holding back those memories of Vivien since her sister died.

She had tears on her cheeks.

Shit. So did I. I had tears on my cheeks too. Shit.

This wasn't just dangerous. It was *embarrassing*!

Leather jacket sleeves are useless for wiping your eyes. So I reached up for a box of hankies I'd seen on a bookshelf, took a handful and skimmed the box over to her.

She pulled one out and blew her nose.

She wasn't sorry. She could see what she'd done to me and she wasn't sorry. Curious. Weirded out. But not sorry. Bitch.

I cleared my throat. "So. The urn's not in the bedroom then."

"What? After that, you still want the urn?"

"You've joined a few dots, Lucy, which makes you very clever, but doesn't change the fact that your family still has a secret that can damage my family, and I have to find it before my family come calling."

"I'm not afraid of you or your family. All I have to do is touch you and you fall down. I'm not scared of you."

I took a deep breath. I had to get on top again.

"I'm *not* scared of you," she repeated.

I had to do this. "Vivien was scared of me. And she was absolutely terrified of the man who strapped her to a chair and jerked her head round so hard that he broke her neck."

Lucy gasped. She grabbed another hankie. "You bastard!"

"Sorry. But you can't stop being scared of my family just because... just because I'm..."

"Just because you're a wimp?"

"Yeah. Ok." I stood up. "Yeah. Just because I'm a wimp doesn't mean the rest of them aren't dangerous. You could shoot hate thoughts at them all day and they

150

wouldn't miss a step. So be scared of them, even if you aren't scared of me. And give me a hand to find this bloody urn. Is it in the bedroom?"

She shook her head.

"So I'd better search your uncle's house next. Now you know I'm a pathetic wimp and I know you're a vengeful cow, I assume we don't want to be a buddy movie any more. Give me the address and go home."

She stood up and stretched. Neither of us were really in control of this situation, we were both too shaken. But she was putting on a good act.

"No," she said. "I'm not letting you go on your own. I didn't mind crossing Winslow with you when I knew you were a burglar and a murderer. Why should I mind a road trip with you now I know you're a fairground freak and a crybaby?"

"No, Lucy. You're not coming with me."

She glared at me. "Yes I am."

This girl seriously wanted to punish me now, so she was a significant danger to me. And there was almost no fear or self-preservation in her any more, so she was a danger to herself too. This couldn't get any worse.

I had to focus. "Where does your uncle live? You said a road trip. Do I need a taxi?"

She snorted into her hankie. "A taxi? I don't think you could afford it. Uncle Vince lives in..." She indulged herself in a dramatic pause. "In... Scotland."

Ok. Now it couldn't get any worse.

"Scotland. Fantastic."

"Yeah. So you can go home to Mummy and Daddy and all your little baby psychics."

"How do you...?"

"How do I know you're Scottish? It's obvious every

151

time you open your mouth and say 'och aye the noo'. You're not hiding your identity very well, you know."

"Where in Scotland does he live?"

"Edinburgh. Where in Scotland are you from?"

"Not Edinburgh, that's all you'll ever know. Now give me his address, so I can get going before the sun is up."

"So *we* can get going."

"No. I'm not travelling to Edinburgh with you. It would take all day. You'd drive me nuts."

"I hope so. A life sentence in Broadmoor might be the right punishment for killing my sister. They're used to people hearing voices in their heads. Someone will study you for their PhD..."

"NO. No! Don't..." I nearly sat down again. She was pressing all the wrong buttons. Curiosity had been her priority before, but now she had a few answers, she'd moved onto the next stage. Punishment, retribution, revenge.

I stepped away from her to the window. I saw the policeman in the car at the front and sensed the matching vigilance of a newly arrived colleague at the back. "They're still out there. One front, one back. We can't go out either door."

"So we're trapped?" she asked.

"I'm never trapped. We can't go out the bottom of the building, but I can go out the top."

"Oh yeah? Now you can fly?"

"No. I can climb. But you'd probably fall and crack your skull, so you'll be safer staying here. Give me the address in Edinburgh, Lucy."

"No. You can't scare me off. I'm not scared of you any more and I'm not scared of heights or spiders or monsters under the bed either. Where you go, I go, until my family is safe and Viv's murderer is behind bars."

I couldn't give away more family secrets if she came along. She knew almost everything already. And this wasn't the best place for a long argument.

So I shrugged and left the flat, letting Lucy lock up behind me.

I walked up the stairs. I didn't wait for her. If she couldn't keep up with me, I'd leave her behind, travel up to Edinburgh without her, and get Roy to find the address for me before anyone else on base woke up.

Perhaps that would be easier. Perhaps I should just ditch her now. I swung round. She was two steps below me, radiating resentment and hate.

Aye. Right. Leave Lucy Kingston Shaw behind in any state of consciousness and she'd be calling her family, the police and her uncle up north before I was on the train. I'd never make it to Edinburgh, and even if I did, the police would have found the urn and read the flash drive before I got there.

No. I needed to keep her where I could see her. Or I needed to silence her. Permanently.

I looked at her. She glared right back.

I could do it. I could silence her. If I had to.

But I didn't have to. Not yet.

So I climbed the stairs and she trailed after me.

When we reached the top landing we saw a wooden access panel in the ceiling and a stepladder leaning against the wall.

"How did you know that was here?" she demanded. "Did you read someone's mind?"

"I just guessed, because most flats like this have

153

shared roof access. It's not all mindreading. Some of it's training, some of it's informed guesswork."

"Some of what?"

"Some of what we do."

"What do you do? What job are you training for?"

Damn. There *were* more family secrets I could give away. She was so nosy.

I ignored her and opened the stepladder, then climbed up and eased the panel across slowly. There were a few creaks, but no more noise than someone would make climbing the stairs.

I grabbed the edges of the hole and pulled myself straight up. Like chin-ups on the bars in the gym. No sweat.

I turned round and watched Lucy climb up. She reached the top rung, grabbed the edges and hauled up, like I had done. But she couldn't lift herself in. Her arms kept crumpling at the elbow.

"Wimp," I whispered.

"I have the address. You have to pull me up!"

"Only if you think about kittens and birthday cakes while I do."

"Why?"

"If you think about prisons and policemen again, Lucy, I will drop you. It won't be deliberate, I just won't be able to hold on."

"Oh. Ok. Sugar and spice and all things nice, I promise."

So I anchored my feet against a beam and after a moment's consideration I took off my leather gloves. Touching her wouldn't be easy, but I didn't want the gloves slipping off or her slipping out of my grasp. She'd make too much noise if I dropped her.

I grabbed her and yanked her up as fast as I could.

As I swung her in, she did try really hard. She thought about tiger cubs at the zoo and chocolate éclairs.

But even in those few thoughts, she couldn't keep away from her sister, like she had no happy memories without Vivien. And even in those few seconds, too much got through and I was shivering when I tried to pull my gloves back on.

She watched me struggle to get my fingers in the right place. "Sorry. I tried not to hate you."

"No. You were fine," I gasped. "You did fine. I just..."

"Is it always like that? Whenever you touch someone? Whatever they're thinking?"

"Yes." I got the second glove on at last. "Yes. Always. Sometimes worse, like downstairs. But always a bit like that."

"So do you ever touch anyone? Can you ever...?"

"No."

"But, when you were little, didn't you get cuddles from your mum? Or anyone?"

"No!" I snapped. "No! Ok! And don't ask any more..."

Now I wasn't just sensing a desire for revenge or curiosity. Now I was sensing pity. Wonderful.

Now Lucy felt *sorry* for me.

I twisted away from her, braced my feet against the beam again, and leant down to fold the stepladder then rock it on its feet back over to the wall. I managed it almost completely silently, with only one metallic click as it fell gently against the wall.

I was impressed.

I don't think she even noticed.

Then I sat up and lifted the panel back over.

155

As soon as the wooden cover slid into place, cutting out the light, I sensed Lucy jerk into a familiar fear. She was scared of the dark. Not spiders, not heights, not me, just the dark. I didn't say anything, but I switched my torch on.

"Walk on the beams," I ordered. "The insulation won't support you." I walked off into the attic.

"Aren't we going onto the roof?" Lucy asked behind me.

"I hope not. If there's access to the next block up here, we can go through their panel, down their stairs and out their door."

I'd hoped for a continuous attic, all the way along the block. But I was balancing on a beam looking at a solid red brick wall. I swung my light left and right. Not even a door I could unlock.

"Ok, let's go with your plan," I said cheerfully. "Out on the roof!"

"It wasn't my plan!"

"Yes it was. You sounded disappointed that you weren't going to do a Mary Poppins, dancing round the chimneys."

I flicked the torch beam up. How did workmen get onto the roof?

There was a small metal-framed hatch, above the access panel we'd come in.

We tottered back on the beams.

The hatch was held shut by a metal bar. Which I couldn't reach.

I didn't want to balance the stepladder from the stairwell on these narrow beams. So I searched the attic with the torchlight. There were lots of fragile cardboard boxes and flimsy rucksacks. Then I saw a pile of solid metallic suitcases. We pulled them over and made a set of steps, high enough that we could reach up and climb out without help.

Before I could clamber up, Lucy stood on the top case and pushed at the metal bar. It screeched rustily, then opened.

"Wait, Lucy! Let me go first. I need to see how steep and slippery it is out there."

"Yeah, then go off and leave me behind in this creepy attic."

"I'm not going to leave you behind. As you keep reminding me, you've got the address."

She didn't argue, she just slid through the hatch then scrambled out.

I held my breath. Worried that I'd hear a scrabble and a scream and her sliding off the roof. Worried that I'd sense her terror and...

No. Satisfaction. Security. She was fine.

I climbed up the cases, slithered through the gap and onto the tiles.

Lucy was perched above the hatch, her heels jammed onto the top of the frame. She was delighted with herself.

I looked round at the map of streetlights, the slabs of tower block lights, the streams of moving headlights.

I laughed.

"What?" Lucy whispered.

"Look at the size of the outside world. And look at me, on top of it all. I wonder if I *can* do it?"

"You wonder if you can do what?"

"Maybe I can survive out here, on my own!"

"You're not on your own. I'm here."

"Even better. You're here and you're mindblind. I've

spent my life terrified of spending time away from my family, out among the mindblind, and here I am. Coping with it all."

"I'm *mindblind*, am I? Thanks. And you're coping, are you? You've spent most of the last couple of hours rolling about on carpets moaning. And you had to wipe your eyes and blow your nose in Grampa's living room."

"True. But that wasn't so different from how I looked last night when my family had finished with me. So maybe I do have a choice."

"A choice?"

"Yeah. I can live with my family and live with... what they do. Or I can leave and live out here. On my own. If I can survive more than a few hours..." I looked down. "And if we can get off this roof and out of this city."

chapter 20

Ciaran Bain, 30th October

Roofs aren't that scary. Anyone who's spent time on a climbing wall or a cliff face won't find a sloping roof with moulded tiles much of a challenge.

"Lucy, have you done any rock climbing?"

"No. I prefer my sports at ground level."

Someone who hasn't been on a wall or a cliff should find a roof this height, at night, quite scary. But she wasn't scared. She was enjoying the view, enjoying the excitement. I sensed her confidence and trust.

She was trusting me to get her down from here.

She really shouldn't trust me. No one should trust me. Especially not her.

I was responsible for her sister's death. She knew it and she'd seen my face, so she could describe me to the police. Really, she should be very scared of me, because I had every reason to pitch her off this roof.

But she trusted me.

And I was keeping her alive.

"Right, Lucy. We'll climb along the lower part of the roof."

"Why?" She might trust me, but that wouldn't stop her arguing every single bloody point with me.

"Shouldn't we be higher up, so we've more time to stop ourselves if we fall?"

"No. If you slip, it's better to hit the gutter slowly so it stops your fall. If you've slid a long way and built up speed, you might knock the gutter off and fall down with it. So clamber along low down."

I took my gloves off and showed her how to move over the tiles. "Like a crab, slowly and carefully."

I moved to our right, heading for the flats round the corner, where the front door wasn't visible to anyone watching Reginald Shaw's door.

I leant my weight into the roof, bare fingers grasping the edges and ridges of the tiles. I slid along slowly, letting Lucy keep pace with me, so I could grab her if she started to fall.

But really, it would be hard to fall off this roof. We might slip, but we weren't going to fall, so long as we didn't lean back and flail our arms about.

I could sense Lucy's concentration. She was doing fine.

Then we got to the corner, where the next block met this one at right angles.

"Good news and bad news," I muttered.

"Mmhm?"

"Good news: we're halfway to the hatch we want. Bad news: this corner looks tricky."

The join was a wide strip of lead, to keep the corner weatherproof. But it was softer and slippier than the tiles - we wouldn't be able to get any grip on it. And we were on the back of the building, inside the right angle of the corner. So to reach the safe tiles on the other side of the lead strip, we wouldn't be able to keep our bodies in close contact with the roof, we'd have to bend round and grab the tiles to the side and behind us.

Basically, we'd have to lean back and flail about. Prime falling-off conditions.

I sighed. How was I going to get Lucy round this?

"I'll go first, then shine a torch to show you where to put your hands."

"What about the policeman down there?" she whispered. "Isn't the light too much of a risk?"

"Not as much of a risk as you falling. Anyway, he's watching the lane and the back door, not looking up at the roof."

"Are you sure?"

"Hey, I'm a mindreader." To be honest, I wasn't sure. But I did know he was relaxed. If he was stretching up to look at the roof all the time, that would make him irritable. I was fairly sure it was ok.

I traversed the join slowly, sliding my body across the lead, feeling carefully for every handhold.

Then I pulled out my torch and lit a route for Lucy, guiding her hands and feet past the broad lead strip. "Don't lean back too much. Keep curled in. Hand up to the right. Yes. There."

I could sense her fear, her desire to grab and leap, but also her trust in my instructions and her determination to do this properly.

"Just a bit more. Up to your right. Perfect."

She was across.

We kept moving along the roof to the hatch. We crawled up and rested above it, our feet on the frame.

We both sat there, staring at it. It was the same as the hatch we'd climbed out.

Locked by a bar on the inside.

We couldn't open it from the outside.

I whispered, "I have no ideas. Do you have any ideas?"

She shook her head, carefully not blaming me. We were high on a roof, after all.

I shook my head too. "I messed up. Sorry. Let me think..."

"I don't want to go back," she said quietly. "Not round that corner again."

"Ok."

"But I don't mind going on. This block goes right along the whole street, so we could get further away from the policeman down there, then climb down or abseil or something."

"Oh good! Abseiling is a great plan! You brought a rope, did you? And some harnesses?"

"No!"

"We're five storeys up. There is no safe way down the outside."

I sensed the spark of an idea in her head, like she'd worked out the answer to a riddle.

"Yes, there is! The local library is in the middle of this block. It's the old town hall, with balconies at the front. We could drop off the roof onto the top balcony. Then we could either climb in a window, or jump down from balcony to balcony."

She waited, impatient.

I grinned. "Great plan! Much better than my stupid locked-hatch plan. How far along is the library?"

"Another three or four buildings."

We crawled along the roof, under three more useless hatches. Then I whispered, "Far enough. Up we go, over to the street side. You first, just to the ridge."

"Why me first?"

"So I can block you if you start to slide."

But she didn't slide. She'd had no training, but she

did have natural flexibility and balance, and she was a fast learner. If she wasn't mindblind, she might be quite useful in a team.

She reached the top and waited for me.

I caught up with her and said, "Lie flat on the top, so you don't make an obvious shape on the skyline, then slither over. Like this."

I pulled myself up so I was lying along the cold ridge of rounded tiles. Then as I let my legs slip down, I felt my phone vibrate in my pocket. A text, at 3 a.m.?

I watched Lucy slither safely over, then I took an angled route down the roof.

The streetlights didn't reach this high. I didn't think anyone on the road, or looking out a window on the other side of the street, could see us. So when I got to the lowest tiles, I balanced my foot on the gutter and used my left hand to wiggle my phone out of my jeans. Lucy couldn't see me. She was above me, still making her way down.

The text was from Roy's phone.

> Where the hell r u? U mal on warpath.
> Keep ur head down. Don't reply.

Oh.

Shit.

Oh shit.

I concentrated on my breathing, on keeping calm, keeping my chest pressed to the tiles.

If my family were looking for me, they'd find me much faster than the mindblind police. And if Roy didn't want me to reply, he must be worried Malcolm might confiscate or check his phone. I couldn't communicate safely with him.

Oh shit.

All my brief confidence about surviving on my own collapsed. I might be able to cope with the mindblind for a while, but it would be much harder to cope in the outside world with my family after me.

I leant back to put the phone in my pocket and felt the gutter lurch under my foot. I suddenly remembered I was on a roof high above a London street.

I curled my fingers round the ridged tiles and pushed forward towards the roof. I had to concentrate on where I was, not what was chasing me.

Lucy was right beside me. I hadn't even noticed. I am so useless.

"You ok?" she whispered.

"Fine. Where's that bloody balcony?"

"Just there, past that lion."

I glanced along the roof edge, to an elaborate stone carving five metres ahead. "Let's crawl past the lion, then see if it's safe to jump to your balcony."

"What if it isn't?"

I didn't answer. My head was jangling with panic, frantically searching for any whisper of my family approaching.

We crab-crawled along until we were past the carving and on the roof of the library, which had older grainier tiles than the flats.

Lucy's balcony was one floor below us. It ran the length of the building, but it was less than a couple of metres wide. It wasn't an easy target from this height.

"The trick is to fall," I said, "not to jump."

"What?"

"If you jump, you push off, so you go outwards and miss the balcony. If you fall, you go straight down, so you'll land nice and safe." Probably.

I kept my voice positive. "Just dangle your feet below the edge of the tiles and slip down off the roof."

I could sense her doubts.

"I'll go first," I offered. "I'll catch you if you want."

"Won't that hurt you?"

"Not as much as landing hard on the balcony will hurt you. See you down there!"

I lifted my feet off the tiles, gave a wee shove with my hands and slid off the roof. I fell for less than a heartbeat, then bent my knees, hit the balcony and rolled.

I called up, "I'm here. It's easy."

I put my gloves on, so I could catch her.

But she was radiating fear, reluctance, frustration. Three emotions adding up to one thought. She didn't want to let go.

"Lucy?"

"Yeah, yeah. I'm just being a wimp. I've spent the last half hour getting good at *not* falling off a roof, so it's hard to decide to fall deliberately. Give me a minute."

I kept quiet. I sensed her get control over herself. Will over mind. Mind over body. Turning terror into determination, reluctance into decision.

Then she let go, so fast I almost missed it.

She slid off the edge of the roof, fell past the windows and crashed into my chest. I didn't really catch her, just provided a softer landing than the stone of the balcony floor. We rolled away from each other immediately.

"We're off the roof. Now what?" she asked.

Now what? I couldn't think of anything apart from not getting caught by my family.

"Now what?" she repeated.

I didn't have an answer. But we did have to get off this balcony, so that I could get further from anywhere my family might be searching for me.

I had to show the same control Lucy just had. I had to stop flailing and get a grip.

I stood up and looked over the parapet. All the balconies below us were exactly the same width. To drop from the upper to the lower balconies, you'd have to swing inwards each time. It was possible, but not easy.

I turned to the door. It had one simple lock, which was probably alarmed, but we should be out within minutes of entering, so breaking in was less risky than an acrobatics display down the front of a public building.

"When I open the door, let's assume I've set off an alarm, even if we can't hear it, so we run downstairs and out the front door as fast as possible, without pauses for argument. Yeah?"

"Yeah." She was getting pretty causal about this breaking in stuff.

"Ready?"

"Yeah!"

I picked the lock and shoved the door open.

Total silence. Total absence of klaxons, sirens, bells and whistles. But there might be a light flashing in the police station.

I leapt in. Lucy leapt past me. I jerked the door closed and flicked my torch on. We ran to the door at the other side of the room, which unlocked from the inside, then we battered down four flights of wide stairs to a round hall with a faded mosaic floor and a huge arched wooden front door.

I ran towards the door, hoping it wouldn't have an ancient lock I'd never met before.

But it was the same kind of cheap lock you get on every council building. Not even screwed on right. There were a million ways to pick this. I had it open in seconds, and we stepped out together.

"Lead us towards the centre of London now," I instructed, "but keep clear of the police station. And walk, don't run."

She turned right and walked down the street. I followed. But as soon as we heard the faint wail of a police siren, Lucy panicked and started to sprint.

"Turn a corner!" I said. "If you have to run, run somewhere less public!"

We veered into a dark alley. I sensed Lucy's fear immediately, just like in the dark attic. I switched on the torch, and the narrow light gave her enough confidence to keep running.

She was a fast runner. An athlete at school, probably. A sprinter possibly, given her speed, but we'd see if she had my stamina. I let her lead, sensing nothing from her apart from the excitement of the chase, now her initial panic had died down.

We leapt over piles of cardboard and heaps of binbags at the back of shops, squeezed past parked vans, and kept running until the sirens died out behind us.

Lucy slowed to a trot. But she wasn't tired, she was elated. "You're right, it is more fun when you're being chased! What do we do now?"

I read the text again as we walked.

Where the hell r u? U mal on warpath.
Keep ur head down. Don't reply.

It didn't look any better on solid ground than it had on the roof.

Should I head home and tell them what I'd worked out, so that Malcolm could search for the copy? Or should I try to find the copy myself and return home as a hero? If I went back now, I'd probably suffer another Q&A; if I kept going, I'd probably get caught and thrashed by Daniel long before I got to Edinburgh. All for a flash drive which was still guesswork on my part.

I looked at the text again, then looked at Lucy. It wasn't just me who might get hurt this time.

"Bad news," I muttered.

"We got past the last bad news."

"Really bad news. My family know I've gone. They're hunting for me and once they discover I've been in the Shaw files, they'll visit your family's addresses."

I realised what I had to do. "We have to split up, Lucy. I'll go north if I can. You just get away. But don't go home yet. Your family's total ignorance of me should protect them, but you know too much and you wouldn't be safe.

"Go to a friend's or a distant relative's. Somewhere my family won't find you. But most important, Lucy, stay away from me. It's me they're looking for, not you, and they'll find me more easily than you. If you don't think about me, they may not realise you've talked to me or know any more about us than you did last week."

It was a slim hope. We'd left an obvious trail. She was missing from home the same night as me, and there was evidence of break-ins at her grandfather's block of flats and at the local library.

Also if Mum and Malcolm questioned me about tonight, no matter how hard I tried to hide her, they'd catch glimpses of Lucy. So if I returned home, or if they caught me, she was dead.

I'd probably killed her already.

But I couldn't tell her that.

"Why will they find you more easily than me?" she asked. "With all your sneaky ninja skills, can't you hide from anyone?"

"Not from my family. They can detect my mind from a distance. As soon as they get close enough, they'll find me."

But they hadn't always found me. Daniel hadn't found me on the golf course, when I'd fallen into Vivien's death. I almost hadn't climbed out, though. It was too risky, I couldn't do it again. I just had to run.

"Goodbye Lucy. I'm going this way. You're going that way. Goodbye. And good luck." Though with Malcolm and Mum out hunting, luck was unlikely to save her. Or me.

Chapter 21

Lucy Shaw, 30th October

He said goodbye, then he actually flapped his hands at me like I was a pigeon or a stray dog he was trying to shoo away!

I folded my arms and stood my ground. "You can't just get rid of me. You need me."

"Aye, right. I need you like I need a kick in the teeth."

"You do need me, because I know where my uncle lives and you don't."

"I don't need you any more. Edinburgh isn't like London. It's a small city. There won't be many black English intellectuals called Vincent Shaw living there. If you won't give me his address, I'll still find him."

"How do you know he's an intellectual?" What was he reading from my mind? I had to stop *thinking* near him.

"Don't panic! It's not me mindreading. I just worked it out. Your nana was a research scientist, your grampa's a writer, your dad's an optician. You all have exams and degrees. What's your uncle? A lawyer? A doctor?"

"I'm not telling you!"

"Fine. I'll find out tomorrow. Now off you go, Lucy. I'm on the run and I need to move fast."

"I'm not slowing you down! I can run as fast as you."

"No, you can't, not for hours. And you do slow me down, because I have to argue every bloody decision with you." He scowled at me. He stood with his legs apart, chin out, fists tight, like he was ready for a fight. "I don't need you. I don't want you. You're a danger to me. I'm a danger to you. Now *goodbye*."

I didn't move. Neither did he.

I didn't say anything. I just stood there. Refusing. Solid. Negative.

It's quite fun arguing with a mindreader. You don't even have to speak.

He almost smiled. "Very impressive. I can hear you thinking 'No' as loud as you can. But it would be stupid of me to take you and it would be stupid of you to come. Why do you *want* to come?"

I didn't answer that. Because I didn't really know.

He laughed. He knew how confused I was. I couldn't keep secrets from him. Maybe it's not so much fun arguing with a mindreader.

He turned and walked off. I followed.

"Why are you following me, Lucy? What's floating around in that wild hairy head of yours?"

I put my hands up to my hair. I'd lost a clip on the roof, or when we were running, and half my hair was bouncing loose over my left ear.

He kept talking as I tidied it up. "If you want revenge on me, then relax. I will be in *so* much trouble with my family if they catch me before I find that flash drive, and they really know how to hurt me, even more than you did in the flat, much more than the police ever could.

"If you want protection, don't be fooled by me staying between you and gravity on that roof. I'm not on your side, Lucy, I'm not your guardian angel. I'm

171

trying to protect myself and my family. Don't trust me to protect you and yours."

He paused and concentrated on something, like a dog sniffing the air, then started walking briskly again.

"If you want answers, I'm not going to tell you any more about us or about Vivien's death. And you won't get to read the flash drive, either, because if I find it I'll destroy it.

"If you want distraction from your grief, then travelling with Vivien's killer, looking for what she tried to hide, that's a stupid way to escape her death. You'd be better reading a good book or having a night out with your friends."

He stopped at a corner and faced me. "Whatever you think you're getting from following me, all you're doing is annoying me and risking your life. So *go away*!"

He turned his back on me and peered round the corner.

I wasn't sure how his mindreading worked. He seemed to know so much, but he missed really obvious stuff too.

He'd nailed most of my reasons for not letting him out of my sight. But he missed a few too. I needed to stay with him to gather as much evidence as I could. Also, I was kind of having fun tonight. And when I could forget his involvement in Viv's death, I actually almost liked him.

He swung back round. "Give me the address if you want to help me, Lucy. Then just go."

"But don't you need to keep me with you? So I don't call the police, tell them what you look like and tell them you're going to Edinburgh?"

"Come on, Lucy. I caught you when you were

dropping off that roof. You wouldn't drop me in it now, would you?"

I didn't say anything. Just looked daggers at him, made my anger burn as hard as I could.

"You would as well!" He laughed. "Ok. If you're giving me the choice of you tagging along or you grassing me up, then please tag along. But remember I can't keep you safe from my family. I can't keep myself safe from them."

He walked fast round the corner. I jogged after him. "So what are we doing?"

"We're getting away from Winslow, away from the first places my family will look."

"Won't they know you're going to Edinburgh?"

"Yes, of course, they'll work that out eventually, so we need to get there before them. Stop asking obvious questions!"

"Well, *sorry*, but I can't read minds, so I have to ask questions. If I know what we're doing, I can be helpful."

"And what skills do you have that will be helpful in this situation, Lucy?"

"You tell me your skills first."

"I'm not telling you anything else about me."

"I already know that you can read minds, move like a cat burglar assassin, and kick like a horse. And I know that you're part of some weird Scottish circus mafia, so probably you can also juggle, walk the tightrope and tame lions. But I've no idea if you can score a hat-trick in extra time, bake muffins or play the piano."

He snorted. "Those are your skills? Football and cakes. Very useful."

"I speak fluent French too."

"Really? You could give me a hand with that. My French is merde."

"You do ordinary stuff like lessons and exams?"

"Yeah, whatever subjects Mum thinks are relevant. Languages, IT, business studies."

"Do you go to school?"

"Not really. We move around a lot." He shook his head. "Stop prying. You can ask about the journey, in case you have any bright ideas, but don't ask about my life or my family."

I shrugged. "I was just being friendly."

"I don't do friendly."

"I can tell."

"Anyway, you weren't just being friendly. You were digging for information."

But I don't think I was digging. If I'm not sure of my motives, how can he be?

"We don't need cakes just now, Lucy, but your local knowledge should be useful. Where can we get a taxi?"

"We can phone one."

"Hailing one is harder to trace."

I nodded. "There's a 24-hour rank ten minutes from here."

"Lead the way, please."

I took the next right. "Where do we want the taxi to take us?"

"Euston or Kings Cross, for a train to Edinburgh."

"Flying is faster."

"You have to show ID to get on a plane," he said. "Trains are anonymous."

"But if your family fly, they'll get there much faster."

"Only once they work out where I'm going. They don't even know I'm working this job yet, and when

174

they realise, they'll try the Winslow addresses before they think of your uncle in Edinburgh. If we get an early train, we could be there before lunchtime, while they're still searching down here."

As we walked through the empty streets, he kept checking his phone and frowning. I got my own phone out to check train times. He peered over my shoulder suspiciously, but nodded when he saw my screen.

"The first train is just after 5.30, from Euston, via Glasgow," I said. "Do you have enough money for a ticket?"

"Yes. I'll pay for yours too. We'll use cash rather than cards."

Cash? For two train tickets? Murder must be profitable.

I had so many questions:

How did his mindreading work?

Did he know everything I was thinking all the time? I didn't think so, or he wouldn't have had to check what I was doing with the phone.

So was his mindreading fuzzier at a distance, and clearer close up?

Was that why touching me freaked him out?

What did his family do for a living?

Why had Viv been so scared that she used Nana's urn as a hiding place?

And why did they kill her?

I knew he wouldn't want to tell me, but I hoped I might get answers when we were stuck on a train together for five hours.

So I kept quiet and kept walking. He kept looking at his phone like it might bite him. Though surely he knew the real danger was walking beside him.

chapter 22

Ciaran Bain, 30th October

It was my duty to contact my family.

Now I knew they were following my trail, it was my duty to warn them about the surveillance teams.

But if I told them not to go near the Shaw residences, they would know I was working this job and they'd realise the next logical destination was Edinburgh. We would lose our headstart.

Lucy led us onto a walkway over a bypass. The noise of the traffic below was constant, even at 4 a.m.

The noise in my head never stops either. Except when I climb mountains in weather too wet and miserable for anyone else to be within miles of me.

I didn't let the traffic noise distract me. I had to decide. Our headstart versus my family's safety.

I wasn't trying to find the flash drive just to prove I could cope outside. I was also doing it to protect my family. It would be pointless to win the race to the urn if half my family got arrested on the way.

I had to warn them.

I thumbed a text to Malcolm.

Don't worry. Not gone rogue. Tidying

> up shaw job loose ends. Alert all teams
> – don't go near shaw residences cos
> staked out by plainclothes police. Bain

I took a deep breath and sent it.
He replied within two minutes.

> Mission not authorised. Report back
> to base now. U r not up to this Bain.
> U r putting us all at risk. Come back in
> or we take u out.

Take you out, not take you in. I shivered.

But now I knew where I stood. I knew they were after me. If Malcolm had said, 'Ok, go for it, I trust you to sort it out,' I wouldn't have known if I could believe him. And at least I'd warned them about the police. They'd check out the Winslow houses anyway, but they wouldn't blunder in, and if they knew there were police about, they'd be unlikely to harm the Shaws.

My phone buzzed again. A text from Mum this time. I sighed and opened it:

> Come home now Ciaran or I'm not
> sure I can protect you any more.
> Please! Mum x

I put my phone on silent and slipped it in my pocket. There was no point in replying to Malcolm. I'd nothing to say to him now until I succeeded. Or failed. There was no point in replying to Mum either, because as usual I couldn't do what she wanted me to do.

We were walking through a built-up area, surrounded by offices containing a handful of almost awake people. Probably cleaners or security staff, going through familiar routines.

Lucy's presence was much clearer, sharper. She was a tired mess of emotions: hate and concern, curiosity and pity, excitement and revenge. At least she wasn't asking questions.

Then suddenly I was assaulted by an increase in volume, a crashing wave of emotions, hundreds of people lurching into my head without warning, crowds of them feeling pain, fear, grief, panic.

I stopped. I couldn't move any closer.

I realised I was sitting on the pavement. I scrabbled back a few metres, past where the volume had first risen, until the emotions were faint enough for me to breathe and think.

Lucy turned round. "Come on. The taxis are this way."

"Where is this all-night taxi rank?" I gasped. "It's not a train station or a... Shit. It's a hospital, isn't it?"

"Yeah. People come and go all night to A&E. There are always taxis."

"And always people in agony, people dying. I can't go any closer to all that pain."

"Sorry." She wasn't sorry. "I didn't realise it would bother you. You really can't survive in the real world, can you? But could you crawl to the taxi rank? It's just round the corner. Or I suppose you could stay here, and I could bring a taxi back for you."

"Would you come back?" I asked.

She shrugged. "Would you still be here?"

I shrugged.

She laughed. "Well, you look like death warmed up,

so you'll fit right in at the hospital. Grit your teeth, get round that corner, get into a taxi and I'll tell the driver to take us to Euston. You'll be ok once we drive further away, won't you?"

I nodded. "Give me a minute, and I'll try to get round the corner."

We were far enough from the Shaw houses that there weren't likely to be any of my family or a surveillance team nearby. It was probably safe to try out my weakest skill: stopping other people's emotions from polluting my head. Could I manage it well enough to walk round a corner without falling over?

I sat with my head in my hands and tried, like I had in the van with Vivien, to build a wall round my mind to stop the world getting in.

Uncle Greg says positive emotions work best as building blocks. He suggests love. Aye, right.

Or happiness. Which I've never been much good at.

Or good memories. Or hopes and ambitions. All too fluffy for me.

The only thing which works for me is building a wall of hate.

I've managed it a couple of times with a smooth cold silver wall of hate. Invading emotions can't get a grip, they slip off.

So, on the gritty pavement, with Lucy hovering, I built a wall of hate.

I hated Malcolm, who never hides his contempt for my weakness.

I hated my mum, who brought me into this family.

I hated my dad, who didn't take me when he left.

The wall wasn't high enough. The hospital emotions were still lapping over the top. Who else?

I hated Roy, who could get out and leave me behind.

I hated Daniel, because he enjoys using his skills.

I hated Vivien, for pulling my mask off and for having to die.

I hated Ivy Shaw, for experimenting on Billy Reid.

I hated Lucy for... for what? None of this was her fault. But I could hate her for seeing me collapse. For seeing me cry. Yeah, I hated her too.

And I hated myself, most of all, for being so bloody useless...

All this good strong hate ringed round my mind, pushing away the fear and pain of the hospital.

I'd built a wall to protect me. But now I couldn't sense anyone approaching, I couldn't sense any threats. Now I was mindblind.

I hauled myself up, holding tight to my hate.

Lucy jogged along the road then round the corner towards a massive white hospital. I lurched like a zombie after her, legs sliding out from under me. I staggered over a flowerbed on a roundabout towards a row of black cabs.

Hate. Weakness.

Hate. Contempt.

Hate. Resentment.

Hate...

I got there.

I fell into the front taxi and collapsed onto the seat. I heard Lucy saying, "Euston please, going by Egham, not by Winslow."

Clever route, I thought. That momentary admiration put a crack in my hate, the silver wall crumbled and the hospital misery slithered in.

I sensed someone near death.

I sensed someone lose hope.

I felt someone die...

I slipped off the seat onto the taxi floor.

"Is your boyfriend ok?" I half-heard the taxi driver over the sound of the engine starting up. "He won't throw up, will he? He's not infectious, is he?"

"He's just been up all night," Lucy said. "He'll be fine."

I could sense the driver's reluctance. He didn't want me in his taxi. But I desperately needed him to drive away.

I dragged myself onto the flip-up seat behind him. I pulled out a £50 note and passed it to him. "Just get us to the station," I said as clearly as I could. "Thanks."

Then I slammed the shutter closed, fastened the seat belt to hold myself up and dropped my head down. I let go completely, sliding under the waves of pain thudding out of the hospital.

The taxi drove off, and the emotional chaos drained slowly away.

When, finally, I could think enough to move, I sat up.

Lucy was shaking her head. I sensed sharp claws of curiosity and a twinge of amusement. "You're not exactly a superhero, are you? All that muscle and kick and cleverness, but you turn to jelly every time someone gets a little emotional."

"A little emotional! Lucy, there were people dying in there. I felt them die."

"Poor you, you're so sensitive! But that didn't stop you killing my sister, did it? Did you have a little cry after she died?"

"Keep your voice down!"

The barrier was closed. The intercom light was off. The driver had switched his radio on. But even so, words like 'kill' and 'die' have a way of making themselves heard.

I checked his mind was on the road, not on us, then I looked at Lucy. She was generating hate far better than I just had, almost exploding with it.

"Did you lose it like this when Viv died?"

She wasn't going to stop asking questions and I didn't have the strength to distract her.

"Did you lose it like this?" she asked again.

"Yes."

"Did you care? Did you try to... stop it?"

"Yes. Yes. I did. Both." I spoke softly. I wasn't proud of my answers.

"I can't read your mind. I don't know if you're lying. I don't know if I can trust you."

"You can't trust me. But I'm not lying."

"Did you fight them? When they were killing her?"

"No."

"Why not?"

"It was too late."

"Why did she die?"

"Because..." I stopped. If I said Vivien died because she saw my face, then Lucy would know that she was almost certainly dead too. "I can't tell you."

"Why not?"

"She died because of what she knew. And I don't want... you to... em..."

"You're trying to protect me?"

I shrugged.

"Don't bother. Don't you bother protecting me! Why would I want your protection when all you did when my sister was dying was whinge a little? Is that what you did? Then what? What did you do next?"

I didn't say anything.

"Did you have a wobble, did you run off because it was all too heavy? Did you run off and leave her to die?"

I closed my eyes. I felt it all again.

My face in her head. Her terror. Her panic. Her mind switching off.

But I didn't fall into her death. Lucy's hate and contempt battered me back into the taxi, anchored me to the present, pulled me away from the nothingness of Vivien.

"You did! You ran off! You left her to die! You weak wimping wobbling pathetic scum. That's worse than having the guts to kill her yourself. I hope it hurts. I hope all the pain and death in the world hurt you for ever..."

I couldn't defend myself.

Was she right?

Was I worse than Malcolm?

I'd never actually killed anyone. But I'd been involved in grabs before. I knew what could happen to the targets. And even after feeling Vivien's misery and fear, I'd been ready to do it again the next day, to track an undercover cop and betray him to his death, if I'd been allowed to go along.

I'd always known I was crap.

But now I saw myself through Lucy's eyes.

And I wasn't just crap.

I was a wimp.

A coward.

Weak.

Evil.

I hated myself. I hated myself so much I could

probably block out the world, but I let it in. Let it rip me apart.

Lucy stewed in her grief and hate, ignoring me, looking out the window.

And we drove steadily through London. Towards the train, towards Scotland, towards the urn, the ashes, the answers.

chapter 23

Ciaran Bain, 30th October

It was a quiet journey.

Lucy was concentrating on not crying.

And I couldn't think of anything to say that wasn't a pathetic excuse for my behaviour. A pathetic excuse for my life.

We were starting to drive through bits of London I recognised from the telly.

Then I sensed a hunter. Focussed. Searching. Ready to attack. Patient, but burning with anger. Malcolm.

"Stop!" I slammed the plastic shutter open and screamed at the driver. "*Stop!*"

He slowed down. Slightly. "But I thought you had a train to catch? We're nearly *at* Euston!"

"Turn round," I insisted. "Drive away from the station."

"He hates being early," Lucy explained. "We can't go to the station yet. Please, turn round."

At last, as I felt my uncle's rising spikes of interest, the driver U-turned on the empty street and drove away from Euston. Shaking his head, wishing we were out of his taxi.

Lucy looked at me suspiciously. "What's going on?"

I moved to the back seat and whispered, "My family are at the station. Staking it out. Waiting for me. I sensed their concentration."

"Did they... sense... you?"

"I don't think I was near enough for them to sense me. But I'm not sure. This bloody driver drove on for at least a couple of blocks after I detected them, then hung about far too long..."

"We were near enough for you to sense them, but not for them to sense you?"

"Yeah."

"Can you read minds further away than they can? Are you better at this than them?"

I choked on a laugh as the taxi stopped at deserted traffic lights. "Better? No one else collapses when they're reading, so 'better' is not how I'd describe it."

I moved back to the seat behind the driver. I could think more clearly when I wasn't right beside Lucy. I asked her to check bus times to Edinburgh on her phone, while I worked out what to do.

"Bus times? But no one takes the bus!"

"Precisely. That's why we're going to take the bus." I remembered what I knew about exit routes. "The buses go from Victoria, which is a nice long way from here."

I took my own phone off silent and checked my messages. I ignored four from my mum, but opened a very recent one from Roy:

> Keep moving. U came 2 close.
> They're on to u.

Shit.

"Lucy. They know I'm here."

She looked up. "The first bus from Victoria isn't until nine o'clock."

"You have to go to the bus station on your own. Buy our tickets." I hauled out a handful of notes and gave them to her. "Then buy a book, something totally unlike our night, no chases or police. Buy a romance or something historical. Find a dark corner, get your head down and read the book. Lose yourself in the story completely. Don't think about me or my family or being on the run."

She was going to argue. I put my hands up. "Please, Lucy. I'm going to lead my family to Kings Cross as a decoy, then I'll get away and join you. Just do what I say. Please."

She wasn't convinced.

"Do we trust each other?" I asked.

We both shook our heads.

"But will you be there, waiting?" I asked.

"Yes."

"Then I'll find you." Which sounded more like a threat than a promise, but I couldn't do any better.

I handed the taxi driver another note. "Take her to Victoria Coach Station. Thanks, mate."

Then I turned back to Lucy. "See you there?"

She nodded, still surprised by the speed of our changing plans.

I jumped out of the taxi, to run straight back to my family.

I sprinted away from Lucy and her on/off hate, towards Euston, towards Malcolm and his constant anger.

My family knew the exit routes out of London too. They'd know that once I realised they were at Euston, the next obvious place for me to go was Kings Cross, not far away. So I'd lead them there, then run like a rabbit north, as if I was looking for another station on the route to Scotland. Then when I was out of range, when they couldn't sense me, I'd circle south to the coach station.

And I'd try not to worry that I was on foot or paying taxis, and couldn't get either a train or a plane, and that my family had unlimited cash, and cars.

Lucy Shaw, 30th October

He sprinted towards the station.

Running straight at danger, as fast as he could.

Idiot.

At least he was getting to do something.

I, on the other hand, had been ordered to sit in a corner and read a book about corsets and tapestries.

What if his family caught him?

What if he changed his mind and joined up with them again?

What if he was planning to get the train to Edinburgh on his own and reach my uncle before me?

I had no idea what he was going to do. Which was unfair, because he always knew what I was going to do.

But I could find out what he was doing.

I wasn't sure how his mindreading worked, but if he could detect his family and the police on the other side of buildings, he'd detect me if I followed behind him in a taxi.

However I knew where he was going. Or at least,

where he said he was going. So I could get there first.

I wouldn't even break my promise to him. I'd plenty of time before the bus was due to leave, so I would still get to Victoria before him.

I leant forward and spoke to the taxi driver, whose face, never mind thoughts, I could read easily. "Don't take me to Victoria, please, take me to Kings Cross, but go the long way round."

I wanted to know if I could trust this boy, if this family existed. So I'd go to Kings Cross and watch what happened. I'd even use his advice to hide my mind in a story. If it would work on his family, presumably it would work on him too.

The taxi driver was shaking his head. "You kids just can't make up your minds, can you?"

"I'll get out at Kings Cross and you can keep all that change."

Ciaran Bain, 30th October

I couldn't run straight at them. I had to give the impression of sneaking past, of fear, of incompetence.

From where I was now, getting to Kings Cross meant going right past the entrance to Euston.

So I walked slowly along the pavement towards Euston. Like I was uncertain about what I'd sensed. Like I was hoping the fright five minutes ago was a mistake.

I could sense them, waiting and searching, but they couldn't quite sense me yet.

I was glancing around me like a rabbit in the middle of a field, looking for boltholes.

189

I had to be nervous, on the verge of panic, not checking my surroundings efficiently because I was too scared to concentrate. Then it might be plausible that I wouldn't notice them. And when it became so obvious they were onto me that I couldn't ignore it, then I could panic and bolt.

I let the questions I'd been forcing down all night crash to the surface.

What the hell was I doing?

Why was I disobeying Malcolm?

Why was I undermining Mum?

I allowed myself to be a mess of perfectly genuine doubts and fears. I was moving erratically, acting conspicuously, letting my emotions overtake my training.

I was that idiot boy, Bain, making a mess of it again, being exactly as useless as Malcolm always knew I was.

But while I walked I was also scanning for my way out.

I sensed a spike of interest from Euston. At last. They had noticed me. I tried to ignore it for as long as possible, giving off nerves and uncertainty. I sensed a hunter homing in, but I kept the panicked questions circling round my head.

Would I ever be able to go home?

Would I have to keep running all my life?

Then more hunters, a pack, all grasping after my trail of emotions.

When I reached the red circle of Euston Square Underground, I couldn't ignore them any more. The spikes of interest from ahead were too strong. They were starting to organise. They were coming for me.

So I acted like panicking prey, and decided that it was just as fast to keep running forward to Kings Cross as it was to turn round and run away.

I changed direction like that terrified rabbit, hurdled the railing and sprinted to the other side of the road, which wasn't the direct route to Kings Cross but would give me a little distance from the hunters.

I ran faster than I'd ever run round our track at home. I ran for my life. I didn't care if they knew it. I wasn't pretending at all. I was being hunted. So I ran.

Of course, they could run too. And they could use their cars. But I had a headstart and I wasn't faffing about giving orders like I could sense Malcolm doing.

So I ran at a hellishly fast pace along the wide road. The family hadn't posted anyone on the outer perimeter, they all had to get out of Euston past a row of shops, the parked buses at the stances outside and a narrow park. Someone got tangled up. Roy was falling over again.

They were so close now I could even hear Uncle Paul yelling. Now I was past Euston and on my way to Kings Cross. But I was too visible, the only person on this early morning pavement.

I heard a car screeching round a corner. I didn't look. I just kept running.

They were chasing me as I ran towards Kings Cross, which was the first part of the plan. But I couldn't let them catch me, so I took the first right-hand turning and hurtled down it.

I'd got their attention, now I had to get away.

Lucy Shaw, 30th October

Kings Cross was quieter than I'd ever seen, because there weren't many trains this early. But the newsagent was open, taking delivery of papers, so I bought a book, just like I'd been told.

I didn't read in a dark corner, because it isn't good for your eyes. I sat under the edge of the curving triangles roof, where the boy would cross my eye-line when he came in. I couldn't *think* about searching for him, I had to concentrate on the book, so that anyone reading my mind only saw glimpses of lovelorn maidens in inconvenient skirts.

I lost myself in a story and waited to see if he had been telling the truth.

Ciaran Bain, 30th October

I turned left, parallel to the main road, heading in the direction of Kings Cross. This was definitely the centre of London. Even the back streets were filled with curved white windows and black iron balconies, blurring in the corner of my eye as I ran.

Malcolm and Daniel were excellent at pinpointing the location of a mind, but I hoped I was running fast enough that I was hard to pin down.

I hurtled around corners, past posh shops and little cafes, sensing screams of mental annoyance behind me as my pursuers got snarled up in the maze of back streets.

I was also searching, under all the erratic rabbit running, for my real way out.

I heard a couple of cars screeching one block over, past the heaving of my breath and pounding of blood in my ears. I was in good shape, but I couldn't keep up this pace much longer.

I was running towards a pub with flower baskets hanging over its windows, when I sensed them getting closer. Not the hunters on foot, they hadn't a hope of catching me. But the hunters in the cars were ignoring one-way streets and red lights, trying to cut me off.

Then I sensed the mind I had been hoping for, my way out.

But I also sensed...

Shit!

I also sensed what I should have anticipated.

I wasn't just running from Malcolm's team at Euston. I was running towards another team at Kings Cross.

Of course. They had both obvious boltholes covered.

The family must have sensed my genuine shock. Now I could legitimately turn and run north, like I was trying to run all the way to Edinburgh.

So I headed for the mind I'd detected a moment ago. A patiently waiting mind, a working but resting mind.

I could win on foot for a short distance, but for a race halfway across London, I needed wheels. I turned a corner and found the black cab of a taxi driver hoping for an early morning fare.

As I got in the taxi, Malcolm noticed my change of direction, my change of intention. He went into Sergeant Major mode, new orders exploding around him.

I told the driver to head north, on the same bearing as the train line, so the family would think I was searching for the next station any Leeds or York or

Edinburgh trains would stop at. But as she drove off, I sensed one more thing.

A single mind. Past the chasing tail from Euston and the waiting ring at Kings Cross. A familiar mind, but not family. A mind muffled by second-hand emotions like someone reading a book or watching a film.

It was Lucy. Hiding in a story, but not at Victoria. At Kings Cross.

I yelled, "Stop!" at the driver.

What was Lucy *doing*?

I couldn't go and get her. I had to get away myself.

She'd chosen to ignore my advice. She'd chosen to put herself in danger.

I had to leave her.

I nodded to the driver and repeated my instruction to head north.

Then I felt a jolt of recognition. Someone had recognised Lucy.

Was she sitting in the open?

Idiot.

So that was it. She was already dead. I couldn't do anything. I had to leave her. I sat back as the taxi drove off.

chapter 24

Lucy Shaw, 30th October

I suddenly felt like an antelope being watched by a pride of lions, with warning tingles across my shoulders and up my neck. I kept my nose pointed at the book, but raised my eyes to glance round.

Was the boy here? He would probably be seriously pissed off if he'd seen me. But I wasn't scared of his anger. He always calmed down pretty fast, and he hadn't actually attacked me since I tried to stab him.

But it wasn't him.

There was a line of people looking at me, over by the brick entrance to Platforms 0–8.

A line of people, moving towards me.

Striding forward, in the middle, was a slim woman in heels, with bright blonde hair and too much make-up for this time in the morning.

I recognised her. She was the Irish reporter who'd interviewed us about Nana.

"Lucy Shaw!" she called cheerfully. "What are you doing here, dear?"

They were spreading out like a net.

There was the reporter, a skinny man in jeans, a shorter woman and a couple of teenage boys, a ginger spotty one and a handsome darker pony-tailed one, both tall and muscly, both with the same sour scowl that the blond burglar had when he was trying to sense the surveillance team.

This must be his family.

I was caught in a trap meant for him.

I looked round in panic. The station was almost empty. No police or rail staff, just a few sleepy passengers. No one who could help.

Could I run? His family were fanning out, blocking the nearest exit. They were walking towards me, staring at me. Were they reading my mind already?

I was shaking with fear and with anger at my own stupidity. They had *killed* Viv! What would they do to me?

The pony-tailed boy was reaching out his hand to me, staring at me with his dark eyes.

What could I do?

"Get up. Run."

A voice, in my head. Could I get up? I was too scared to move. Anyway, what was the point? If they could recognise my mind, they could follow me, I would never get away.

"Get *up*, you idiot. Get up and run."

I felt a fist punch my shoulder. It was his voice. The blond burglar. Not in my head. Behind me. I got up and I ran.

I ran round the back of the bench and followed him away from the train lines.

I glanced back. The Irish woman was falling behind, talking on a phone. The two teenagers, taller than us, with longer legs, were chasing us.

We sprinted towards the exit leading to St Pancras.

But there was a man in the way, between two wide white pillars, arms spread to halt us. The photographer who worked with the Irish reporter.

I slowed down.

The blond boy kept going, launched a kick at the man's stomach and muttered, "Sorry, Uncle Hugh," as the photographer crunched to the ground.

I sprinted out of the station, and the boy grabbed my sleeve and pulled me into a taxi. He spoke fast to the driver and the taxi accelerated away as I was closing the door.

I looked back. The short woman was bent over the injured man on the ground. The teenagers were running after the taxi, the dark one reaching out to grab the door handle.

"Don't look in his eyes!" the boy beside me shouted.

But I already had. His cruel narrow brown eyes. Nothing like the failed burglar's bright blue eyes. He laughed as he ran alongside the taxi, trying to get the door open. But the taxi was too fast, too heavy, and he lost his grip as we swerved round the corner.

The taxi driver said, "You're in a rush, love."

The boy said calmly, "Just a bit of family trouble. Nothing to worry about." He slid the barrier shut.

I stared behind me at the pony-tailed boy as he waved his phone at us.

The blond burglar slumped into the seat beside me. "Did you look in his eyes just there, Lucy?"

"Em. Yes."

"And when he was walking towards you in the station? Did you look in his eyes then?"

"Em." I remembered noticing how dark his eyes were. "Yes."

"Shit." He slumped lower. "What were you thinking when you made eye contact?"

"What?"

"Were you thinking about buses? Or Victoria?"

"No. I was just thinking: How stupid am I? How scary are they? Are they reading my mind already?"

"Great. Now they know you know about the mindreading. And when we got in the taxi, were you thinking about where we were going?"

"No, I was leaving that to you, you were talking to the driver. I was just hoping he didn't get in the taxi and thinking his eyes were a different colour from yours."

"Why were you comparing our eyes?"

"Looking for a family resemblance."

"So he knows I've told you we're cousins. Great. Thanks."

"You didn't tell me that some of you read minds with eye contact. That might have been helpful."

"Eye contact, skin contact, voices. We do it all, between us. One great-uncle even used to walk into a room and sniff out vague thoughts from people's B.O. My mum jokes that the next generation will be able to read by tweet and text." He grinned, then looked at me seriously.

"Lucy, think back. Did you think the words 'bus' or 'coach' or 'Victoria' at any point from when you first saw Daniel until he was out of sight?"

"No. I didn't."

"Alright. It's a risk, but we have to chance the bus..."

His phone buzzed and he pulled it out of his pocket, looking at it like it was a cockroach, the way he always did. Presumably he didn't have friends who sent him invites to parties and rude pictures.

I grabbed it off him, suddenly, before either of us knew I was going to.

The newest text read:

> She's pretty but u don't get to keep her. And she isn't worth the thrashing u'll get when I catch u, wimp. She knows 2 much. Does she know what my dad does to girls who know 2 much? C u very soon. Daniel

I handed the phone back.

"His dad kills girls who know too much," I said quietly.

"Yes," the boy said, dropping his phone on the taxi seat. "But you don't know too much, do you? You don't know anything at all, or else you wouldn't have done something so... *stupid*! Why didn't you go to Victoria like I told you to? Why were you sitting right there, right where I was leading them? Of all the stupid, misguided, ridiculous, dangerous, pointless..."

I let him rant at me for a couple of minutes, because I knew he was right. But I didn't know why he'd arrived at the last minute and saved me. I wonder if he knew himself.

He stopped at last and turned away. Then he turned back. "Ok. Just tell me what you thought you were doing, once, without excuses, and I'll try not to mention it again."

"I wanted to see if you were telling the truth, see if your family really existed and if you really are on my side rather than theirs."

"I'm not *on your side*, Lucy. I never claimed to be." He shook his head in amazement. "Were you just waiting for me to turn up, hoping I'd be pleased to see you?"

"I didn't think you would see me. I was hiding in a book like you said. I just wanted to see what you would do at Kings Cross."

"I wasn't going *into* Kings Cross, I was only going *towards* it. I was leading the pursuit to a bolt-hole, I wasn't planning to get trapped inside. You nearly got trapped there on your own."

"But I thought it'd be safe, hiding in a book. I didn't think they would find me. I didn't even think *you* would find me. I didn't think it was dangerous."

"We're not just mindreaders. We've got ordinary eyes too. They recognised you from photos in the files. My mum and uncle have even met you in person."

"Oh. The reporter is your *mum*?"

"Yes."

"But she's Irish."

"No, she's not. She can do loads of accents. Teaching her to do accents is the only useful thing my dad ever gave her, she says." He looked at his hands, clenched fists inside his gloves.

"You're not useful then."

"Apparently not," he said.

"You got me out of there, so I think you're useful. Sometimes."

"Just as well I'm a mindreader or I wouldn't know that was a thank you."

He leant forward and spoke to the taxi driver, then leant back and spoke to me. "My family think we're going north by taxi, so if we get out and hide now, they'll drive right past us."

As the taxi pulled over, he shoved more cash at the driver and we leapt out.

I was determined not to do anything else stupid

until I knew more about this family's powers, so I followed him up a side street, over a fence and down a ramp into an underground car park. He crouched in an oily corner behind a van, his back against the wall. I crouched beside him.

"We've hidden our bodies from them, now we need to hide our minds until they've gone past." He pointed to the book, still clutched in my hand, my fingernails almost embedded in the girl's face on the cover. "Read your book and that'll hide you from them, just like it did until Mum recognised your face."

"You don't have a book. Do you want to share this one?"

"No, I don't have time to get involved in the story. I'll have to take a risk and lose myself inside... em... inside somewhere kind of dark. But it's not easy to pull myself back out. So in... What time is it?"

I looked for my phone, to check the time. "I've lost my phone!"

"No, you haven't. I took it out of your pocket and left it in the taxi. I left mine too."

"You stole my phone!"

"Phones are easy to trace. You can buy a new phone. But if my family find you again, you won't be able to buy a new life." He handed me his watch. "In fifteen minutes, please shout at me. Like in the hospital taxi, be angry at me, hate me. But please wake me up or I might stay in the dark for ever. Will you wake me up?"

This was my best chance to bargain with him. So I folded my arms. "What's your name?"

"What?"

"If I'm going to drag you back from 'somewhere kind of dark' I'll need to call you by name."

He glanced at the car park entrance.

"Are they near?"

He nodded.

"Do you trust me with your name?"

"My name is Ciaran. Ciaran Bain. Now read your bloody book."

So I did. I glanced up once and saw him fall back against the stained wall, eyes closed. Then I flung myself passionately into the night before a battle. Even though I knew the English would win, I let myself care about which dashing officer the girl would give her lace hankie to, because obviously the soldier who got the hankie was bound to die...

I reached the end of a chapter, and realised what year this was and who I was. I looked at the boy's watch. I'd been reading for twenty minutes. I hoped his family were out of range by now.

Ciaran Bain was collapsed in the corner beside me, eyes closed, breath fast and shallow.

I could leave him in whatever psychic coma he was in forever, or until the van driver came back.

I could tie him up with my shoelaces and call the police.

I could kick him black and blue.

Or I could wake him up. Like he asked me to. Like he trusted me to. Even though I'd made a right mess of the last thing he asked me to do.

If I woke him up now, I could take my revenge later. Somewhere less dirty and cold.

"Ciaran," I whispered. "Ciaran Bain."

Nothing.

I spoke louder. "Bain! Wake up! We've got a bus to catch."

Nothing.

I touched his forehead. It was cold and clammy.

I curved my hand along the width of his smooth forehead and I did what he'd asked. I hated him. It wasn't hard.

"You are scum, Ciaran Bain. You are a creeping sneaking thieving piece of scum. You are a murdering lying sister-killing..."

He moaned.

I lifted his hand, I pulled off that stupid glove, wrapped my fingers round his palm and hated him.

He had taken everything from me.

My perfect sister.

My normal family.

My safety.

He gulped one deep breath.

I thought about everyone else hating him:

My mum and dad demanding justice.

His dyed-blonde mum screeching at him.

That long-haired cruel-eyed Daniel kicking him and laughing.

The police running at him with handcuffs, pepper spray and arrest warrants.

Viv's voice haunting him.

All calling his name. Ciaran Bain.

"Whoa! Enough, Lucy, enough!"

He jerked his hand out of mine and sat up. Then he threw up under the van.

I moved out of range.

When he'd finished, I asked, "Are you ok?"

He coughed. "Do you care?"

I didn't answer. I just gave him his glove and his watch. And we went to the coach station.

chapter 25

Ciaran Bain, 30th October

I didn't want to pay another taxi fare, because I'd been spending money too fast and using a cash machine could reveal our location. We had enough time to take a red London bus towards Victoria Coach Station.

We climbed to the top deck, sat on the line of seats at the back, one at each window, and ignored each other.

Lucy's levels of hate were subsiding. Perhaps she couldn't maintain an absolute desire for revenge for long.

Halfway to Victoria, Lucy swivelled round to face me and put her feet up on the seat. "So, how does hiding in a book work? Why did it hide me from your family, but not from you? Don't you use the same tricks as them?"

I didn't answer.

But she was determined to have a friendly conversation. "Were you trying something new? Something your family don't do?"

I shrugged. "Kind of. I've noticed people's minds are harder to grasp when they're reading a book or watching a DVD than when they're listening to music or playing with their phone, because they're lost in a story. I thought it was worth a go, to protect you."

"So you were guessing? You were experimenting on me?" She almost smiled. "Now I'm not a skinny stray cat, I'm a guinea pig."

"It was not an experiment!" What did she think I was, some kind of sadist, who would *experiment* on her? "I would *never* experiment on a person. That would be sick."

"But you did experiment on me. You had a theory, that your family wouldn't detect someone if they were reading a book, then you tested your theory, by telling me to lose myself in the story, and now you have a result, because you detected me and your family didn't. Your experiment worked. So you *did* experiment on me."

"No I didn't! I was just trying to keep you safe!"

"I know you were trying to keep me safe. I'm just saying it *was* an experiment."

"No it wasn't! Experiments are torture, like rabbits with shampoo in their eyes or dogs smoking cigarettes. Experiments are scientists in white coats, with electrodes and flashcards. I would never do that."

Her family would though. Her nana experimented on Billy Reid, with wires on his head and chest. I bet her family would still experiment on me. I bet her Edinburgh uncle is a doctor or a scientist, wearing a white coat and cutting up frogs.

Lucy was just as bad, with her constant curiosity about how my powers work. Curiosity leads to questions, to tests, to experiments.

"I didn't experiment on you. And *no one* will ever experiment on me!"

"Calm down. It's not a war crime. It's only science. And that thing you did in the car park, was that more guesswork?"

205

She just wouldn't stop pushing me!

"What was it? What did you do?" She leant forward eagerly, keen to find out more with her nasty scientific mind.

So I told her. "I went into your sister's death. I jumped into the last moment of her life, when her terror shut down, her thoughts broke off and her mind went dark. I hid in the shadows of her death. So Vivien kept me safe. Thanks, Viv."

I turned away. But I sensed Lucy's shock and revulsion, I heard her sudden gasping tears.

Served her right for asking too many questions.

Lucy Shaw, 30th October

He used her. He used her terror and pain to protect himself. He wrapped himself up in her death like an invisibility cloak.

That's so *low*. Almost worse than killing her. Like he was sucking up the last moments of her life to make himself stronger. What a disgusting slimy creep.

We were nearly at Victoria. I had to decide. Was I travelling north with him? Was I going to sit in a bus for nearly ten hours with him, knowing he was keeping Viv's fear and death like a trophy, knowing he was using her murder for himself?

Could I even bear to be near him?

I wanted to protect Uncle Vince and I wanted revenge on Ciaran Bain. And now I knew more about Bain, I had a clearer idea how to get revenge. Also I didn't want to stay in London, near his brassy mum and scary cousin.

So I'd get on the bus, but not as his travelling companion. I'd get on the bus as the devil on his shoulder, as my sister's revenge, as his worst nightmare.

Ciaran Bain, 30th October

What an idiot! Telling her how I had hidden my mind, telling her how useful her sister's death was to me.

I'd wanted to punish her for going to Kings Cross, for pushing for answers, for winding me up about experiments. I'd wanted to shock her.

I'd done all that and more. I thought she hated me before. But now she was boiling over with disgust and contempt.

This bus journey was going to be fun. A whole day in a metal box with someone who would happily wind my guts round my neck and watch me choke to death. Also the toilets would probably smell and there would be old ladies talking loudly about their bladder problems. I should just have gone to bed last night and not got involved in this Shaw job at all.

We didn't talk when we arrived at Victoria. I checked for any surveillance teams or hunters, but apparently no one thought we'd travel by bus, because I didn't sense anyone watching for us. So we walked together, still not talking, to the ticket office.

I bought my ticket. A single to Edinburgh.

She bought hers, with my money and not a word of thanks. She got a return. Optimistic.

Then she headed round the station towards the gate, while I bought supplies at the newsagents. More chewing gum, because after throwing up, my mouth felt the way Roy's dirty-washing heap smelt; water and chocolate to keep us alive; a few more books; an *A–Z* of Edinburgh. Then I found the right gate and sat at the other end of the bench from Lucy. No one watching us would know we were together.

We weren't together. We'd never been further apart.

I should just leave her here. Right now, she was a danger to both of us.

But before I could work out a way to leave her behind safely, the bus arrived and she was showing her ticket. I let the few other passengers get on, then I followed.

Lucy was sitting a couple of rows from the front. She smiled like a hyena and patted the seat beside her. I shook my head and walked towards the back of the almost empty bus. I chose a seat far enough from the toilets not to be overpowered by air freshener, and far enough from Lucy not to be overwhelmed by her simmering hatred.

As the bus drove off, I was checking the other passengers and the driver for problems and scanning as far as I could outside the bus for any hunters.

Had we left the surveillance teams behind in Winslow? I caught the odd whiff of police pursuit as we drove through the city, but nothing that related to us.

Where were my family? Were they still heading north? Would we be travelling on the same motorway as them? I had to stay alert.

I'd bought a book for myself. Something I'd never normally read, a book with dragons and swords and elves. I wasn't sure whether my family would recognise me if I was lost in a story, but it might be useful to find out. It wasn't an experiment though.

I'd bought Lucy a couple more books, to last her all the way to Scotland. But she wasn't reading, she was sitting still, wrapped in her hoodie and her hate.

I balanced down the bus and leant over her seat.

"Read," I whispered. "Please. They might be driving up to Edinburgh too, or they might be waiting by the motorway to check all the buses going north." I offered her another book.

She shoved it away. "I'm not taking advice from you. Especially untested experimental advice. If they're going to Edinburgh, they're already miles ahead of us. And if they've guessed we're taking a bus, then as this bus has "Edinburgh" in bright orange letters on the front, I don't think reading a book is going to save me. So don't you try to protect me with your nasty little theories."

I staggered back up the bus. Two old ladies showed me their bright plastic teeth as I passed. Sympathy for the nice boy with the grumpy girlfriend. Aye, right.

I read anyway. Not just to protect myself, but also because it was too frustrating to think about the mess I'd got myself into when I couldn't do anything to solve it for hours.

I read a page, then checked inside and outside the bus for problems, then read again, then checked again. Except during battle scenes, when I occasionally forgot to check for a few pages.

There were no problems though. No one was following the bus. No one was searching up ahead. The only person on the bus who wasn't either asleep or bored or chatting about trivia was the one-girl vendetta down at the front.

Then she stepped up the aisle. "Did you buy water?"

"Do you want a bottle?"

"Do I have to ask nicely? I don't think I can be polite to you."

"Here. No please or thanks required." She grabbed the bottle and the chocolate I held out. She turned to go. Then she turned back and sat down beside me.

I moved my leg and shoulder so we weren't touching.

She gulped a mouthful of water. She was grateful, but didn't say thanks. She glared at me, because she knew I could sense her gratitude. It was quite fun reading someone who knew they were being read. She knew she couldn't hide anything from me and she really resented it.

Her hatred of me was building and sharpening, then I sensed her make a decision. With a flash of fear I wondered if she had a weapon.

But she wasn't focussed on anything about her body apart from her hands holding the bottle. She wasn't concentrating on a weapon. I was safe.

Then she shifted. Away from the aisle, right up against me. Shoulder to shoulder, thigh to thigh.

And I saw a picture of Vivien. Alive. Laughing.

Lucy was remembering her sister.

I jerked away, pushed myself against the window.

So that's what she had decided on. A bus journey full of punishment, of guilt, grief, pain. Like in her grampa's flat, but for a whole day.

She put her warm hand on my cheek.

Her parents crying, gulping and snottering.

I shoved her hand away.

Should I fight her off? But we couldn't spend the whole day wrestling at the back of a bus. Someone would notice.

She grabbed my wrist and wrapped both hands round it.

Her parents telling her that Viv was dead.

Her shock.

Her disbelief.

Her frustration...

"Fight me, Bain. Don't just sit there, fight me." She let go. "Wimp. I know it hurts, so fight back."

She was sitting so close. The seams of our jeans were touching. I had no space to move.

I could feel her breath, her heat, her hate, her anger at me, at herself, at her sister, at her parents. She *really* wanted a fight.

"Fight me, Bain!"

"You want me to fight you? I could break your neck right now." I lifted my hands.

I sensed her sudden shocked terror. How could she keep accusing me of murder and forget that I could easily kill her?

I lowered my hands. "I don't want to fight."

"Well I *do*!"

With all the confidence of someone who'd just seen their enemy surrender, she ripped off my left glove, held my hand tightly and...

And I realised she had stronger weapons now than in the flat last night, weapons too strong for me to bear.

Lucy Shaw, 30th October

Wimp.

Wilting sodding pathetic *wimp*!

He'd just given up. Wimp.

211

So I hit him with everything I knew about him, everything that hurts him most.

I locked him in a bright white room, and added equipment from my dad's clinic. Opthalmoscopes and retinoscopes on a shelf. The huge many-eyed refractor head hanging from the ceiling. The black leather chair with its motor and levers, and extra straps and buckles.

I mixed in a dentist's surgery, with probes, needles, tubes, sinks and the smell of disinfectant. Then the science lab at school with Bunsen burners, goggles and glass containers.

He was shaking, gritting his teeth. Trying not to move, trying not to make a noise.

He'd be *screaming* when I was done with him.

I thought the word *experiment*.

Experimenting...

Proving...

Testing...

Theories...

Facts...

Science...

I thought of wires, stopwatches, pulses, temperatures, doctors, consultants, researchers and professors.

Then I had a better idea.

An MRI scanner. Lying flat in a metal tube, trapped, unable to move while doctors, nurses, researchers, professors, *scientists* studied his brain. Read it, scanned it, printed it, stored it on a computer.

I pinned scans of brains, all the colours of the rainbow, on the white walls inside my head.

He was gasping for air now, his eyes were tight shut. The left hand, the one I was holding, was hot and shaking. His right hand was clenching, gripping, loosening.

Why wouldn't he *fight*, the coward?

Ciaran Bain, 30ᵗʰ October

I tried to build a wall against her. I really did try.

The wall that had worked at the hospital:

solid
      smooth
           high
                silver
                    hate.

She was forcing pictures and noises, words and ideas into my head. Clinical cold flat voices speaking my name, then lists of theories and experiments and conclusions.

I had to hate someone.

Hate Vivien for dying?

Hate Mum for protecting her family?

Hate Malcolm for doing his job?

Hate Daniel for being better than me?

Hate Lucy for seeking justice?

I couldn't.

Faces peering at me, bright white lights.

I was shaking too much to hold onto the hate.

Cold metal touching me, white coats around me.

I tried harder. I hated myself, for being cowardly and cruel and selfish and useless. I could hate myself easily enough. But I hated myself for the same reasons Lucy hated me. So my sweet silver hate just built a ramp for her crusading hate to storm up and attack me.

Wires on my chest.

Needles in the backs of my hands.
Lights burning my closed eyes.
I couldn't build a wall.
I wouldn't fight her off.
I just had to bear it.

Lucy Shaw, 30th October

Coward. Wimp. Loser.

I'd been imagining cartoon scientists wearing big glasses and white coats, in expensively equipped labs, for half an hour.

And he still hadn't lifted a finger.

I needed a rest. But if I stopped, could I start again?

I pulled my vision out into a wide shot. Not just Bain in a chair, but his whole family, in a long line, like butterflies pinned onto a collector's table. All being experimented on.

He groaned and whimpered. It was the first noise he'd made apart from stuttering breathing since he'd threatened to break my neck.

Then his arm went limp. He'd fainted. *Wimp*.

I let go. Now I could take a rest. I shifted away, nearer the aisle, and grabbed the water and chocolate.

I checked the time on the clock at the front of the bus. We weren't due in until late afternoon, so I could re-run that experiment horror film a dozen more times. That still wouldn't pay him back one millionth of the pain he'd caused Mum and Dad and me.

I tried to take another bite of chocolate, but I was holding an empty wrapper. I'd eaten a whole Wispa in two bites. I was shaking.

Could I do it again?

I looked at him under the blue-ish bus light. He'd bitten his lip. He was bleeding.

Viv hadn't bled when she died. But her blood would have drained out at the autopsy.

I wondered how he'd enjoy a post-mortem scene. Or the dissection of a living brain.

He moaned and stirred.

Could I do it again?

I thought about him wrapping himself in my sister's death, and thought, *hell* yeah, I can do this all day!

I grabbed his hand again.

Chapter 26

Ciaran Bain, 30th October

She dragged me up out of unconsciousness and started again.

Steel tables. Blood-pressure cuffs. The sound of taps dripping and the smell of sharp chemicals.

I realised I was holding her hand as tightly as she was holding mine, like I couldn't let go of my punishment. But I wasn't going to pull away. I wasn't going to fight or run. I was going to take it, all day if I had to.

Then, past the experiments she was placing carefully into my head, I sensed a hunter, a searcher.

Waiting. Watching.

I forced my eyes open. Through a blur of tears, I saw the bus was moving slowly, caught between lorries.

A traffic jam.

Past the nausea and shaking, past the wires and test tubes, I sensed them again.

Hunters, ahead of us. Stuck on this road or waiting just off the motorway? Checking all the buses as they went past?

She was pressing against me. Clinging to my hand. Taking her time. Building elaborate experiments, her scientists using Latin words I couldn't understand, chanting scientific magic over my head.

I had to escape from this imaginary laboratory, or when we got closer, the hunters would recognise my overreactions.

I didn't want to fight her, but I had to.

I couldn't move. My body really believed I was strapped down, immobile in a lab.

I tried to move my fingers, to break her grip.

But she just had the scientists move nearer, talk louder, wave more equipment. Sensors on my forehead, lights in my eyes, thermometer in my mouth.

"No!" I spat. "No! Stop!"

"Yes! At last, you're fighting!"

She leant over me, pushing at my chest.

My brain lit up on a screen. Cells under a microscope. Slices of me, magnified in her eyes.

"No!"

The bus lurched forward.

I lurched too. Shoved at her. Pushed her off me.

I gulped a clean breath of reality while I could.

She pounced and grabbed me again.

I fended her off with my elbows, safely jacketed in leather.

"Lucy!" I croaked, "No, not now. My family —"

"Oh yes," she hissed, "your family too, all of you, in a laboratory."

She had my hand again.

"No!" I tried to say that my family were nearby, but I couldn't get the words out. She was pushing me through the swinging door of a lab, blinding me with science.

I couldn't go under again. Not now. I had to protect us.

I dragged the picture of the lab from her head. Through her neck, her arm, her hand, I dragged the picture right into me and –

Blew it up.

All those Bunsen burners and test tubes and computers. I took the gas, the electricity, the sparks, the chemicals and I blew it all up.

One massive white-hot explosion in my head.

The explosion blew me out of the black chair and blew the scientists out of windows and doors.

It blew Lucy into the aisle of the bus.

It blew me out of the bus seat.

Suddenly I was crouched on the floor, hard up against the seat in front.

She was on her arse in the aisle.

Just as our hands were torn apart by the force of the explosion, I saw it happen in her head too. We both heard screaming scientists, and saw cables dropping from the ceiling, ruptured pipes squirting water, a storm of flames and blood and broken glass.

I pulled myself back into the seat. She stood up. We stared at each other.

Our minds were surrounded by shattered glass, singed white coats and the smell of burning paper. But our bodies were surrounded by a dozen passengers, listening to music and reading magazines, not even looking up.

The bus seats were tatty, but not ripped; the air was stale, but not smoky; the floor was sticky, but not with blood or ash. The lab had exploded in our heads, but the bus was fine.

"What was that? What did you do?" She looked

dazed and sick.

"I have no idea, but my family are up ahead, scanning the traffic jam. So lose your vindictive little mind in this book. Now!"

She sat down and we both read, the books shaking in our hands. She travelled to a distant war and I went to a land where boys fly on dragons. As we lost ourselves in the stories, the stink of blood and smoke in our nostrils faded.

Lucy Shaw, 30th October

He whispered in my ear, "You can stop reading now. We're past them, so you're safe."

"Safe? With you? I doubt it!"

He was grinning at me. A cheeky, pleased-with-himself sort of grin.

He bounced back so fast. I'd seen him fainting, vomiting and weeping, as well as exploding his own mind, but he always recovered so fast!

He held out both bare hands towards me. "Ready for round two?"

He laughed as I scooted away across the seat towards the aisle.

"Surely your imagination hasn't run out of experiments and scientists? Don't you want to punish me again?"

He reached out to grab my hand and I snatched it away. "No!"

"Are you finished then? Have you had your revenge? Am I a free man?"

"I'm done, for now. But I'm not sorry. You deserved

it. You'd deserve it if you really were locked in a lab for the rest of your life. Because Viv is dead and it's your fault, and you use her death and it's disgusting." I was hissing at him, almost spitting in his face, and still no one in the half-empty bus had noticed. "You deserve everything bad that could *ever* happen to you."

"Yeah." His grin had faded since I refused his challenge. He was slouched in the seat, staring out of the window. "I always deserve everything. Every time Daniel kicks the shit out of me. Every time Malcolm humiliates me..." He whispered so low I almost didn't hear. "I deserve it all."

I wasn't going to let him feel sorry for himself. That was too easy. "Why didn't you fight? Are you a complete coward?"

"I didn't fight because I didn't want to scare the old ladies."

"I don't believe that."

"I didn't fight because I didn't want to hurt you."

"I don't believe that either."

"Have it your way then. I didn't fight because I deserved it."

"No. If you thought that, you'd give yourself up to the police. Why didn't you fight?"

He turned and looked at me, with those ridiculous pale eyes. "I wanted to see if I was strong enough. Strong enough to stand you, anyone, anything and everything in the world outside.

"And I *was* strong enough, wasn't I? I didn't beg you to stop, not like I did when Mum and Malcolm... I didn't beg or whimper. I didn't even fight you, not until I sensed them up ahead, and that wasn't a whimper that was a..."

"Yes, ok, I get it."

Shit. It wasn't just my sister's death that was making him stronger, it was my revenge too. He was like a sponge, absorbing poison, feeding on his crimes, getting stronger on the pain he caused others.

If hating him wasn't breaking him, maybe sympathy would. "What did your mum and Malcolm do, that you begged them to stop?"

"They..." He bit his lip, wincing when his tooth touched the cut he'd made earlier. He wiped the blood with a fingertip.

Then I saw that look. The look from the back seat of the double-decker, when he was going to tell me something I didn't want to hear.

"They questioned me. About Vivien. They read everything in my mind, with Mum's hand on my shoulder, Malcolm looking me in the eyes and my uncles listening to my voice.

"They dug inside me for every moment I'd spent with Vivien. They dragged out what we yelled at each other when I grabbed her, what she was worrying about, like her maths test and her phone and you and how scared she was. They ripped me apart to get my memory, until I was screaming and crying, begging them to stop."

He was speaking in a controlled quiet voice, watching me for my reaction. But his fists were clenched and if it was true, if his own mother had held his shoulder to force answers from him, it must have been unbearable.

"Did you tell them everything or did you try to protect Viv?"

"Oh Lucy!" He laughed, as if this was a joke. "You don't know what it's like. Of course I gave them everything."

"So you betrayed her. You did kill her."

"Not by telling them everything. She was already dead by then. They were only questioning me because they couldn't question her any more."

"They questioned her? Your mum *tortured* my sister?"

He looked away.

"Your mother is a monster. You're all monsters!"

He whirled round. "You're calling us monsters? What about you, Lucy? Perfect law-abiding Lucy? What have you just been doing?

"You used everything you know about me, all my weaknesses and my fears, to put the scariest stuff you could think of straight into my head, and you watched me shiver and sweat, and you would have kept doing it for hours if I hadn't blown that hellish lab up in your face. You'd do it again if you weren't scared of what I'd blow up next time. You don't think that was torture? You don't think that was monstrous?

"Don't you dare call my mother a monster! Don't you dare judge what my family do to survive in a world that would call us freaks and lock us up, until you look at what you've become."

He grabbed a bottle of water, and as he drank about half of it in one gulp, I tried to think about his life, rather than my sister's death or my revenge.

I whispered, "You have a horrible life with your family, don't you?"

"No! No, it's great most of the time. We have exciting jobs, real training not pointless exams, and we can head off into the hills or fishing or whatever when we're not working. Where else would I be safe? Where else would I be happy?"

"But you've never tried anything else, have you?"

"This is trying something else." He pointed at me and the rest of the bus. "And it's making me quite nostalgic for the loving arms of my family."

"So you think I'm worse than your family."

"Oh yeah. Lucy, you're my worst nightmare."

He held up his book between us. Conversation over.

I moved to the empty seat in front, to give us both space.

Was I worse than his family? Was I worse than him? Would I have kept going with those experiments all the way to Edinburgh?

Would I have stopped if he had stopped breathing?

I didn't know.

Which made me a potential killer, just like him.

Only he wasn't a killer. Not really. It wasn't a life he'd chosen. Was there a way to give him other choices? Not just a life of crime or a life in prison?

I was startled by a gentle voice from behind me. "Don't feel sorry for me, Lucy. I'm not worth it. I'm not a stray puppy you can take home, it's far too late to house-train me. But at least now we know you're as vicious as me. This book is boring me. Wake me when we're over the border, and I'll check for hunters again."

When I glanced back between the seats five minutes later, he was asleep.

chapter 27

Ciaran Bain, 30th October

When Lucy woke me at the Scottish border, she was still feeling wretched.

Good. She deserved it.

Even after a rest, I felt rotten too. But I couldn't let Lucy see that, because if she thought I could recover from her attacks easily, she wouldn't try again.

But really, I was pretty shaken.

I was shocked by how stupidly I'd given her all the information she needed to attack me. I was shocked by how easy it had been for her to defeat me.

And I was appalled by what I had done to stop her. Getting into her head, pulling out her thoughts, then exploding her vision. I had no idea what I'd done, no idea if I could do it again, nor if I wanted to.

But I grinned and made out that I was indestructible, and she was so miserable in her new self-image as the most evil person on the bus that she didn't notice I kept biting my cut lip open and couldn't stop my hands trembling.

We even managed to be almost polite to each other. As we got closer to Edinburgh, I asked, "Can I have your uncle's address now, please?"

"Not until we get there."

I traced the bus route on the map. "I need to know if your uncle's house is near this route, in case my family are already there. It's going to be hard enough here," I pointed to the city centre, "where we drive right over the train station, because my family will definitely be there. But our books should protect us, so long as the bus doesn't get stuck above Waverley station for ages."

"I thought your book was boring."

"It's alright really. So, do we need to be careful before the train station?"

She shook her head and jabbed her finger at the blue water north of the city. "My uncle lives in Leith. This bus won't go anywhere near his house. We'll have to get a taxi."

"Let's walk. I'm sick of sitting down."

She glanced out the window, which had been streaked with rain since the Midlands, and made a face.

I was worried about the train station. But I was more worried about the bus station. I'd never been there, so we would be stepping off the bus into an unknown space, possibly surrounded by enemies.

I split the last of the water and chocolate between us. I stood and stretched, then walked up and down the aisle. I wanted to be limber enough to run.

"Nervous?" Lucy asked, when I sat down again.

I nodded. "I don't know who's there and I don't know the terrain. Do you know Edinburgh?"

"Not really. My uncle usually comes home for visits, I've only been up three or four times. With... Viv..."

We both took a deep breath. "I'm sorry," I said. "But

we have to concentrate. And when we get off the bus, please do what I say immediately. I'll sense my family before you can see them, and I'm trained at evasion and escape, so do exactly as I say."

"Ok."

That was too easy. But I couldn't detect any duplicity. If she really did think I was good enough to get us past my family, she had more confidence in me than I did.

As we reached the city centre, I pointed to our books. "Read, we're nearly over the station."

Even past the excitement of a dragon-back battle, I detected my own hunters below as we crossed the bridge over Waverley. But they didn't notice us.

Lucy nudged me as we drove into the bus station. I dropped the book and scanned the area. I sensed the hunters at the train station, only three blocks away. But I didn't sense any familiar minds nearer. Malcolm must have thought that using one team to check the buses going north was more efficient than using three or four teams to watch all the exits at Edinburgh bus station.

So we got off the bus and headed through the station towards the main exit.

It was dark, windy and raining. The few people who were outdoors were walking fast under big umbrellas.

I jogged a couple of steps, then took shelter by a big department store window. Lucy joined me, and I laughed. "Welcome to Scotland."

"What?"

"Well, it's pouring with rain and they've put on a pageant of my family history. Look!" The bright window behind me had a fairground theme, with

226

carnival booths, a big top, mannequins in ringmasters' hats and a red rollercoaster painted in the background.

I used the light from the store window to read the map. "Let's walk a bit, get a feel for the city, stretch our legs."

"We'll get soaked!"

"You soft southern girl. It's just a bit of rain. But if we walk from here to the top of Leith Walk," I pointed to our right, along the shiny wet pavement, "we can get a bus to..."

Then I sensed someone, watching, waiting. Much nearer than my family.

I stepped away from the bright window, to the middle of the pavement. In the shop doorway, I could see a man. He walked forward, and his thin grey raincoat was lit up by the garish light from another window, which displayed a bearded lady in a cocktail dress and a strongman in skimpy pants.

"Are you kids just off the London bus?" He asked the question in his posh English accent, but he already knew the answer.

"Lucy, run!" I sprinted off down the hill, the direction we'd just decided. But she didn't move.

I sensed her fear and heard her voice at the same time. "Bain. He's got a gun."

I turned. He was pointing a handgun at Lucy's chest.

He wasn't going to shoot her. He wasn't going to shoot either of us. The gun was just to scare us, he had no intention of using it in public, though none of the handful of people walking round the square had noticed anything beyond their wet feet and umbrellas.

I walked back towards Lucy. "Get behind me," I ordered.

"Why, are you bullet-proof as well?" But she did what I asked.

The man was totally confident. He'd found who he was looking for and he thought he had us under complete control.

I knew he wasn't a local policeman. Not because of the accent, because of the gun. Scottish police don't use guns that casually.

Then he decided to contact the rest of his team.

I was concentrating now, so I could sense a wide ring of his colleagues outside every exit from the bus station. *Now* I could sense them. Five minutes too bloody late.

I had walked right into this.

When we had got off the bus, I'd stood there grinning at a stripy tent in a window and chatting to Lucy, so I'd forgotten to scan for police surveillance as well as family. Now this grey man was pointing a gun at me. But I wasn't going to let him tell all his mates he'd caught me.

I stepped forward. He stopped patting for his phone and put both hands on the gun. I didn't care about the gun. I cared about the phone. That's what could harm me and my family. I took another step towards him. He sidestepped, towards a window with a fortune-teller's rose-painted caravan.

"Back up, boy. I don't want to shoot you. I just have a few questions."

I lowered my head, like I was scared, took half a step back and waited, balanced over both feet. He was reassured at my retreat, so he let go of the gun with his left hand and went for his pocket again.

And I kicked.

I launched off my perfect stance and kicked the gun out of his right hand, then spun and kicked his left hand away from his body. He kept his balance, dropped to a crouch and got ready to fight.

I sensed his confidence. He was bigger, older and a professional, and I'd just got a lucky shot in...

But I was still moving and I was sick of being the bottom of the heap, sick of being chased, followed, questioned and punished. So I aimed a right-footed roundhouse kick at his face.

Finish it. Finish it, Bain.

My foot connected, his head flicked back, his legs crumpled and his head cracked into the sharp stone edge of the window behind. He slumped down.

And I felt his confidence flicker out. Everything stopped. His belief that he could beat this little London oik, his dependence on his mates, his puzzlement at my attitude to the gun. His existence. His life. It stopped. I felt it crack and drain and vanish.

Oh no. Oh no. That wasn't what I meant...

I bit down on my lip, where it was already bleeding. I forced myself to concentrate.

I knelt down beside him, in the bar of darkness against the wall, in the shadow before the splash of light from the fortune-teller's caravan hit the pavement.

I ignored the black endings gathering inside me. I ripped my gloves off, slid my hand into his pockets, found his phone and his wallet.

There was an outraged whisper behind me. "You're not *stealing* from him, are you?"

I opened the wallet.

Ah. Shit.

He didn't have a police warrant card. He had a Home Office identity card in the name of William Borthwick. It didn't say what his job was at the Home Office, but I didn't think their catering staff carried guns.

This card must mean security services. It must mean MI5.

The surveillance teams weren't police. They were MI5. Holy shit.

I sensed growing panic from behind me.

"Is he ok? Bain? Is he unconscious?" Now she was down on the pavement too, her fingers feeling for a pulse.

I already knew, but the shock of her discovery just about knocked me over.

"He's *dead*. You killed him. Oh my god..."

We were the only ones who had noticed. His mates in the ring around the bus station were still bored and wet. The few folk walking past were in their own umbrella-shaped bubbles. And he was hidden in the dark shadow under the window.

But someone would notice soon. I got up and turned round once. Scanning for anyone I needed to worry about, looking for escape routes.

I saw the park across the road.

"Bain! You killed him." Lucy wanted me to tell her it wasn't true. She was going to lose it in a minute. So was I. His mind was switching off again and again and again in my head, like a drum roll. And it was getting louder.

I had to get us away from these bright windows with their caravans and freaks, and from his body in the shadows.

"The park," I said. "Do as I say and it will be fine."

"It won't be fine. He's *dead*."

"Shut up, Lucy. Follow me."

Lucy Shaw, 30th October

That was all he said to me.

"Shut up. Follow me."

And I did.

I don't know why.

I had just seen him kick a man's head nearly off.

I had just seen him murder someone.

Then he said, "Shut up and follow me."

And I did.

I didn't know what else to do. I didn't want to stay with the body. I didn't want to get arrested. I didn't want anyone else to point a gun at me.

Bain seemed to know what he was doing. So I followed him.

I'd been calling him a murderer all day. Now he was one.

But I followed him.

He ran across the road and into the park. I followed. It was easier than deciding to go somewhere else.

He sprinted over the grass to a great column of stone, almost as tall as Nelson's Column. It probably had some Scottish bloke at the top, but I didn't look up.

Bain ran round the base of the column, to a door in the stonework. He'd unlocked it before I got my breath back. He didn't tell me to go in, just held the door open and gestured.

It was pitch black inside. I hesitated.

I heard a police siren in the distance. I ran inside. He

231

followed me into the cramped space, closed the door and locked it behind us.

He pushed a torch into my hand. He slid down the wall and he was unconscious before he hit the floor.

I switched the torch on, then panicked about light showing round the door, and switched it off again.

I sat down suddenly. And waited for Bain to wake up.

chapter 28

Lucy Shaw, 30th October

He didn't wake up.

I crouched on a narrow stone bench and listened to the police arrive outside with sirens and shouts.

As I sat in the cold dusty dark, my wet clothes sticking to my shivering skin, I kept remembering the kick, the crack, the smash. Had it all been one noise or lots of different noises?

The blow of Bain's boot, a breaking bone in the face, a breaking bone in the neck, the smash of the skull on the stone, the thud of the body on the pavement. As I remembered it, sometimes it sounded like dozens of separate notes, sometimes it was one big explosion.

I saw the man's face. Pale. Paler than Bain's golden skin. Paler in that shadow than he had been thirty seconds before when he was pointing a gun at me.

Because he *had* been pointing a gun at me. If I was the damsel-in-distress type, I might believe Bain had killed him to protect me. But I wasn't that stupid. Bain had killed to protect himself and his family. The family who were trying to kill me.

And I heard the blow. The blows. The thump and crack.

I saw the man's face. I felt his skin under my fingers. No pulse, but still warm. No blood, not that I saw. Just like Viv.

These mindreaders were tidy murderers.

Was that Ciaran Bain's first time, I wondered. Or had he killed before?

I wondered when he would wake up. Then I knew he wouldn't. Not for ages. Maybe not ever. Unless I woke him.

Because I guessed what had happened. He was lost in the moment the man died. Like he lost himself deliberately in Viv's death in the carpark. Like he lost himself unexpectedly when he felt someone die in the hospital. If he felt that way outside a hospital when someone died several walls away, then how deep down must he be now, after killing a man and rifling his pockets?

If I didn't wake him up, he might stay there.

His breath was shallow and fast and gasping. He wasn't happy, wherever he was.

Should I wake him up?

I thought about the dead man out there. I wondered if he had a sister or a brother or a girlfriend or a boyfriend or a wife or kids.

What would they want me to do? Would they want me to let his killer rot here? Die of despair in his own head, starve to death in his own body?

What would happen to me if I woke him? I was a witness now. I had *seen Ciaran Bain kick a man to death*. That made me dangerous to him. And it made him even more dangerous to me.

But if I didn't wake him, how would I get out of here? He'd locked the door with his lockpicks or skeleton key or whatever, and I'd no idea how to open it again.

I was locked inside a small stone room. In the dark. With a murderer.

I thought he was scary when I found him in the hall.

I thought he was scary when he kicked the knife out of my hand in the kitchen.

I thought he was scary when he blew that lab up inside my head on the bus.

But now I was truly scared of him. Because now I knew he was a killer. He could kill as fast and efficiently as a tiger. He might get wobbly and depressed afterwards, but that didn't make the man out there any less dead.

And I was trapped here with him until he woke up or until I woke him up.

I heard sirens again. Just one siren, getting quieter. One police car leaving. But the rest of the police must still be out there.

And I realised I wasn't trapped. If I made enough noise perhaps the police would hear me before he did, wherever he was.

Maybe now was the time to do what I'd always planned. Shout for help and let someone else punish my sister's murderer.

Once the police broke down the door, they'd probably arrest me. But at least they wouldn't torture and kill me. They'd offer me a lawyer and a phone, and probably even a toilet and a cup of tea.

But what about him? If I screamed for the police, what would happen to Ciaran Bain?

Well, what about him? I don't think he did kill Viv, not on his own. But he certainly killed that policeman.

If he wasn't locked away now, he would kill again. It was too easy for him. Kick crack smash thump and someone else was dead. Just like Viv.

I stood up and felt my way to the door, then raised my fist.

Ciaran Bain, 30th October

He died surprised.

He felt no fear. I'd kicked the gun out of his hand and his hand away from the phone, but he wasn't scared. He'd been up against much worse than some oik from London. He was lowering his centre of gravity, getting ready to fight, expecting to win. He wasn't even afraid of getting hurt. Not afraid of much more than bruising his knuckles on me.

So when he finally saw my boot coming towards his eyes and realised I was about to smash his face, he wasn't afraid. There wasn't time. He was just surprised.

Then my boot hit his face and his skull hit the stone and he died.

I didn't know anything else about him. He's in my head forever now, but apart from his misplaced martial arts confidence and his assumption I was from London because I got off the London bus, I knew nothing about him at all. I touched him with my feet not my hands and only for three brief moments, three fast kicks. I didn't read a lot from him. Except his death.

But the feeling of sudden surprise, then the sudden absence of anything at all, were pounding at me. The surprise and suddenness and absence were fogging my

236

brain. The crashing rushing blackness of death was suffocating me and I couldn't breathe.

I didn't mean it.

I didn't mean it. I wasn't kicking to kill. It wasn't that hard a kick.

But when you kick a man in the head, you have no business being surprised if he dies.

This felt different from losing myself in Vivien's death. I lose my sense of myself in her death. But I was completely aware of being trapped in this moment of Borthwick's death. Was this the punishment I deserved, for my first real murder? Held forever in the dark and sudden limbo of his surprise.

But I could hear something.

A thump. Not a body landing on the ground, but a hand pounding.

I didn't care. I couldn't breathe past this continuing and constant sudden surprise. It was surrounding me, choking me, darkening my eyes and my brain and my lungs. This was exactly what I deserved.

Lucy Shaw, 30th October

I banged on the door, but there was a screech of car wheels at the same time. No one would hear my pathetic knocking past that noise.

I lifted my fist to hit the door again, once there was silence outside.

I couldn't see anything. Not my fist, not the door. Not the stone bench I'd been sitting on. Not the boy at my feet.

But I could hear him. His breathing was slowing, stuttering.

How long had he been lying there? It must have been longer than the twenty minutes he was inside Viv's death in the carpark.

I couldn't hear him any more.

I knelt down. On one of his hands. Whoops. I lifted my knee and moved his hand away.

He was freezing.

I put my hand out, found his chest and unzipped the leather jacket. Something clattered out, so I padded my fingers around on the floor and found a phone. Probably the phone he had stolen from the man outside. I put it in my pocket.

Then I put my ear to his chest.

No breath. He wasn't breathing.

What should I do?

If I didn't want to be trapped in here with a dead body, I had to get him breathing again.

I didn't want to give him the kiss of life. I really didn't want to. I'd seen him throw up this morning. Also, given his major issues about touching, the shock of my mouth on his might kill him rather than save him.

So I thumped his chest a couple of times and heard a great gasping breath.

Then I grabbed his hand and started talking.

He'd told me hating him worked best, but I didn't have the energy to hate anyone. So I just talked. "I'm scared, Bain. I'm bloody terrified. Will you stop hiding inside your head and come back, please."

His breathing was ragged, but at least he was getting some air. I kept talking, kept thinking, from my hand to his.

"You're the only one who can get us out of here. And you don't want to die here. Inside a statue is a ridiculous place to die. Daniel would piss himself laughing.

"And I'm scared of the dark. I think you know, because you gave me the torch before you went all wobbly. But I didn't put the torch on, in case the police saw the light round the door.

"I'm scared of your family too. They might be creeping up on us right now. I need your weird sixth sense to know what's out there. I'm afraid of the dark in here and the dark out there and I'm afraid of the people looking for me.

"I'll tell you what else I'm scared of."

His right hand was warming up. I found his left hand and rubbed it.

"I'm terrified of you. You nutter. You killed him, then you went through his pockets, like some medieval soldier looting bodies on a battlefield. And you didn't collapse until it was safe, so maybe you have more control than you think. I'm totally terrified of you. But I'd be more scared of you dead than alive, so will you *please* wake up."

His hand moved in mine.

"Bain. Please. Come back."

He coughed and pulled his hand out of mine.

I backed away to the stone bench, hoping he wouldn't remember anything I'd said.

He coughed again. I heard scraping sounds as he sat up.

"If you're..." he gasped. "If you're that scared of the dark..."

He had heard it all. Damn.

"If you are that scared, let's go up the steps a bit and put the torch on. Then it won't shine round the door."

I'd thought I was sitting on a low bench. But he was

right. When I reached behind me, I could feel the start of a spiral staircase, leading up towards the statue.

I crawled up a dozen steps. I heard him coming after me. A murderer, crawling upstairs after me, in the dark. My skin was prickling.

"It's ok," he said. "There's no need to be scared of me. I couldn't strangle a kitten right now. Not even a cute ginger one. I feel like... like death."

I sat on the next step.

"Put the torch on," he said. "No light will leak from here."

I switched it on. It shone right in his face. He flinched.

I laid the torch on the step and angled it at the wall. Not pointing at me, not pointing at him.

No one spoke for a moment. I looked at my hands. He slipped those ridiculous gloves on again.

"Thanks, Lucy, thanks for waking me up. That was... I nearly..." He took a deep breath, got control of himself. "Thanks anyway. That was gentler than last time, and the first time you've said 'please' to me." I saw a flash of his teeth as he smiled. He was recovering already. He'd be at kitten-strangling strength any minute now.

But he put his head in his hands. "I didn't mean it. I wasn't aiming to kill. It was just an unlucky shot, him cracking his skull against the stonework. I've used that move dozens of times and no one's had more than a headache... Do you believe me? That I didn't mean it?" He looked up at me.

"It doesn't matter if I believe you. What matters is he's dead, and you killed him, and all the other policemen won't care that you didn't mean it, they will just care about catching you - catching us..."

"The other policemen? You don't know, do you?"

"Don't know what?"

"I looked in his wallet…"

"Yeah. You stole his phone and his money, you grave-robbing ghoul." I remembered him bent over the body and I moved a step higher up.

"I didn't steal his money! I needed to know who he was, because Scottish cops don't wave guns round like that."

"Was he a London cop?"

"No. This is much worse than a murder hunt. He was MI5. Security Service. Spooks. Spies."

"MI5? Spies? Why would spies be interested in you?"

"Your nana worked for them, didn't she? That's why you only had her notes, not the full report, because the report was for Military Intelligence, for the wartime security service, wasn't it?"

I nodded.

"So what if the official report was destroyed or lost after the war and now the spooks want the same page of the report that my family do? The one with the real names? What if they're searching for these mythical mindreaders, hoping to pick up where your nana left off and use us for experiments…"

"Or spying."

"Or whatever. But we won't be used. That was the whole point."

"The whole point of what?"

He angled his wrist to the light. "It's not even midnight. We can't leave yet, the police are still out there. So I'll tell you my family history and what I think MI5 want. Let's see if your highly educated brain can make more sense of it than I can."

chapter 29

Ciaran Bain, 30th October

So I told Lucy our family history.

"My great-grandfather Billy was a fortune-teller, like his dad and his granny and so on back for generations. In the 1930s and 40s, Billy worked in fairgrounds during the summer and variety shows in fleapit theatres during the winter."

"A fortune-teller? So can your family see into the future?"

I laughed. "Don't be daft. No one can see the future. But if you read someone's mind as they come into the caravan, you can tell them what they want to hear.

"The mediums we've had in the family can't speak to the dead either. No one really wants to know what it's like to die, they just want to believe Auntie Irene is still thinking about them.

"It's not magic, just a secret ability that a few people used to make a living.

"My family scraped by as fortune-tellers for years. When the war started, Billy was too skinny and rickety from a carnie family upbringing to be conscripted. But then he was caught up in a sweep of psychics, mediums and fortune-tellers, taken down to England and experimented on.

"He used to tell us all nightmare stories about it. Our parents still tell the wee ones if they won't go to bed they'll be sent to the braindrainers and the lady in the white coat.

"Most of the psychics the senior scientist tested were frauds. Billy had genuine skill, but didn't want her to realise that, because he knew how dangerous that could be. It was only a few generations back that two of our ancestors had been burnt in tar barrels for witchcraft. Billy used his mindreading skills to make a living, but he was always careful not to be too accurate, not to terrify people."

I told Lucy how Billy had tried to fool her nana into thinking he wasn't psychic so that he wouldn't be sent to mindread the enemy, how those wrong answers had provided the evidence to land him in prison as a conman, and how he'd realised that the criminals he met inside might pay for his skills once he was out.

"But the gangs he worked for never found out how he tracked people or discovered information," I said. "Billy trained up his children, they trained up their children and it became the family business. But now the people who gave him the idea of becoming a spy are catching up with us."

"Maybe they read the article in the *Chronicle*," suggested Lucy.

"Maybe. That's how we found you. Perhaps the spooks have kept tabs on your family since the article, hoping genuine mindreaders would turn up to destroy the evidence. Probably they still fancy having psychic spies doing their dirty work. But we don't work for anyone else, and we certainly don't work for MI5 spooks. My great-grandfather protected his family from that, and I will too."

"My nana tried to protect you as well."

"No, she didn't," I said quietly. "Your nana caused this mess. She experimented on people. She forced us into this business to protect ourselves. Your nana has been our bogeywoman, the monster under our beds, for four generations."

"Nonsense. She protected your great-grandpa's privacy. She put everything in code and she was really angry with Viv for contacting the local paper. She tried to take your secret to the grave with her."

I knew I was offending Lucy, but I wanted to give her as much truth as I could. "She didn't do that because she was being nice. She did it because she was scared. That's why she stopped researching. She wasn't protecting mindreaders to help us."

"How do you know?"

I pulled the letter from my back pocket.

"That's the letter from Grampa's book!" she said angrily. "You stole it! Did you read it?"

"Of course I did! What kind of irresponsible idiot would leave this kind of information sitting there unopened? She was writing to her old assistant, the other braindrainer. I needed to know what it said. Do you want to know too?"

Lucy paused, then nodded and took the letter from me. She picked the torch up and read it.

"He threatened her? He threatened her family? That's why she left the university? She always told us it was because she couldn't get any funding." She sighed. "Our whole family history seems to be sliding out from under me tonight. Nana must have been really scared. This guy Lomond must have been terrifying. But why didn't he just kill her, like your uncle killed Viv?"

"I don't know. Malcolm would have killed her. But Billy was only just starting off as a criminal. Perhaps he wasn't as ruthless then, as he was when I knew him."

"You knew him?"

"Yes. He only died seven years ago. The family must have honoured his promise of keeping watch for any mention of your nana's research. That's why we rushed down here, that's why we interviewed you, that's why we grabbed Viv."

"So your Billy killed Viv, even after he was dead. He carried out the threat he made last century."

"No, I killed her, by letting her see my face. I have to take the blame for that."

"Do you? Really? We've got all night, Bain. Tell me exactly what happened."

So I did. I told it as straight as I could, the grab, the Q&A, the conversations with Roy and everything I'd read in the files. Not to scare or shock Lucy this time, but to share it with her.

Once she'd blown her nose a few times, she started thinking it through. "So that's why she hid the copy in the urn. That never seemed right to me. If she'd wanted to hide it from the family, she could just have hidden it in her sock drawer. But she hid it in that really gross place because she was hiding it from you. She was scared of you, because Nana had told her... How much had Nana told her?"

"We'll probably never know. Enough that Vivien was scared, but not so much that she was prepared to destroy the notes completely."

"I wish she had." Lucy wiped her eyes.

"So do I. Then I wouldn't have her death in my head."

"I don't think you should carry her death around like that, Bain, because it really wasn't your fault."

"Yes it was. She had to die because she saw my face, and she saw my face because I was careless. It was my fault."

"No. Now I've heard the whole story, I think your mum and uncle would have killed her anyway. Viv was making a connection between them and Lomond. She knew too much and was guessing the rest. She was a risk. They wouldn't have let her live."

I rubbed my hand over my face, where the mask had been. "But Mum... but Malcolm... they said..."

"They let you think it was your mistake that killed her, but it wasn't."

"Why would they let me think that? Malcolm might do it to torment me, to get control over me. But why would Mum...?" I shook my head. "Even if the mask thing wasn't what killed her, I still have to take responsibility. I did grab her. It is still my fault."

"If it's your fault, then it's my fault too. Isn't it? When your mum interviewed us, I said that Viv argued with Nana, that she hadn't wanted to destroy the notes. I pointed your family at Viv, didn't I?"

I hesitated, then nodded.

"You already knew that?" She was crumpling the old envelope in her hand.

I nodded again.

"You've said some pretty horrid things to me today, Bain. Why haven't you said that? Why haven't you said Viv's death was my fault as much as yours, or Billy's, or anyone else's?"

"Why didn't I use the strongest weapon I could find to hurt you? Maybe I was saving it, for when I really needed it."

"Or maybe you're not as ruthless as you think."

The torch flickered. The battery was running out.

"But the guy outside," I muttered. "He was completely my fault."

Lucy frowned. "Nothing you've told me explains the man out there. Why were MI5 in Edinburgh too? Are they here protecting Uncle Vince?"

I laughed. "Protecting your family? The spooks were using your family as bait to catch a family of freaks. And the first thing that guy did was point a gun at you."

She paused, dealing with a rush of remembered fear. "So why are they here? Do they know you're Scottish?"

"No. I didn't get much from that spook when I... when I..." I took a deep breath. "When I kicked him, all I got was he believed that I was a London oik, and that he could take me in a fight."

"His mistake."

"His last mistake. He didn't know anything about me or my family."

"So how did they know to look for us getting off that bus?"

"Presumably someone has noticed you're missing from home, and has noticed a break-in at your grampa's flat, so perhaps MI5 have worked out that you're involved with us, and that you might come up to the last family address. They're probably staking out Edinburgh airport and rail station too. So I have to warn my family."

"Your family? But they're trying to kill me!"

"Yes. But you aren't as much of a threat as MI5. Once I let them know the surveillance teams are spooks, you'll slide right down the list of priorities."

Then I had an idea. Only a glimmer of one, but the first bright thing I'd had in my head since the black suddenness of Borthwick's death. "No, you're right. Let's not warn my family about MI5 yet."

"But then you risk MI5 catching your family."

"Don't underestimate my mum and Malcolm. I'd back them against a handful of spooks in raincoats any day, especially when the spooks don't yet know exactly what we can do. And perhaps while everyone is confused, we can sneak through and get ourselves a bit of leverage."

"Leverage? What do you mean?" Lucy asked.

"The information everyone wants, the page that links the codename Lomond with Billy's surname."

"But you want to destroy the report to protect your family. How can you use it as leverage? What do you want that either MI5 or your family will give you in exchange?"

"Life. Not death. There's been too much death this week."

"Life? Your life?"

"No, Lucy. Your life. If we find the flash drive, I can use it to persuade my family not to kill you. I can threaten to give the codename page to MI5 unless Malcolm promises to leave you alone."

Lucy was almost as surprised as William Borthwick had been.

chapter 30

Lucy Shaw, 31st October

If I was choosing a knight in shining armour, probably he wouldn't be a violent Scottish teenager with a scuffed leather jacket and scary blue eyes, who had a habit of throwing up and fainting in public.

Probably he wouldn't have kidnapped my sister and kicked a man to death in front of me.

But Hollywood heroes and fantasy princes can't read their enemies' intentions round corners or answer my questions before I ask them.

"I'm not doing this because I *like* you, obviously."

"Obviously."

"I'm doing this because I'm struggling to cope with the number of dead people in my head already. You're irritating enough when you're alive, Lucy. You'd drive me nuts if I had your last breath in my head."

Delightful. He's got some crazy plan to take on his family and MI5 to save my life, not because of my sparkling wit and stunning good looks, but because he doesn't want me to haunt him.

Still, at least he's trying.

We got out of the stone column quite easily.

We waited until Bain couldn't detect any police or

family or surveillance teams. Then, in the very early morning, we left. We opened the door, walked out and walked away.

The plan we'd agreed in the cold dark hours under the statue, after the torch battery died, was that we would go to Leith and see who was staking out Vince's house.

"Always do the recce," Bain said. "Preparation is never wasted. Forewarned is forearmed."

Before he could think of any other clichés, I agreed. Partly to shut him up, but mainly because I'd been useless at giving him information about my uncle's flat and the surrounding streets. If we were going to get in and out without being identified by MI5 or captured by his family, we needed more useful facts than: the door is blue, he has a real snakeskin in a drawer and I think the hall carpet is red.

So we walked from the centre of Edinburgh towards Leith and its docks. The rain had stopped, but it was still cold and windy.

We didn't talk much as we walked. We had talked ourselves out, sitting in the huge stone column. He knew I was afraid of the dark, so he'd just chatted like a normal human being, to keep me calm.

We'd talked about films and books. And the difference between team sports like football and lone sports like running and climbing, then the difference between people who enjoy the former (me) and people who enjoy the latter (him).

There was lots of stuff we didn't talk about. Mothers and sisters, uncles and fathers. And once it was dark, we didn't talk about death either.

But now we were back to business, on our way to recce the site, to devise a plan for getting in.

I already had a plan. But it was so silly I was trying not to think it, in case it made him laugh.

"Go on, then," he said eventually. "What's your plan?"

"How do you know I have a plan?"

"You're bursting with it, Lucy."

"I don't want to tell you. It's silly."

"Silly is fine. A laugh will do us both good."

So I said, "It's Halloween."

"Yeah. Ghosts and spooks and witch burning. Not my favourite time of year."

"You go trick or treating up here, don't you?"

"We call it guising. Dressing up, in disguise. Guising."

I nodded. "That'll work. We have two problems to solve before we can get to my uncle's house. One is getting past your family. The other is getting past MI5."

"Yes. And I would add getting out again as a top priority."

"I have no idea how to get past your family in either direction, but I think we could get in and out past MI5 quite easily."

He made a hurry-up gesture with his gloved hands.

"What are they looking for?" I asked.

"If they've asked about passengers on buses that arrived just before Borthwick was killed, they're looking for two teenagers, one black, one blond, going to your uncle's house."

I grinned. "Tonight there will be dozens of kids, toddlers to teens, going to my uncle's house. We stayed with Uncle Vince one Halloween and there's a real community feel in his terrace, with kids knocking on every door, singing songs and telling jokes, then getting an apple and some sweets. All we have to do is -"

Bain laughed in delight. "All we have to do is dress

up, knock on a few other doors before we go to your uncle's and we'll blend in. Brilliant! So after we've finished this recce, we buy ourselves cheesy costumes, hide up for the rest of the day, then knock on his door tonight. And you can say: *Hi Uncle Vince, rather than a sweetie, can I have Nana's urn?*" He laughed again.

I was ridiculously pleased that he liked my idea, even though it was only the middle bit of a plan.

We reached the foot of Leith Walk and Bain turned to face me. I knew what he wanted. With MI5 and the local police and his family after him, he didn't have time to search Edinburgh for a Vincent Shaw. He needed me to give him my uncle's address.

But once he had the address, I was more use to him dead, unable to give evidence against him.

And even though he said he would use the flash drive to keep his family away from me, I couldn't be sure...

"Don't you trust me, Lucy? Aren't we a team now?"

I didn't answer.

"Yeah. Why would anyone want me on their team?" He stamped on an empty crisp packet as it blew past. "I know I've done some horrible things, but I'm trying to do the right thing now, and I just need you to give me the address."

"But then will you still need me? You're starting to survive pretty well out here on your own."

"Of course I'll need you. Your Uncle Vince is more likely to give the urn to you than me. You're his beloved niece, I'm either some weirdo he doesn't know or someone he suspects of kidnapping both his nieces."

"You didn't kidnap me! I followed you."

"I know that. But your family don't. They just know you've vanished."

I must be either completely self-centred or completely stupid, because I hadn't thought about that all the time we'd been on the run. I'd been away from home for more than 24 hours! Mum and Dad must be panicking, thinking that I'd never come home, that they'd lost both of us.

I sat down on a wet bench. "Oh no. I'm so selfish. I never even thought."

"It'll be fine. If we get the flash drive this evening, I can negotiate with Malcolm tonight and you'll be home tomorrow."

He lifted his head, like an animal sniffing a scent.

"Your uncle lives that way," he jerked his arm to the right, "doesn't he?"

"Yes. Can you sense them? Are they there?"

"They're all there, family and spooks." He pointed urgently down another street and we walked briskly for a block, ducked round a corner, then jogged into a wide tree-filled park. We stopped by the wooden fence round a kids' play area.

"How can we do a recce when we can't get near?" I asked.

"I can work out where they're stationed by circling round just close enough for me to sense them. I need to know the layout of the street too, but you can give me that."

"How? I've told you all I know."

"No, you haven't. Have you ever been here before?" He waved at the climbing frame.

"Yeah. Uncle Vince brought us when we were kids."

"But you didn't mention a play park to me. You didn't remember it until we got here, did you?"

I shook my head.

"You have more in your memory than you realise. So, show me the way from this park to your uncle's."

"You want me to talk you through it?"

"No, I want you to think it. So I can read everything in your head."

He took off one glove and held out his right hand.

"But won't you go all, you know, sweaty and wobbly, then collapse?"

"Probably. But if you promise not to draw a moustache and glasses on me if I faint, I'm prepared to take the risk. Give me your hand."

I felt him jerk away in revulsion as soon as we touched. But he held on tight and looked me in the eye. "Think about walking from here to your uncle's. Take it slow. Don't worry about me."

I closed my eyes and I remembered the way.

I walked through the park, past a roundabout and up a hill. A raincoat on my back and a sister by my side. Up the hill, past a new school and an old school, then turning into the terraced streets that locals called 'the colonies'. One long narrow dead-end street led to half a dozen even narrower ones, branching off like ribs from a spine. I walked past cars parked tightly against the pavement, little gardens, thin houses. I turned left into my uncle's terrace, climbed the outdoor stairs, then opened the blue door with the snake knocker. I stepped onto the red carpet and heard Viv demand the hot chocolate Uncle Vince always made...

Bain dropped my hand and leant against the fence, his fists clenched, one gloved and one bare. He dragged great lungfuls of air into his chest.

But he stayed on his feet. Then grinned at me. "That worked. I must be getting better at this. Or better at you, anyway." He stood up straight. "So, only one way in and out of the colonies. They can't chase us by car in there; we'll be much faster on foot. And you're right about a real community feel. With houses so close together and tiny gardens, anyone hanging about all day will be very obvious."

"I didn't tell you all that."

"No, because you didn't know you knew it, and you don't see it the way I see it. So now let's find out where my family and MI5 are waiting for us."

Ciaran Bain, 31st October

I was boring Lucy. She was knackered and cold and we'd already walked a wide uneven loop around the colonies twice.

I walked down streets until I sensed my family and the spooks, then moved back, to get away from the intensity of their emotions, marked their locations on the map and moved further round.

By the time we saw the first uniformed teenager heading to school, Lucy was ready to drop. "You've proved you can sneak up on your family, so can we have breakfast now, please?"

I had all the information I was going to get, so we clambered on a bus, returned to the city centre, found a café under a church, and bought a hot drink and a croissant each.

When she was warm enough to pay attention, I showed her my carefully marked map. "See these two sets of dots? The red ones are MI5 spooks, close to your uncle's terrace. They're mostly in parked cars, but there are a few floating around on foot, probably dressed as BT engineers or other workmen.

"But they don't know that my family are out here on the main road - the blue dots - watching the only way in and out of the colonies.

"The family know the surveillance teams are there, that's why they aren't any closer to the target. But I don't detect the level of fear and caution there would be if Mum and Malcolm knew the surveillance teams were MI5 rather than police. They're watching the watchers, but they're waiting for us."

"They're *all* waiting for us."

"Yes. The spooks want us for the death of their pal, and because they assume I'm one of Lomond's descendants. But they don't know they're surrounded by a whole team of the mindreaders they're searching for.

"My family want to kill you because you know too much, and they want to teach me a lesson. Though from the emotions I detected when we were walking round Leith, I suspect that Malcolm has given up trying to teach me anything and just wants to get rid of me."

I took a sip of cold hot chocolate, remembering how familiar Malcolm's emotions had felt. As we'd walked round the colonies, I had recognised the decision to kill someone. The decision my family had made just before Vivien's death. Now Malcolm was making the same decision about me. I took another sip, and focussed on our plan.

"Mostly, though, my family want to get the copy of the report. But they don't know for sure that there is a copy, where the copy is or what form it's in. So I *might* be able to persuade them to let us go in and find the copy then give it to them on our way out." I rubbed my cut lip again, the pain a useful reminder of my weakness, while I wondered if that plan would work.

Lucy was already convinced it wouldn't. "So you're going to ask your family nicely to let us past and promise them they can catch us on the way out once we have the prize. But if everyone knows they're going to punish you and kill me, they'll never believe you would agree to that; they'll think you're planning to double-cross them."

"So I'll tell them I'm planning to double-cross *you*."

She shivered. She found that very easy to believe.

I thought for a minute. That could work. "Yeah. I'll tell them that if they let us in, you'll get the copy from your uncle, then on the way out, I'll give them the copy *and* you, if they promise not to punish me."

"You'll promise your family they can kill me, if they don't hurt you?"

"Yeah."

"And they'll believe that?"

I grinned. "Well. Do you believe it?"

She picked at her croissant. "I don't know what to believe."

"Lucy, I've told you, I don't want you dead. You see how I react to death. I admit I'm being selfish rather than heroic, but I really don't want you dead. I want you safe, alive and in Winslow. So, let's have another hot chocolate then get out of here..."

But she didn't trust me. I'd shown her how easy it would be for me to protect myself and my family for the price of her life. And I'd realised it myself too.

If I could get the secret, elude the spooks, save my family, impress my mum, change Malcolm's mind about me, and all I had to sacrifice was one argumentative girl from London, that was a rational decision. Wasn't it?

But I needed Lucy on my side until the end, or the plan wouldn't work.

So I had to convince her I was double-crossing Malcolm, convince Malcolm I was double-crossing her, and keep in mind whose side I was really on.

Mine. My side. No one else's. I wasn't trying to be a hero. I was just trying to survive.

chapter 31

Lucy Shaw, 31st October

"You can't dress up like that!"

"Why not? This was all they had left, apart from wizards and vampires."

Bain was dressed as Death. Skull mask, black cloak, scythe over his shoulder. He didn't seem to think it was tasteless.

He'd offered to buy me a costume too, but I stopped letting Mum buy me clothes years ago, and I wasn't about to let someone else take over. So I'd gone shopping as well.

Now I was a witch, with a warty mask, nylon gloves with silver nails, a long cloak, a tall hat and a large plastic cauldron to put apples, chocolate and dead relatives in.

We were comparing disguises in my room in a backpackers' hostel in the touristy centre of Edinburgh. We'd bamboozled the receptionist with Bain's dodgy ID and a handful of cash, and rented a couple of single rooms for the day, so we could sleep and shower.

Now it was after 4 p.m. and the light was already starting to fade in this cold northern city. Time to go guising. But first we had to negotiate our passage through the family from hell.

Bain showed me the cheap new phone he'd bought. "We'll call Malcolm once we're on our way, so if they trace the call we're already moving towards them."

We left the hostel with our masks perched on top of our heads and our thin cloaks blowing behind us. As we walked down the steep cobbled hill, I said, "In this phone call, you're going to offer to give me to your family if they let us past to get the urn?"

"Yes."

"And I'm supposed to not know this."

"Obviously. Or you wouldn't be daft enough to play along."

"And I'm not daft, am I? And because you've told me what you're planning, I'm supposed to believe you're double-crossing them and being honest with me."

"It would be handy if you could read minds, Lucy, because then you'd know I'm telling the truth. Though how could you not trust me, when I'm dressed like this?" He whirled his plastic scythe over his head.

But I couldn't trust him. Not completely. I'd also bought a phone while I was out, and kept it hidden. If he did betray me, I could dial 999 and land everyone in the cells until the police sorted out the goodies from the baddies.

And that wasn't the only phone I had in my pocket. I could call MI5 too.

Ciaran Bain, 31st October

So Death and a witch walked down the Royal Mile, phoning a man who'd happily kill us both.

I dialled Malcolm, but he wouldn't answer a call from an unknown number in the middle of a complex job.

I texted:

> Take call from bain re getting
> lomond codename copy

Then dialled again.

"Bain! Where are you? What the hell are you doing?"

"I know where the copy is, Malcolm, and I can get it, if you let me past to the uncle's residence."

"You can't *get* at the uncle's, you stupid boy. It's surrounded by plainclothes. We'll get past when one of them dozes off tonight, or in a few days when they run out of overtime. Stop distracting me."

"I *can* get there. The girl can get me in and she knows where the copy is. Let us past and we'll bring you the copy."

"Why would I trust you with that? You've made a total arse of it so far."

"I've made an arse of it, have I? I got all the way from London to Edinburgh without you laying a finger on me."

"Then you killed a man outside Harvey Nicks and brought the whole Scottish police force down around us. Just like you brought the Surrey police down on us when we had to kill the older girl because you couldn't keep your mask on.

"You're a threat to this whole family and we should have drowned you at birth. Bring yourself in now or I'll send Daniel after you with instructions to bring nothing back but your over-sensitive skin."

I lowered my voice. "Malcolm, I won't just bring you the report. I'll give you the girl too."

"What?"

"She thinks I'm on her side. She's helping me get the copy so you won't kill anyone else in her family. But she knows too much about us now, it's not safe to let her go. If you allow me past to get the report, I'll give you them both. The copy and the girl."

"Why?"

"Because I'm sick of being on the run, Uncle Malcolm. It's scary out here on my own, and I want to be back with my family. So if we find the report, then I give you the girl and the copy, will you let me come home? You know, without...?"

"Without a Q&A?"

"Yeah."

"You're such a wimp, Bain. Letting your girlfriend die, just to save yourself a bit of discomfort."

"She's not my girlfriend!"

"Alright, Bain. This is how it's going to work. I'll order everyone to let you and the girl past. Then when you come out with the copy, you come straight to me. Not to your mother. If you bring me the copy and the girl, then I will welcome you back to the family without question or punishment.

"But if you make a mess of this, or if you try to cheat me, then I will let my son loose on you and I will not tell him to stop. Not until he's finished what he's started so many times. Do you understand me?"

I did understand. I had just heard my uncle pass a death sentence on me. I said politely, "Thanks for making it so clear. See you soon, Malcolm."

I switched my phone off and turned to Lucy. I even managed to smile at her. "He went for it. He believes I'll give him everything just for a warm welcome home."

"You didn't tell him how we were dressed. They won't recognise us."

"They'll recognise our minds. That's why I had to negotiate a way past."

She shrugged. She was getting nervous about the whole idea. Presumably she was going to ask more about our tactics...

"So who did he think was your girlfriend?"

"What? No one!"

"No, I suppose not. The fainting and the throwing up when you hold hands isn't very romantic. What you need is someone on the internet in Kazakhstan."

"It's not funny, Lucy."

"This whole thing is hilarious, Bain. You're a murderer dressed as Death and I'm about to ask my uncle to dump my nana's ashes into a witch's cauldron. It's completely absurd."

That was certainly a more cheerful way of looking at the evening than the picture Malcolm had just put in my head. So I smiled at her again and agreed it was absurd.

As we walked past the palace at the bottom of the Royal Mile and turned left towards Leith, Lucy finally started to think about tactics.

"We have a free pass through your family and the disguise will get us past MI5. We might even get past MI5 again on the way out, if Uncle Vince doesn't blow our cover. But how do we get past your family again? Without giving them... everything. We can't go in without a plan to get out."

"I have a plan, but I'm not going to tell you, because I don't want any hint of it in your mind as we go past my family."

I had to be careful about what they sensed from me too.

It was alright for Malcolm to know that I was genuinely keen to be back with my family. With Uncle Greg, who was trying to teach me to read minds without losing my own. With Roy, who was as close to a normal friend as I'd ever have. With my mum, I suppose.

But I couldn't let him realise that I wanted to be back on my terms. With respect for my abilities, as well as understanding of my weaknesses, and if possible without the death of another Shaw girl in my head.

I had to make sure they didn't pick up any of that on the way in.

"Nearly there, Lucy. Don't think about an escape plan, just think about what we're doing now. Being nervous is fine. Nasty thoughts about me will work too."

"That'll be easy." She pulled the witch mask down over her face. "What will you be thinking, Ciaran Bain?"

"I'll be thinking about saying goodbye to you, Lucy Kingston Shaw." And I pulled down Death's mask.

Lucy Shaw, 31st October

As we started up the hill towards the colonies, Bain nodded at two men in a four-wheel drive. Further on, I noticed his mum, smoking a cigarette and slouching at a bus stop, dressed much less elegantly than at Kings Cross. She frowned at Bain and beckoned. But we stayed on the other side of the road.

I kept thinking, *I don't trust him, I have to trust him, I don't trust him, I have to trust him.* Like I was ripping petals off a flower. Or legs off a spider.

Then a boy stepped out right in front of us. He wasn't in a Halloween costume, just jeans and a t-shirt. He was tall, with dark red hair and a squint nose like a boxer or a rugby player. He looked ready for a fight, but he gave Bain a genuine smile.

Bain stopped; so did I.

"How you doing?" the tall boy asked.

"Surviving."

They both laughed, quietly.

"Can I help?"

"Maybe later. Just go with the flow, and don't let Malcolm detect you expecting anything unusual."

"Anything unusual? You're dressed like a skeleton and you're hanging out with a hag. I can't possibly expect anything *usual*."

The tall boy turned to me. "Hello, Lucy."

This must be the cousin who wanted Bain to test his survival skills, the one who'd wanted to rescue Viv. I nodded from behind my warts. "Hello, Roy."

Roy glanced at Bain. "How much does she know?"

"Everything."

Roy shook his head. "You idiot, Bain. That's not fair on her..."

"Leave it, Roy. Read me the moral lecture when this is over. Come on, Lucy."

Roy looked back at me. "Nice to meet you, Lucy. Don't worry. This boy is brighter and better than he thinks he is."

We were passed by a gang of tiny witches, with orange plastic pumpkins already filled with jelly worms and smarties.

"We have to go," said Bain. "You'll be in trouble for speaking to us."

"I'm a big boy. I can take it."

They slapped hands, then Roy went downhill and we kept going uphill.

When we reached the corner of the narrow entrance to the colonies, I saw a tall man in sports kit with a baseball cap shading his face, standing by black recycling bins on the other side of the road. He had a box full of newspapers and was slowly feeding them into the bin.

Bain whispered, "Malcolm. Don't stare."

We walked towards the first terrace, past a clean black car, with a man and a woman in the front. Bain jabbed his elbow into my side. "Spooks."

Then he dropped a bit of paper into my cauldron. "Roy's number. He just passed me it. I know it off by heart, so he must have meant you to have it. He might be angling for a date, which is unlikely with those warts, or he might be offering to save your life. Put it in your phone."

"I don't have a phone. You stole it, remember."

"You'd have to be a complete idiot not to have bought a pay-as-you-go when you were out. Put Roy's number in and remember he's the nearest thing to a decent human being in my whole family."

As I saved the number into my new phone, we saw a group of guisers heading towards us. The tallest guiser was dressed in two foil-covered cardboard boxes and a pair of silver wellies so he looked like a 1950s robot. Walking beside him were a couple of witches, a plump boy in a tiger onesie and a small pink fairy.

We joined the group as they passed us.

"Can we go round wi' you?" Bain said in a stronger Scottish accent than I'd heard him use before.

"Aye, no problem," rumbled the robot, as we turned right into the first terrace.

The tiger lifted the fairy up to press the first doorbell and I realised I'd forgotten one vital element of my plan.

chapter 32

Lucy Shaw, 31st October

"Lucy? What's wrong?"

"I don't have a song or anything. For at the doors."

"Just do a joke."

"I don't know any jokes!"

"You were full of poisonous jokes when we first met. Ok, here's one: Why couldn't the skeleton pay his bus fare?"

"I don't know."

"Because he was skint!"

"I don't get it."

"Don't worry. Everyone else will."

So we all stood there, in black cloaks, orange fur, silver foil and pink lace, facing a woman with a toddler on her hip.

The fairy skipped forward. "I've got a joke from my gran. What do you call two burglars together?"

The mum smiled. "I don't know, petal, what do you call two burglars together?"

"A pair of knickers!"

The mum laughed and the fairy ran back to the tiger, who asked a riddle about a towel. What gets wetter the more it dries? I wished I'd thought of that.

The two little witches sang a song about a black bat and the robot made his eyes flash, which made the toddler giggle. Then it was our turn.

I stood at the back and asked the skeleton joke as quietly as I could. I was surprised when everyone laughed. "Good one," said the robot. I still didn't get it.

Then Bain sang in a clear voice about a goose getting fat and an old man's hat.

The mum said, "We've all heard that one before," and brought out a big box of sweets. We each took a couple. Bain dropped his into my cauldron. The robot put the sweets straight into his belly, posting them through a hole in the box round his middle.

We knocked at six more doors, doing our party pieces in the same order each time. Then we walked up to the next terrace, past another dark car with adults in both front seats, and I stopped at the corner. We'd done enough to be identified as guisers, so I said, "I'm taking a break, because my witch's shoe is coming off. You go on, but can you do me a favour, fairy princess? For some of my magic sweets?"

She looked up at the tiger, who nodded his stripy head. I held up a folded note, carefully drafted earlier in the hostel.

"When you get to the blue door with the snake knocker, please give this note to the man. Don't say anything, just give it to him, when you do your joke. You can have all my jelly worms."

She gave her wand to the tiger, then grabbed the note with one hand and the tangle of sticky worms with the other. I bent down to re-tie my laces while the robot and his gang moved away.

"Well done," whispered Bain. "We'll visit another

couple of doors on the way to your uncle's, to give him time to find the urn."

We stood and watched as the fairy's group climbed up my uncle's stairs.

I saw the door open, saw the fairy step forward and my uncle crouch down to listen to her joke. I saw her pass the note to him. He put it in his pocket, rather than read it while the tiger did his riddle.

Once my uncle had closed his door, Bain and I did our usual party pieces at three more houses, collecting sweets at each one. Then we did the last door before my uncle's, singing the fat goose song together this time, to make the whole thing quicker, and we took an apple each.

"Quite right," the man at the door said to me, "you want to avoid sweeties with skin like yours!" Bain laughed at that, but I couldn't.

I was *so* nervous. It was my plan, so it was my fault if it all went wrong.

"Don't worry," said Bain as we approached the bottom of the steps. "It's a great plan. We'll be fine."

We walked up to my uncle's. Hearing laughter and songs all along the terrace, I grasped the snake knocker and banged three times.

Ciaran Bain, 31st October

She was so nervous. So was her uncle behind the door. I'd sensed his shock when he read the note. I knew Malcolm could sense our emotions all the way down the road, but nervous and shocked were fine. Anyway, I wasn't concerned about what my family thought right now, so long as the spooks didn't pick up anything suspicious.

I was finding it hard to stay calm around so many kids I didn't know, but at least their emotions were all positive, nothing grating or draining. As we stood at the door I sensed a couple of cheerful guisers behind us. I turned as Lucy knocked for the last time. A short pirate and a tiny grey bat were trotting up the stairs.

"Come and join us," I said, and let them get in front of me.

Then her uncle opened the door.

I knew he was grieving and confused, but he smiled at the children on his doorstep anyway. A nice man. From a nice family, I suppose.

Lucy sang a song. Not one she'd sung at any other door, a couples of verses, with a Caribbean rhythm. I could sense his nostalgia, and his desire to grab her and keep her safe.

But he nodded, then said in a croaky deep voice, "What do the rest of you have for me?"

I did the skeleton joke and he laughed, clearly having lived in Scotland long enough to understand the language. After the pirate and bat sang a nursery rhyme, he said, "Sweets for you all, and the young lady can have this." He handed me a bowl of sweeties to pass round, while he placed a black and gold urn carefully into the witch's cauldron.

"Thanks," she whispered behind her mask.

"Go home safely, all of you. And don't leave it a year before you come back."

"Do you want us to come back soon, Professor Shaw?" asked the pirate.

"Is that little Liam from downstairs? Yes, Liam, you and your mum can come and knock on my door whenever you like."

"He has a snakeskin in a drawer he can show you and he does really nice hot chocolate," muttered Lucy through tears that must have been audible to everyone. "Bye." She almost ran down the stairs, the cauldron banging against her leg.

Vincent Shaw gave me a very hard stare, before I turned away and chased after Lucy.

We jogged towards the narrow road linking all the terraces, then stopped on the corner.

"It's ok, Lucy. You did brilliantly. You'll see him again soon. Now we have to get out of here."

She took a deep breath. "Tell me your plan."

"I can't tell you in case Malcolm senses us plotting. Just follow my lead, and don't ask questions. Can you manage that?"

If she did ask questions, I wasn't sure I could justify my plan, because it relied on guesswork, variables out of my control and chaos.

First, I had to draw attention to myself. Not something I enjoyed doing. Then I had to draw attention to my family. Which was something I was hardwired to avoid. Then I had to escape using a route that I'd only been able to recce at a distance and therefore wasn't even sure was viable.

But it was the only plan that offered a slim chance of protecting my family permanently, and an even slimmer chance of keeping Lucy alive.

Lucy sighed. She wanted to ask questions, she wanted to be involved in the decision-making, she didn't want to be a follower. I knew all that from the emotions I was sensing. But I was fairly sure I would have known it anyway, because I'd spent two nights and two days with her. Not by reading her mind, but by knowing her as a person. Presumably this was how the mindblind always had to work out what was going on.

As I pulled an empty rucksack from under my cloak and put the urn in it, Lucy said, "Just get us safely out of here. I won't argue with that."

So I shouted at the top of my voice, "Sweetie thief!" Everyone swung round to look at me.

"Sweetie thief!" I pointed at Malcolm, down by the recycling bins. "He stole my little sister's sweeties!"

All the guisers in sight swung round to look at Malcolm. Most of the spooks' heads turned too. The group we'd been knocking doors with appeared from a nearby garden.

"He's hidden the sweeties in that box," I shouted even louder. "He's been taking them from all the little kids."

The robot and the plump tiger walked towards us, and I almost staggered backwards as their anger and aggression crashed into me. Tigger asked, "Really? Has he been nicking sweeties from the wee kids?"

I nodded. "Aye. I'm not sure if he's a mad dentist trying to protect their teeth or if he's going to eat them all himself, but they're hidden under those newspapers."

I could sense concern from Malcolm, who didn't like being the centre of attention, but who didn't want to move away because he was trying to keep me in range.

The pink fairy was poking inside a glittery bag. "Did the sweetie thief take my sweeties?"

I could sense Lucy's doubts about this tactic, but she crouched down beside the fairy. "Yes, my love. He took lots of chocolate. You hardly have anything left."

The little girl burst into tears, prompting a wave of guilt from Lucy that I'd never sensed when she made me cry.

I shouted, "Look, this wee girl's crying. Let's get her chocolate back from the sweetie thief..."

And three streets worth of guisers started to march towards Malcolm. The robot and tiger had been joined by more tall boys in onesies, including a kangaroo and a white rabbit.

I sensed my uncle's struggle to control his fury.

The fat tiger and tall kangaroo barged right up to Malcolm. "Is that true? Are you nicking the kids' sweeties? Are you a mad dentist? Show us what's in your box!"

As Malcolm tipped the box of newspapers on the ground, saying reassuringly, "I'm not a dentist and I don't have any sweeties," the whole army of guisers blocked the narrow entrance to the colonies. I could sense increasing confusion from the spooks.

Now there was a bottleneck at the junction. The rest of the family couldn't get in past the guisers, and the spooks were temporarily watching dozens of other kids.

So I ran. Away from the only way in and out. Lucy, stifling guilty laughter, ran with me.

Malcolm was backing off, retreating from a fight he didn't need, trying to work out what I was doing. It wouldn't take him long. We had to be fast.

We sprinted up the narrow road towards the last terrace, turned right, ran to the end and through the gate of the last house.

A couple with a baby stood in the doorway, being entertained by zombies singing the fat goose song. I waved as we ran past and in the surprised silence I used a trellis to clamber onto their garden shed.

I sensed a shift in everyone's emotions. The guisers, who presumably hadn't found stolen sweeties, were losing confidence in their crusade. Malcolm was focussed on giving new orders. The spooks were regrouping too. I heard car doors slam and sensed the start of a search. Perhaps they'd finally worked out that the teenagers running away might be the teenagers they were looking for.

"Keep going!" I yelled at Lucy as I scrambled from the roof of the shed onto the high wall separating these terraces from newer houses on the other side.

I leant down for Lucy, but she climbed up without help, though her gloves were off by now and her mask was squint.

"Keep your mask on. MI5 will be checking any CCTV camera signals they can access."

The kids on the doorstep started singing again, as we balanced along the wall. We turned a corner to walk along the back of the terrace, looking for a safe place to jump down.

In the light from house windows I couldn't see any sheds on the other side. Not even any soft compost heaps. Just hard winter ground or decking.

And I knew all the hunters were coming for us now. The spooks through the colonies, the family round the outside. We only had minutes to get clear of these narrow streets before they became a trap.

The wall was no longer above gardens on both sides. We were balancing along above a road on our right, and there was a blue van parked up on the pavement. I jumped off the wall onto its roof and Lucy followed me, rocking the van on its wheels.

We slid down the windscreen to the bonnet, then onto the road, and we kept running. "As fast as you can!" I called. "If we can get clear of these streets, then the spooks will never find us again."

"What about your family?" she gasped, her first question in five minutes.

"They will track us down eventually, but if I'm right about what's in that urn, we have something to bargain with."

As we ran through the maze of small streets, Lucy felt safe enough to ask more questions. "Where are we going?"

I didn't answer. We were still moving at top speed.

The chaos behind us was dying away. The family were calmer. Malcolm must have escaped the guiser army, because he was concentrating entirely on hunting us down. The spooks were still confused but starting to follow familiar routines.

We had to keep ahead of any attempt, from either side, to find us again. Before I wanted them to, anyway.

As we ran across the park, Lucy asked again, "Where are we going?"

"The docks."

"The docks? Why? Why not the city centre, where we can get lost in the crowds?"

"Because I need witnesses for what we do next, witnesses who can't stop us or attack us. And I can find that in the docks." I didn't explain any more. She kept pace with me, as we ran past warehouses, building sites, scrapyards, then into Leith docks.

I slowed down, at last.

Lucy was nearly out of breath, but she wasn't going

to follow me unquestioningly any longer. "Don't shut me out, Bain! Why do you need witnesses, what are you planning to do now?"

I was about to answer, when suddenly it was too late. There was no time to explain the whole plan.

Because we were no longer alone.

I'd sensed what I'd been hoping for, but what I'd also been dreading. The approach of a hunter.

I started running again. I had to find the right location, before they found us. "Now," I called behind me, "now I'm going to destroy the flash drive."

She ran after me. "But I thought we were going to use the flash drive to bargain for my life. Why do you want to destroy it?"

"The spooks are still too close. If they find us again and grab the flash drive, my whole family is in danger."

"Hold on, Bain. You can't change plans like that."

I kept running. I could argue with her later.

She chased after me, but I stretched out into a burst of serious speed and she couldn't keep up. She stopped to catch her breath, which was the opportunity I needed. I stopped, took off the rucksack, crouched in the tangled shadow of a crane and pulled out the urn.

Would I find anything inside at all, apart from Ivy Shaw's remains? Had the last two days been worth it?

I could sense the hunter getting closer. I twisted the lid off the urn and, with Vivien's gritty fingers scratching the inside of my mind, I put my hand in the ashes.

Yes! I felt it. The long smooth shape of that flash drive. My guess had been right all along. Vivien had led me to the right place.

Lucy kicked me in the ribs. "You bastard, leave my nana alone."

I pulled my hand out of the ashes and twisted the lid back on. "Calm down, Lucy, and help me find two things: moving water and a camera."

"Why would I help you, when you're clearly not trying to save me?"

"It might still work out for both of us, if we hurry. Come on!"

Then I sensed the hunter again. Far too close. Far too fast. Far too much like Daniel.

chapter 33

Lucy Shaw, 31st October

Bain was running towards the water with my nana's ashes. My sister had died because of what was hidden in there. I was not letting him destroy it.

So I ran after him.

We reached a concrete-banked river flowing into the deep water of the docks. Bain ran onto an old railway bridge. The rails were covered over with boards, and the sides of the bridge were a complex pattern of rusty blue girders, framing the dark oily water.

He stopped right in the middle of the bridge. He looked down at the water, then up and round at various lampposts on the bridge, and at the roofs of nearby buildings.

I crashed into him and grabbed the backpack. "No, you bloody don't, not without a better explanation."

"I thought she wanted to be scattered in the sea, Lucy."

"The open sea, not this ditch." I had a tight grip of one of the backpack straps.

"Let go, Lucy. I have to destroy the copy now or it will be too late."

"But if you do, it will be too late for me."

"I'm sorry, Lucy, but it was probably too late the minute you saw my face."

I couldn't believe it. I thought I could trust him. Not completely, not with my bank card details and stuff. But I thought I could trust him with my *life*. I had believed he was sorry for killing Viv. I had believed he didn't want my death in his head.

I must have been wrong. I should have concentrated on getting revenge and not tried to understand my sister's killer.

But if he was going to betray me to his family, why hadn't he just handed me and the flash drive over to Malcolm back at the colonies? And why was he so keen to find water and cameras?

"Lucy, let go!" He hauled on the backpack, but I held on. I saw panic in his eyes. I looked behind me.

In the dim industrial light of the docks, I saw the cousin who'd chased the taxi. He was wearing a black-and-white *Scream* mask, but I recognised the long hair underneath and the confident stride as he walked towards us.

Ciaran Bain, 31st October

I let go of the rucksack without warning Lucy, because it's easy to forget how little the mindblind know, and she fell backwards.

I jumped over her and took three steps towards Daniel. Keeping myself between him and the urn, between him and Lucy.

We both kept our masks on. I'd counted at least 3 CCTV cameras aimed at or around the bridge, so it was safer to keep our faces hidden. Especially on the one night of the year when masks aren't immediately suspicious.

I could sense his anticipation and he could definitely sense my fear.

But my plan could still work. I still had the witnesses I needed.

"Lucy, open the urn and tip the whole lot in the water."

"No."

"Please! I'll explain later, if I'm still breathing later."

"No, I'm not tipping Nana's ashes into that filthy water."

"Lucy, I don't have time to argue. Please do as I say, before Daniel rips both of us apart..."

"Why? Can't you kick him to death too?"

I didn't answer.

"You can beat him, can't you?" Lucy asked. "I've seen you knock down everyone else who's stood in your way in the last couple of days."

I sensed Daniel's satisfaction at the way this conversation was going. There must have been a massive smirk under that mask.

"You can beat him, can't you?" Lucy repeated.

"I suppose there's a first time for everything."

Lucy was confused. She no longer trusted me, she didn't want to do what I asked with the ashes, but she didn't want to see Daniel pulverise me either.

I had never managed to beat Daniel in a straight fight. But I could probably keep him busy for a few minutes. So if I could persuade Lucy to ditch the urn while I held Daniel off, we might both make it out of this. "Lucy. If you have any desire to keep us both alive, please pour the contents of the urn into the water. Now!"

Daniel interrupted, "I want that urn and whatever is in it. Don't you dare pour it out, little girl..."

Oh good. If Daniel told her not to, she might do it simply to annoy him.

"No," she said. "I'm not destroying anything of my nana's, on the orders of either of you. Beat each other to death if you like, but this urn is staying on dry land."

I sighed. If Lucy wouldn't dump the ashes, I'd have to do it myself. I'd have to knock Daniel to the ground and keep him there while I poured the ashes out. I'd have to fight him and win. I took another step forward.

Daniel hadn't told the rest of the family he'd found us. I could sense no desire to delay until an audience got here. I couldn't sense any other family nearby either. He'd want the credit for getting the copy, once they finally found us. But in the meantime, he could have fun kicking people weaker than himself, even without his gang of cousins cheering him on.

Daniel was loving my demands and her refusals, our matching fear and anxiety. But even though he was enjoying the ads and the trailers, he was keen to get to the main feature.

So he crouched.

And I braced myself.

Lucy Shaw, 31st October

Bain didn't even look like he was going to defend himself.

I knew he could do this stuff. I'd felt the strength

of his kick on my wrist. I'd seen him knock down his uncle on the run. I'd seen him kill an armed man.

But he wasn't even squaring up to his cousin. He was just standing there. Was this a double-cross? Was this a bit of theatre before they grabbed the urn and got rid of me?

I stood up, slowly. Should I try to get away? Should I let them have their family tiff, and save myself and these ashes? Decide what to do with the secret once I was safe?

But I'd no idea how to get out of the docks. It was dark, there was deep water everywhere and Bain had the map.

Then I saw Daniel leap at Bain. Was this for real? I watched.

As Daniel leapt, Bain fell. Before Daniel could hit him, he just fell to the ground. Daniel stumbled, then turned round to find Bain.

Bain was up again. Still looking casual, not defending himself.

Daniel attacked again, with a high kick at Bain's head. Bain fell away again, but this time Daniel was expecting it, so he pulled the kick short and landed hard on Bain. Stomping on him, two-footed, like a red card foul.

Bain rolled out from under, but I'd heard the smash as Daniel's boots hit his chest. That must have hurt.

They were both up again.

Daniel leapt once more, but Bain didn't fall this time, he whirled away, and got behind Daniel, his hand reaching out for the ponytail.

But Daniel was too fast, and he ducked and turned, got his arms round Bain's chest and started to squeeze.

Bain's elbows jabbed back, he stamped down at his cousin's feet, but Daniel held on. He shifted one arm up to Bain's bare throat.

Shit. Maybe Daniel really was better at this. Maybe he was going to kill Bain.

Daniel said quietly, "I can feel your fear, Bain. You know I'm going to kill you. And you know no one will care that you're gone. Not even your mum."

Bain was kicking at Daniel's knees, pulling on Daniel's sleeves. But pressed hard up against Daniel, reading his murderous thoughts, Bain must be losing his mind as well as his breath.

Daniel laughed. "Little Lucy knows you're dying and she doesn't care either."

How dare he lie about how I felt?

Before I could think, before he could be warned, I stepped forward, swung the urn-filled backpack and crashed it into the side of Daniel's head.

He dropped Bain and turned on me.

Bain just lay there, no help whatsoever, as the tall boy with the screaming face picked me up and flung me against the girders...

Ciaran Bain, 31st October

I sat up in time to see Lucy crash into the side of the bridge, fall hard and awkward on her left leg, then collapse. The rucksack landed on the wooden planks and the urn rolled out to bump against her feet.

I scrambled up, pulling my mask straight. To hide my face from the cameras, and to keep my eyes hidden from Daniel. But I hoped the cameras were catching this: these masked teenagers fighting over an urn. Because those cameras were our witnesses.

Lucy didn't move. I couldn't sense anything from her. But it wasn't the nothing of death, more the blur of sleep. He'd knocked her out.

I owed her a lot for that whack on the head. But she couldn't help again and I wasn't helping myself much either.

My first tactic had been to annoy him by refusing to engage, hoping he'd make a mistake. But Daniel didn't make mistakes. My next tactic had been to go for that stupid ponytail to get control of his head, but he'd guessed what I was doing, let me get close, and nearly strangled me for it.

I needed to try something else. But I couldn't use flashy high kicks. Not because I was wary of them since I'd killed William Borthwick, but because they're positively dangerous against a better opponent. Daniel could get under a kick, grab my leg and use my own momentum to tip me off balance.

I had to aim low. And I had to get him on the ground. The first one to hit the ground and stay there for more than a heartbeat was going to lose this fight.

We were walking slowly round each other. Then he came at me with a punch to the head, a kick to the stomach, a spin and kick to the thigh. They didn't connect, but they drove me back.

He was too fast. I could only keep backing away. Soon he'd have me up against the girders and he could take me apart. I wasn't ducking out now to annoy him, I was retreating because I couldn't get the space or time or angle to fight back.

And our emotions were exploding out at each other.

When mindreaders fight, it's like fights in films where actors talk all the time. People don't do that in real life. They're thinking about defence and attack, not quick one-liners.

But my family communicate with each other even if we don't want to. Daniel's pleasure and confidence were overwhelming me, my fear and frustration were giving him even more confidence.

If I wasn't careful, we could read each other's intentions too. In a fight no one could concentrate on covering their thoughts. He could read me if we made eye contact and I could read him if we touched. But if he read me, he got lots of information. If I read him, I got lots of information plus added overload and nausea.

So I didn't want to read him and I didn't want him to read me. Which meant I couldn't look him in the face. I had to fight him looking down, like a submissive dog. But then, my eyes down, I saw an opportunity.

I acted before he could react to my spike of hope. I launched forward and stamped on the end of the loose board I'd noticed. It lifted his left foot suddenly into the air, and as he lost his perfect balance I kicked low and knocked his right foot away too.

For a split second neither of Daniel's feet were on the bridge. He was in the air, unsupported, crashing to the ground on his back.

As he fell, I kicked at his head. I connected, but only with the side of the mask, because he'd turned away just far enough to protect himself. He was too fast for me.

I flung myself down, to pin him to the ground before he could recover. But he had his long left leg bent and his foot in the air already, and as I crashed towards him, he kicked me in the chest and pushed me up and away.

It wasn't a strong kick. I landed on my feet. But it moved me far enough out of the way for him to leap up.

We were both on our feet again. I'd blown the best chance I was likely to have.

He laughed. "Good boy. Don't make it too easy."

I didn't answer. No breath. Nothing to say.

Lucy Shaw, 31st October

I heard them thumping and gasping, and I was sitting up with my mask off and the urn in my arms before I remembered what was going on.

Bain and Daniel were still fighting.

Bain wasn't dead yet. I wasn't dead yet. That was good news.

But there wasn't any other good news. Mostly I could see Bain backing away from Daniel.

I watched them kicking, jumping, punching and spinning, and I reckoned that half of Daniel's shots were smacking against Bain, and only one in five of Bain's were getting near Daniel.

They were slowing, their dancing circles getting looser. I could hear Bain's creaking breaths and Daniel's low laughs.

I tried to get up. I wasn't sure why. I didn't want to go near Daniel again. Maybe I would run away, maybe I would even chuck the ashes in the river, so I didn't have to carry the urn.

But I couldn't get up. My legs were too shaky and my left ankle was flaring up with pain.

I heard Daniel's voice. "Hello Lucy. Are you back with us?" And he turned to face me...

chapter 34

Ciaran Bain, 31st October

I sensed Lucy wake up. I hoped Daniel was enjoying himself too much to care about her. But he guessed tormenting her would weaken me, so he started to chat to her, from behind that screaming mask.

"How disappointing for you, Lucy. I can sense your lack of confidence in this pathetic idiot. He's not going to save you. He can't even save himself.

"She knows you can't win, Bain. She's expecting to watch you die, then watch me walk towards her. What will I do then, Lucy? You'll find out soon, but Bain won't be alive to know, so I'll tell you both."

I found a tiny bit of energy and flung a spinning kick at his belly, but he stepped back so it missed by a hair and kept chatting to Lucy, as if my attacks weren't worth noticing.

"I will look in your eyes, and enjoy your fear and pain as I twist and dislocate every joint in your body. Starting with your fingers and wrists, then your toes, ankles and knees. I might leave your neck until after my dad has questioned you. Then I'll watch you die, just like I watched your big sister die. But first Bain..."

He smashed both hands together in a crashing blow

that was meant to crack my temples. I fell back from it and made a weak attempt to kick his knee. I missed. Again.

Lucy Shaw, 31st October

I couldn't just lie here waiting for that animal to savage me.

I tried to stand, but my left ankle was in agony, so I slid back down. I tried to think, past the bruises on my body and the growing terror in my head, what I could do to save myself. As I shifted position to take the weight off my ankle, I felt something in my pocket under the ripped cloak.

Phones. I had two phones in my pocket. Mine, with Roy's number in it. And Borthwick's, with lots of MI5 numbers on it.

Ciaran Bain, 31st October

I knew Lucy was coming up with a plan. I wasn't sure if she was trying to save both of us, or just herself, but I was beyond caring.

Daniel knew she was up to something too. "Don't even think about it, girl!" He took a step towards her.

But now I had a short-term plan of my own. Keep Daniel away from Lucy, while she tried to spoil his victory.

I used the last of my energy to stay between him and her. He landed even more punches, on ribs that were already cracked, but he didn't get past me.

Lucy Shaw, 31st October

Bain was almost on top of me, and he didn't look like he had much fight left in him. But he gave a yell of defiance, and drove Daniel back in a blur of punches and kicks.

As they circled in the centre of the bridge, I tried to stand again. My right leg was working now, but I still couldn't put any weight on my left ankle.

If I couldn't run, the phones were my only chance.

I could call Roy. He was as big as Daniel and could probably pull his cousin off Bain. But would he come alone or with the rest of the family? That was a huge risk to take. For me, and for Bain too.

I could call MI5. Text my location to every number in this phone's contacts. Then the spooks would drive up and save me. But would they save Bain? Would it be a kind of safety he'd accept? Probably not.

Neither of these were perfect solutions. So, I could just stay here, watch Daniel kill Bain in front of me, then watch Daniel walk towards me.

No, I wasn't going to let it end like that. I had to make a decision.

I had always planned to discover what Ciaran Bain had done to my sister and why, then call for someone to help me and to punish him. So this was always how it was going to end.

I picked up the silver phone I'd stolen from Bain in the statue, after he'd stolen it from the man he murdered.

And I switched it on.

Ciaran Bain, 31st October

I saw her holding a phone. Not the cheap one she'd put Roy's number in. It was the spook's phone that I thought I'd dropped on the run through the park. Lucy must have lifted it from me when I was unconscious, and kept it as insurance against me betraying her or failing her. Fair enough.

But this was too soon. I didn't want MI5 to know where we'd been and what we'd done until we were well away. If she brought them here now, they could get the flash drive, and could even grab me, grab Daniel, trace our family through us...

But if she left it much longer, Daniel would already have beaten me and be tearing her apart.

I wondered if I could still salvage something from this.

"Lucy, empty the urn!" I yelled. Daniel jabbed at my face but I swung out of the way. "The urn, Lucy. Look up..." but before I could explain, Daniel jabbed again, his stiff fingers caught me in the throat and destroyed the rest of the sentence.

I pointed up at the cameras, but Lucy ignored me, and I couldn't get any more words out until I could breathe again.

Lucy Shaw, 31st October

He was waving at lampposts and demanding that I tip the urn into the water.

But the flash drive was too powerful and too useful to destroy.

291

So I whispered, "No, Bain, not my nana's ashes." But really I meant, *No Bain, not the flash drive that will save my life.* Not even if it would save him.

And I pressed 'send':

Lomond's family at Leith docks now

Ciaran Bain, 31st October

She did something decisive with the phone.

So it was too late. It had probably been too late the minute she switched Borthwick's phone on.

I gasped, "Daniel, MI5 might be here any minute. We have to get out of here..."

"Spooks? Really? They won't get here first..." I knew what he meant. Suddenly I could sense it too.

My family had detected the fight. They had sensed our anger and aggression, my fear and pain.

My family were heading this way.

Now I was getting more witnesses than I could handle. And I was trapped here. From the waves of pain every time she tried to stand, I knew Lucy was trapped here too.

Then I sensed Lucy's spike of hope.

She believed her cavalry was on the way.

Lucy Shaw, 31st October

I opened the text which had just arrived on Borthwick's phone:

Are you Lomond descendant? We can
keep recent deaths out of court if you
come and work with us

I choked back a few rude words. How dare they offer to cover up my sister's death? But I hoped MI5 would protect me if I was still alive when they got here. I didn't answer the text, because I thought a mystery would get them here faster.

Bain looked almost as wobbly on his feet as I was, and Daniel was now managing to land almost every kick and punch.

But I managed to stand up, at last, holding onto the bridge with one hand and the urn with the other.

Ciaran Bain, 31st October

If I was right about who Lucy had summoned, then my slowly approaching family were in danger.

I could sense the family getting closer, creeping up in the shadows on the east side of the bridge. Mum's growing panic, Malcolm's proud satisfaction, Roy's depressed certainty of loss and the rest of the family's nervousness. None of them could risk coming too close.

Then Daniel's heel hit hard and sudden, against my hip. I fell backwards, but managed to stay upright.

Now I could sense the spooks too, approaching cautiously from the west, still at a distance.

"Daniel, we need to leave. MI5 are on their way, and if they grab either of us or any of the family watching us right now, then they won't need the codenames."

Daniel laughed. "I don't care about the spooks or the

Shaw report. This is the best chance I've ever had to get rid of you. Dad's not going to stop me this time."

He was right. I could sense caution from both sides of the bridge. No one was going to move into clear sight. No one was going to step in and save me. Not even Lucy, who was finally on her feet again behind me.

I tried a kick to Daniel's thigh, but I couldn't raise my own leg high enough. I wasn't going to be able to stay on my feet much longer, let alone fight.

Daniel took the risk I couldn't take, because he was still strong and I was weak. He spun round, leapt up and kicked high, hitting me on the shoulder. I didn't react fast enough to grab at his leg. I didn't have the balance or strength to resist the power of the kick. I flew backwards and landed on the ground.

And he jumped on me, pinning me down.

I was on the ground. I couldn't get up. I had lost the fight. But Daniel wasn't finished.

He leant down and stared through the tiny eyeholes in his mask, looking into my eyes.

He knelt on my right hand so I couldn't move it, then he pulled the glove off my left hand, flung it in the water and wrapped his fingers round my wrist.

"Let's do this man to man, mind to mind. I want to enjoy this."

He thought about what he was going to do. How he would strangle me. And how, before he choked me to death, he would break my nose, break my teeth and crush my chest.

I tried to be brave and defiant, but that's pointless when your enemy can read how hard you're trying to be brave and defiant.

I tried to block my thoughts. I dragged a dark fabric

of privacy up behind my eyes, around my mind. But I was in too much pain to create a strong screen and the fabric ripped under Daniel's sharp eyes.

It's easier to control your words than your thoughts, so I started talking. "You've never killed before, have you?"

"Not yet. You'll be my first. What a privilege. I'll always remember you, Bain. Sniffling and struggling and begging."

"I've not begged yet."

"You will."

He punched my chest. When he had hit me while I was standing, there was air behind me to fall into, to absorb some of the blow. But now I was lying on the bridge, my body took the full force. The pain was so overpowering, I was sure his fist had gone right through my ribcage.

I sensed his pleasure and knew his thoughts. Hit again in the same place or hit my face next?

I sensed Lucy, determined to move, to escape, despite the pain in her injured leg.

I sensed the spooks, still slightly confused, wondering if they had found the wrong kids, because a fight probably wasn't what they'd expected.

I sensed Malcolm, calm and analytical, looking for an advantage from this situation. He could sense MI5 too, that's why the family were staying in the shadows.

I sensed my mum's panic and desperation, her frantic attempts to fight free of the uncles holding her back. I sensed Paul and Hugh's determination to keep her quiet and out of sight.

I sensed Roy, frustrated and angry and already mourning me, and the circle of cousins stopping him running over to help me.

And I sensed my own death. Right above me.

"If you've never killed, how do you know you'll like it?"

"You don't like it, do you? You cry. You suck your thumb. You wet the bed. You run to Mummy. The family doesn't have room for weaklings like you."

He punched again. Same place, same thunderous crash, same unbelievable pain.

I sensed the spooks edging closer, clarifying their options, perhaps planning to surround the docks and arrest everyone, then work out what was going on later.

Malcolm sensed it too. He made decisions, gave orders, and some of the family moved away.

No one was paying any attention to us. No one was going to notice my death.

Daniel aimed his fist at me again.

Lucy Shaw, 31st October

I was steady on my feet now, so if I held onto the railing, I could probably hobble away. But Bain couldn't get away. He was trapped under Daniel, who was landing hammerblow punches on his chest.

It was clear from Bain's attempts to talk Daniel out of killing him that their family, and probably MI5 too, were close by. Why weren't his family stopping Daniel?

Even if they didn't care about Bain as a son, a cousin or a nephew, surely the family realised that he was far better at mindreading than them. That he had skills and talents they didn't. That he was way beyond fairground freakery. Surely they must realise his value, his abilities, his power?

But perhaps they didn't know. Perhaps Bain hadn't quite realised himself.

Perhaps that could save him.

"Use Viv!" I yelled. "Take him to Viv. Use Viv as a weapon!"

Ciaran Bain, 31st October

Use Viv as a weapon? What did she mean? I didn't have the strength to wield a weapon.

Daniel was staring into my eyes, he had his hand round my wrist, and we were reading each other more closely than we ever had.

I knew he planned to take as much time as the spooks and Malcolm would give him, to cause me as much pain as possible. And he would relish every jolt of agony, every pang of despair, every shiver of fear.

I really was crap, and I was dying in such a crap way...

"Hey Bain, this is how it feels to die. Are you enjoying it?"

"You have no idea what it's like to die."

Then I realised what Lucy meant. How I could use Vivien as a weapon.

All I had left was how crap I was, how weak I was, how sensitive I was.

I whispered to Daniel, "If you want to feel death, if you want to be a murderer, this is what it's really like..."

I dived deep into Vivien's death and felt her panic. I kicked Borthwick again and felt his sudden stop.

As I thought about their deaths, Daniel laughed,

because he really didn't care. He was pleased they were dead.

Then I thought about how I felt when they died. I embraced my guilt and my regret and my horror, and I stretched out to feel the absolute freezing black nothingness of death. I found Vivien's terror, still there like a scar in my head, and Borthwick's surprise.

Then before they overwhelmed me, I took the blackness of their deaths and the wretchedness of my feelings, my pathetic weakness, my shakes and sweats and screams and moans, and I forced them out. Out of my mind, along my arm, into my wrist, through my skin, into Daniel's grasping hand, and into his mind.

He screamed...

Chapter 35

Lucy Shaw, 31st October

I heard a scream. I wondered if I'd heard Bain die.

Then Daniel toppled over. Bain crawled out from under his cousin, stood up and lurched towards me.

"Lucy, I can't argue or explain..." He coughed. "We don't have time. Give me the urn."

I clutched the urn to my chest. "But the flash drive is my only chance to be safe!"

He held out his hands. "Trust me. Please."

And I did trust him. I gave him the urn.

I watched as he scrambled onto a low girder, untwisted the lid and shouted loud enough to be heard in the shadows by everyone watching and waiting. "The only copy of Dr Ivy Shaw's page of codenames is on a flash drive in this urn. Once it's gone, there will be no link between Lomond and anyone alive today."

He held the urn high above his head, he tipped it up and, in the lights of the docks, a stream of black curved down to the smooth surface of the river. A line of silver, like a fish, dived out of the mouth of the urn, through the darkness, and dropped with a tiny splash into the water.

The flash drive was gone.

Bain jumped back down, groaning as he hit the boards of the bridge.

I heard a muted cheer from the family. Or it might just have been Roy.

Bain stood beside me, bent over with pain, and mumbled, "Get out of here, Lucy, quickly."

"But won't your family come after me? Now that I can identify you and Daniel, and all the rest?"

He straightened up. "No, it would be too risky to come after you again. Now MI5 know for sure Lomond's family exists and that we have attacked your family, the spooks will keep a very close eye on you all."

I shook my head. "But you got past the spooks before. The mindblind are no match for mindreaders, are they? I thought you were going to use the flash drive to bargain for my life, but you just threw it away. Now you're throwing me away too."

Bain pushed his mask up onto his forehead. I could see his face dimly, but it was hidden from the cameras high above. "Lucy, just go, now. You will be safe, I promise."

"How can you promise? And how can I believe you?"

He grabbed my hand, pressing something hard and rectangular into my palm. Then he pulled his hand and the object away, and slid his hand in his pocket.

"What was that?"

"The flash drive."

"You dropped the flash drive in the river."

"No. I nicked a spare from your house the night I broke in. I dropped the blank one in the river." He coughed again. "An old carnie trick, sleight of hand. I've got the real one, Lucy. The one with the codenames. If my family think about coming after you again, I'll threaten to post this straight to MI5."

"But I thought you wanted to protect your family."

"I've already protected them. MI5 think their only lead to us has gone. But I can take that protection away if my family decide to come after you. That's what I always planned, to use the flash drive to keep you alive. So that's how I can promise you'll be safe. And if threatening them isn't enough to stop them, then I'll warn you, give you time to get away."

"But how will you know? How will you be able to threaten them? Are you going back to your family? Ciaran, don't go back to them!"

"We don't have time to argue." He pointed behind me. "You go that way to MI5 and let them ask their questions, then take you home. They're no danger to you, because it's not you they want, it's us. And I'll go that way, back to my family."

In the middle of the bridge, Daniel moaned and rolled over. I saw a couple of the cousins creeping from the family side to pull him away.

"Why would you go back, when you've been running from them all this time?"

"Because now I know what I can do and so do they. I have a choice, for the first time. And I choose to be with my family. For now, anyway."

"But Daniel tried to kill you and the rest of them just watched! You won't be safe with your family."

"I think I will be. I beat Daniel, so Daniel and Malcolm now know I'm as strong as them, in ways they don't understand. Malcolm is a practical businessman. If he can use me to turn a profit, he'll keep me alive. He might even be polite to me, to persuade me to stay with the family, now they know I can cope outside, too." He smiled very slightly. "I survived two days with you,

Lucy Shaw. I think I can survive my family!"

He looked around. "This is your last chance. Everyone is getting closer. The spooks are just round that corner. Go now."

He turned away and took one step towards his family. Then he turned back. "Remember, if they do come after you, I'll be in touch, to warn you. I promise."

"So I should hope I never see you again?"

"Yeah. You should hope that. Do you?"

I didn't answer, but I didn't have to. He grinned and walked away.

Then I turned my back on him and limped off the bridge.

Ciaran Bain, 31st October

As I struggled to walk in a straight line, I could sense everyone around me.

Ahead, just beyond the bridge, I could sense Daniel's grogginess. A little further on was Roy's relief, and Mum's exhausted happiness.

The rest of the family were backing off, keen to get away fast.

And in the midst of them all, I could sense Malcolm's calm reassessment of the situation, and his grudging respect. Respect? For me?

On the other side of the river from my family, I sensed MI5's accelerating intent to rush the bridge.

So I walked faster, trying to ignore the pain jarring up my body with every step.

I sensed people getting on with routine lives in the buildings by the river, and the excitement of genuine guisers a couple of streets away.

And I could sense Lucy...

As I walked away from her, I sensed Lucy's mind, which had become almost as familiar as my own over the last two days.

She was still worried. I sighed. I'd done all I could for her. What was she worrying about *now*?

Ah. She was worrying about me...

She didn't need to worry. I could handle my family. I was getting used to being the sensitive one.

As I walked off the bridge, I grinned. We'd all been worrying about experiments conducted last century; now I was ready to think about experiments in this century. I was ready to discover how far my powers could stretch and what I was really capable of. Not for my family, not for some shadowy spies, but for myself.

Lucy Shaw, 1st November

"Come on, Lucy. He must have told you something.

"Where he lives?

"Where he goes to school?

"The name of someone in his family?"

"No. Sorry. He didn't tell me anything at all. We barely spoke. I don't even know his name."

If I just kept repeating the same story, eventually they'd let me go home.

After all, they couldn't read my mind.

Lari Don has worked in politics and broadcasting, but is now a full-time writer. Born in Chile, she travelled round the most exotic parts of South America before she was old enough to notice any of it, then she grew up in the north-east of Scotland. She now lives in Edinburgh with her children and two cats, who enjoy distracting her by walking on the keyboard and chasing the mouse in a bid to write themselves into her books (the cats that is, not the children). She is the author of more than twenty books for younger readers including the award-winning *Fabled Beast Chronicles*, which were inspired by Scottish folklore and legend. *Mind Blind* is her first novel for teens.

Visit Lari's website at www.laridon.co.uk,
or follow @LariDonWriter on Twitter